KILLER POSE

Andy Phillips

To female athletes for their dedication, perseverence, and achievements against all odds. Their stories were a source of inspiration for this work, and a powerful reminder to never give up on personal dreams.

CHAPTER ONE

Scandalous

Monique Garneau had a task to complete. That was all she focused on while riding her sleek navy-painted motorcycle along the dual carriageway.

The setting sun was low in the evening sky, but her helmet visor negated the hazardous orange glare. For a professional racer with years of experience, driving at seventy miles per hour was no problem. Monique swerved between lanes to overtake traffic. The other vehicles were only a mundane distraction. Best to save her mental energy for the private meeting to come.

As she approached York's outer ring road, her target came into view. The modern skyscraper sign was visible over a mile away. Thirteen shiny metallic blue letters contrasted with black, six-sided background spokes. Every character line was straight, either along the edge of a hex, or between a corner and its central point. Spotlights shone inward from supporting frames, illuminating the angular company logo.

HEXAGON SPORTS.

Tonight, you get what's coming to you, Wilson.

Her unvoiced threat reduced the monotony of the long ride, if only slightly. A dark-coloured minivan sped by, but the middle-aged driver didn't give so much as a sideways glance. The guy may have done had he seen Monique's face, but underneath her all-black leather outfit and thick boots, she could have been anyone.

A five foot ten biker with her brunette hair tucked inside her helmet would be easy to mistake for a man. But that suited her. She wasn't interested in attracting the attention of random motorists.

Monique continued her course without slowing. She was almost at Poppleton Business Park. The houses and small offices of the quaint Yorkshire village were tiny compared to the twenty-three-story tower that dominated the Hexagon Sports complex. The disappearing dusk sun cast a faint orange tint over the fence-enclosed grounds. Beyond the front gate and security station, nearly every parking space was vacant.

The uniformed guard working the evening shift was a curly-haired blonde in her late twenties. What was she called? Janice? Josie? Monique had spoken to her a few times, but the name didn't matter. She was only a minor player, unimportant in the grand scheme of things.

Monique unbuttoned her leather jacket and presented her Hexagon employee badge. The guard hesitated to open the gate.

"You know the procedure, Miss Garneau. No entry without visual ID."

Her tired recital of the company rule book suggested she

was already bored.

"You've a long night ahead," Monique said. "So I won't give you any trouble. Best do what the big man wants."

She raised her helmet visor and angled her face towards the guard station spot lamp. It was hard keeping her tone pleasant when referring to Wilson, but discretion was essential.

After the woman let her through, Monique drove into the parking lot. She chose a space near the building and shut off her motorcycle engine. Except for ambient sounds – fluttering birds and the whirr of security cameras – it was eerily quiet on this Friday April evening.

One camera was stationary, with Monique's bike in the centre of its view. She didn't need to see surveillance footage to verify that, and her parking spot was a deliberate choice. Brad – Hexagon's gatekeeper – would be on duty at reception, so why waste the opportunity to hone her seduction skills?

Monique began her speed strip routine by unbuttoning her jacket top, then lowered the zipper to expose her sleeveless, short-skirted black dress and silver necklace. It took about a minute to slip off the leggings, readjust the clip-on stockings underneath, and neatly fold the biker leathers.

She swapped her practical boots for the high heels she had stored in a lockable box behind the seat. There was also a leather ladies' purse, which Monique collected and slung over her shoulder. She tossed her long hair back, completing the transformation from faceless motorcyclist to attractive sports model.

Monique placed the helmet beside the bike and strode towards the building. The double plexiglass entrance doors slid open, and she entered the lobby.

Her heels clacked on the smooth floor tiles. Inevitably,

they were hexagonal, but so was almost every feature in the enormous hall. Crystal light fittings, partitioned seating booths, posters of sporting legends – objects without six sides were the exception. The dividing wall behind the glossy reception desk bucked the trend, but the stainless steel logo did not. The scaled-down version of the exterior signage even replicated the spoked frames.

Silver plastic mannequins of famous clients were dressed in licensed company sportswear, notably an American baseball star and a four-time women's singles Wimbledon champion. They were shiny but soulless creations. Every object in the welcome area existed to promote the Hexagon brand.

The rough-faced, balding man at reception was fixated on the woman who had just arrived. Brad's dirty thoughts were obvious from his creepily thin smile. Such blatant misogyny would unnerve most young females, but Monique prided herself on being a person in control.

She casually stroked her hair and walked to the front desk. As expected, it was Brad who flinched first.

"Evening, Moni—" He caught his tongue and started over. "Miss Garneau."

Nearly every talent agent Monique had worked with complemented her athletic physique. Her outfit didn't conceal the muscular arms, nor did the transparent stockings hide her powerful thighs, but male observers were usually interested in other features. Tonight was all about tits and ass – to use that derogatory phrase – and Monique's tight dress only enhanced her sex appeal. Spiral gold patterns stood out from the black cloth material around the curves that mattered.

Brad's eyes shifted sideways. An awkward pause followed while he wiped sweat off his forehead. Monique said nothing as she leant across the desk. Her breasts were right under the guard's face, temptingly close, but he wouldn't dare touch them.

"You know, Brad. This could be considered sexual harassment."

His reaction was priceless: a horrified grimace, hands tapping nervously, drooling lips. Give him a few more seconds, and he would break down and beg for mercy.

"How naughty of me," Monique said. "Someone in a position of power taking advantage of a vulnerable employee."

She glanced down at Brad's crotch, where a noticeable bulge had formed in the zipped trousers. He squirmed in his cushioned seat, at a loss how to respond.

"One day I'll try out that big dick." Monique ran her tongue along her lower lip. "And see how it compares to all the rest. Unfortunately, I've made other plans this evening. Money talks, I'm afraid. Far more profit in screwing the boss."

She checked the security monitors behind Brad's desk: nine small screens split between three slanted control panels. And there was the director, pacing impatiently about his office.

"Inform Mister Wilson his eight o'clock has arrived."

Monique circled around the divider slab. Ever alert, she heard the dejected guard comment under his breath.

"Lucky bastard."

She had her back to Brad, so he wouldn't have seen her triumphant smile. The dim-witted guy was so easy to manipulate that it bordered on insulting, but this seductress was just getting warmed up.

There were four lifts behind reception, so Monique only had to wait briefly after tapping the call pad. She stepped inside and selected the topmost floor from the zigzag chain of hexagonal buttons. There was a security camera in the stainless steel box, and two more along the plush upper level corridor. Brad was doubtless monitoring her steady progress.

Nobody was in the waiting area. The executive secretary's curved desk was unmanned, and the computer screens dark. To save energy – and money – most ceiling lights were switched off. Monique walked past the glass tables and company brochures without a glance, and through the unlocked tube-handled oak doors ahead.

If the foyer was about Hexagon Sports, the director's office was decorated to promote the man in charge. Seven gold-framed pictures and informative plaques chronicled Wade Wilson's life story. Photographs spanned decades from his education overseas at Harvard, through middle management years, to his current position as managing director. Some shots had him posing with politicians, including a former Prime Minister, and another with wealthy celebrities. The album took up an entire wall, a vanity project where only one person mattered.

The floor-to-ceiling windows at the far end were as black as the night sky. Antique brass lamps were dimmed, leaving Wilson shrouded in gloom. The director stood beside the mahogany desk, talking excitedly on his mobile phone. His oily skin reflected what little light fell, and Monique could smell his body moisturiser from twenty metres away.

"I don't care about the deadline!" he protested.

The reply was inaudible, but the one-sided conversation was easy to interpret.

"So move it. Why do you think I hired your sorry ass? … The start of the season isn't until next month. That should be all the time you need to negotiate."

While he continued his rant, Monique studied the environment. The office furniture was high end: a rectangular shaped conference table to match the desk, hardback chairs with velvet cushion seats, a giant television screen, and glass cabinets full of corporate award trophies. The ceiling fan was purely for show, since the ventilation system was more than adequate.

Monique walked round the table, ignoring the picture wall and her boss' tracking gaze. She stopped by a well-stocked refreshment bar and poured brandy from a decanter.

Two glasses were on a polished silver tray. Getting his model drunk could be a plan to make her compliant, but she could handle her liquor. Monique downed her beverage in a single gulp and refilled the glass without looking.

"I'm late for another meeting," Wilson said. "So we'll have to pick this up later. But I expect a report, and a better one than you just gave me."

He ended the call and turned his full attention to his visitor. Wilson's clothes were expensive: tailored maroon suit, plain silk tie, monogrammed cuff links.

Monique kept a neutral expression. The contract negotiation had started, and neither party wished to show weakness.

"Miss Garneau. Dressed to impress."

"And are you? Impressed?"

"A new contract is an opportunity. This could be a lucrative arrangement for both of us. How lucrative depends on what you can offer the company. What you can offer me."

The blatant innuendo wasn't lost on Monique. She slipped off her purse, dropped it beside the tray, and opened the fastener.

"Thought you'd appreciate my skills by now."

She took out a lipstick tube and applied ruby red gloss until her mouth felt sticky. The finishing touch, but also a distraction. Wilson was captivated by her parted lips, so he didn't notice her switch on the digital recording device. Its lens pointed through a tiny hole in the purse, cleverly concealed as part of the pattern.

Wilson picked up a remote control from the desk, aimed at a camera above the entrance, and deactivated it with a button press. Monique couldn't resist smirking at his illusion of privacy. A careless visual tell, but he didn't seem to notice.

"I'm a very talented rider," she boasted. "That's why you signed me."

"Much more competition now." Wilson moved closer. "Two million is a lot of money. Are you still worth the investment?"

"What do you think?"

She discreetly closed the purse, took her glass, and walked to the window. His blatant demand for sex was unsubtle, but she made him wait. The more difficult the catch, the more appetising it became.

Liquid sloshed as Wilson poured himself a drink. Monique sensed his eyes were glued to her ass. The bait was ready to be hooked.

The model sipped her brandy as she looked down on Wilson's sports empire. Structures extended from the central tower, notably an Olympic size swimming pool with an enormous glass roof. Hexagonal windows and steel frames created a hive-like pattern. The panes were so immaculately clean that classical-style white marble columns and turquoise blue water were unobscured.

Another extension housed an open-air tennis court, and

a third an athletic track. Those weren't visible from the front side, but Monique had used the complex facilities enough to know the layout.

The view from the director's office was spectacular. At night, the dual carriageway to York resembled an airport runway. Rural homes were pinpricks of light in dark fields. The village station and railway lines looked like a model train set from this height.

Wilson's reflection appeared in the window. He groped Monique's behind. A tight, firm grip that dispensed with small talk.

The predatory man moved his hands up her back and pulled the dress shoulder loops aside. Monique let her frock fall away and slipped out of her high heels. Now half-naked, she tugged free with ease and spun sharply around.

"Yesterday, three of our partners were adamant they wouldn't sign new deals," Wilson said. "What did you do to change their mind?"

"I can be very persuasive."

"What's your strategy?"

Monique stepped back to the conference table and sat with her legs spread wide.

"First, I get myself into a strong negotiating position. Next, I add a sweetener."

She unclipped her bra, finished her brandy, and slid both objects along the polished wood. By the time they stopped moving, Wilson had forced himself between Monique's stockinged thighs.

"Then I complete the deal," she said.

Wilson gave into temptation and caressed her breasts. She turned to smile at the hidden camera. Some people would pay six figures for this sex video, but Monique wasn't doing this for money. Power was far more satisfying, and right now, she was in charge.

She reached under the table and flipped the switch that activated the ceiling fan. Her hair fluttered in the current of cool air. She undid the stocking straps, enticing Wilson to pull them off and expose her thighs. She exhaled, hard enough for the device's audio receiver to pick up. This was all an act, but it needed to be convincing.

Wilson removed his belt, then his trousers. He was about to take off his underwear when Monique grabbed his wrist. A vice-tight hold that resisted all attempts to break away.

She smiled and reached into her panties. Her mark's struggles ceased as she produced an unused condom she had taped inside.

"I came here expecting you to go in hard," Monique said. "So you'd better not disappoint me."

* * *

Wade Wilson ticked off Monique Garneau's name in his appointment book. Hers was the last listed under today's date, and a definite high note to finish on. He closed his diary, deposited it in his desk drawer next to the fountain pen, and leant back in his leather chair.

The contract negotiation couldn't have gone better. As expected, the girl had used her sex appeal as a weapon. That had given her a temporary illusion of power, a bold streak of misplaced confidence, yet Monique was like any other employee. Money influenced career choices. Offer enough, and she would choose Hexagon over the competition. For all her passion and physical strength, the model had conceded to Wilson's demands.

Beauty alone was worth an extra hundred thousand on

the deal, small change compared to millions in potential sales revenue. But Monique's real value was her profession. Female motorcyclists weren't usually head turning attractive, so filling that niche in the sportswear market was a crucial advantage.

Wilson polished off his brandy, savouring every heart warming drop as he relived the encounter. The sexy model's powerful thighs had been crushingly tight around his waist, giving a sense of achievement to each penetrating thrust. Those firm, natural breasts were a pleasure to lick. An hour later, he still recalled how her sweat tasted.

Most women would call him a monster, but should he feel guilty? Monique knew how the meeting would play out and even arrived prepared. But ultimately, victory was his. Another leading model had signed a three-year extension.

A familiar ring tone interrupted Wilson's thoughts. He was alone in his office, listening to the *Top Gun* theme. The director sat up sharply when he read the caller ID: *Monique.*

"Have you seen the news?" she asked before he gave the customary introduction.

Not the opening Wilson expected. Somewhat hesitantly, he pressed a button on his remote. The giant TV screen – opposite the wall with the pictures – came on.

A high-resolution image showed him groping Monique's naked body, sensitive parts censored by blurry squares. He froze upon reading the caption.

BREAKING: HEXAGON SPORTS SEX SCANDAL.

"...still a developing story," the newscaster narrated. "Despite no official word from the company, a reliable source has confirmed this footage is genuine. Wade Wilson, one of the UK's most influential businessmen, is shown sexually molesting a model..."

Wilson stabbed the mute button. He watched the report

unfold, unable to stop trembling as more explicit snapshots appeared.

"You insolent bitch," he said through clenched teeth.

"Careful with the language," Monique warned him. "You never know what's being recorded."

"How much do you want?"

"Money? You're hoping to outbid the press? Too late for that."

Wilson stood up and gazed through the window. No activity outside, but how long before reporters showed up at the front gate?

"You think you can use people, replace them whenever you like."

There was venom in her voice. A merciless rant that Wilson wanted desperately to shut off. But he needed to know why she'd betrayed him.

"Directors can be replaced too," Monique said. "When shareholders lose faith in them. Scandals are bad for business, and nobody likes dirty old men. How long before the board decides you're expendable?"

"Someone put you up to this. Who was it? Harris? Cole? Now you're acting like the victim. You wanted to…"

"Screw you? Yes, I did enjoy that. But not all your women are so appreciative. They would rather you kept your dick zipped away."

Wilson's legs trembled. Were other models involved in this?

"I don't know… what…"

"Do you think they'll keep quiet?" interrupted Monique.

He was considering how to respond when something dropped over his head. A noose tightened around his neck, cutting off his air supply. He clutched at the rope. The discarded phone landed face down on the floor.

"How many people did you use during your career?" Monique asked, oblivious to his plight. "Were they nothing more than stepping stones?"

The attacker pulled on the cord. Wilson's flailing feet scuffed the carpet beneath him, then lifted off the ground. The bitter caller carried on talking, her voice muffled. Couldn't she hear the struggle? His strangled gasps?

"How does it feel to be the victim?"

The commentary was so unnerving in context it could be the killer taunting him. Were they working together?

Wilson swung back and forth, suspended in mid-air. He momentarily glimpsed a black-clad figure, gloved hands clutching the rope. Something metallic screeched above him.

The fan.

A terrifying picture formed in his head. Tomorrow morning, they would discover his dead body hung from the ceiling. The assumption would surely be suicide, and everyone would believe it.

Wilson clawed at the noose, then grabbed the cord above. His legs knocked over the leather chair below, depriving him of a foothold. He tried to swing over to the conference table, but his feet slipped on the smooth edge.

He spun around to get a better view of the mystery attacker. The intruder was tall, face hidden behind a black plastic mask. Wire gauze covered the nose and mouth, leaving only the eyes visible. Narrow slits, skin and brows coated in dark makeup. Their gender, age, and ethnicity were all unknown.

A tripod-mounted cellphone was on the table, its light and camera switched on. The assailant was recording this?

The tense rope creaked, and Wilson's gasps were becoming fainter. He kicked out, but his shoes bounced off protective rubber pads. The killer had shielded their body and limbs.

"Do you even remember them? All those you stabbed in the back?"

Monique's ongoing rant triggered a disjointed set of flashbacks. Wilson saw fearful executives, corporate rivals, and reluctant models. He had made many enemies throughout his illustrious career, and any of them could be the person under that mask.

"What about that swimmer?" Monique asked. "The model you abused and threw on the scrap heap. It ended in suicide. Do you remember?"

Wilson recalled a blonde, teary-eyed woman sat at the conference table – a hazy event from long ago. Who was she?

He drew a blank, and his willpower was fading fast like the light. Even if Monique heard his strangled cries, she only wanted to lecture him. Reporters were after his blood. The camera was still switched off. Brad – too low paid to work harder than necessary – wouldn't check the offices until morning. Nobody was coming to help.

As darkness clouded Wilson's vision, reality sunk in. His career would end in disgrace, and there was nothing he could do to stop it.

CHAPTER TWO

Setting a Trap

Dan Turner had almost finished his round. Four further patrols of the sports centre remained, but it always felt good to complete the first hourly check.

Campus security wasn't the most glamorous job, but the monthly salary made it bearable. University was an expensive commitment considering tuition and maintenance fees, and student loans were a massive financial burden. Dan was sure he'd been up against prejudice when applying to Oxford. Working class, black, and a comprehensive school education was a triple whammy. Juvenile offences and former gang affiliations were grounds for automatic rejection, but those records had been officially sealed, and while he couldn't prove any bias, he would always be suspicious.

Studying at York wasn't all bad, but did the contractor have to purchase such crappy uniforms? The dull grey shirt itched Dan's forearms, the pants were tight, and his equipment limited to a bundle of keys and an electric torch.

Something hummed nearby, breaking the silence.

"Anyone there?" Dan yelled. Then he realised it was just the air conditioning starting up.

With the recent attacks, student safety should be the number one priority, but the sports facility was always short staffed outside term time. Most members who hadn't gone home for Easter would be out partying, and public training sessions were during the day.

That made patrolling the beige-painted corridors and deserted gyms a lonely task. Most checks were uneventful, so anything odd – no matter how trivial it seemed – was cause for concern. The neon strip lamps were glaringly bright, and every section reeked of cleaning fluid. At least there was no danger of falling asleep.

Dan was short of breath when he returned to the office. He really needed to lose some weight.

"Where were you?" his friend asked.

"Making my round. You know, the job I'm supposed to be doing. Can't see Lyle Norton listed on the roster." Dan tapped the wall-hooked clipboard to make his point. "Some people have to work, and don't have time to watch their girlfriends on TV."

Lyle was a handsome, thick-necked blond wearing a casual shirt, jeans, and brand trainers. Slouched in the swivel chair by the monitors, he looked totally out of place. He had the build and stamina for guard duty, but no incentive. With some rich City of London banker for a dad, money wasn't an issue. Dan was a cockney native himself, just from a different social circle.

"I miss anything?" he asked. "Besides the gymnastics?"

With the system rejigged, every screen showed the

practice hall where Cassie was doing her nightly workout. Surveillance footage covered multiple angles, including two wide panoramic shots and various close-ups of equipment.

Dan was no gymnastics buff, but he recognised the vault. The talented young lady pulled off a twist and landed gracefully on the mat with barely a stumble. Judges would probably award high marks, except this athlete was alone and vulnerable. And Lyle still hadn't answered the question.

"So I haven't missed anything. Great. Another no show. It ever occur to you this stalker might exist in your girl's head? And what she's doing is really dangerous. I told you that, right?"

"Every night for the past week."

Lyle hooked up an external monitor that wasn't part of the usual system and connected a portable modem. An image appeared on the screen. Dan saw wooden lockers, shower cubicles, and ghastly pink porcelain tiles.

"You put a camera in the women's changing room!?"

An obvious statement, but he couldn't think what else to say. Was it getting hotter in here, or merely his imagination? He needed some fresh air, so he switched on the desk fan. Except nothing happened. The blade wheel remained still inside its wire cage. Yet another broken item to add to the growing list.

"Jeez! Do you get the trouble we'll be in if they find out? Does your girl even know we're watching her in there?"

"It was her idea," Lyle replied. "And a good one. We need to keep Cassie in sight. Which means no blind spots. If this creep makes a move, it's going to be somewhere private."

"That's the important word here. Private. We're breaching about a dozen ethics violations. This is lawsuit territory. You realise that?"

"The camera's not there during the day."

"Great," Dan said. "And if some other girl decides to use the gym at nighttime?"

"Then we'll delete the footage. No harm done. And you're one to talk about ethics. How many laws have you broken?"

"None that involved assaulting women."

He regretted choosing the student project on inner city gangs, and sharing first-hand experiences with his peers. Now Lyle had ammunition every time he fancied a dig. He was so wrapped up in Cassie's scheme he couldn't foresee any problems, and it was hopeless attempting to dissuade him.

Dan walked to the crooked table and pulled the newspaper from under the wobbly leg. *The York Gazette* was a student union publication, but an external story had dominated this week's headlines. The latest banner was *HEXAGON SPORTS FALLOUT CONTINUES*, and page three featured an article about the ongoing criminal investigation.

"The Wade Wilson files," Dan said. "They even have a catchy name for them now. So Cassie sees this Garneau woman as an inspiration? She's a fucking blackmailer, pun intended. A professional who knew what she was doing. And what's our setup? Strictly amateur."

Lyle was doing the whole concentrate and not respond thing again. Cassie had moved onto the large blue mat to perform tumbling exercises. Still no sign of any trouble.

Dan dropped the folded newspaper in the bottom drawer of the battered filing cabinet. He kicked the compartment closed, and the analogue clock on top wobbled. His outburst achieved little, but made him feel better.

"Remind me why I agreed to this shit again."

"Three rapes on campus in the past year. No arrests. Ring any bells? Imagine if we catch this bastard and break the story."

In principle, it was difficult to argue with the goal, but Dan couldn't shake his apprehension. The two-man (plus one woman) band were out of their depth. That electric torch wouldn't be much use if some guy pulled a knife. A hypothetical situation to Cassie and Lyle, but not to a childhood survivor of assaults and muggings.

"Better do another round," Dan said. "In case I see something that gets me in trouble. Cassie's on board with this peepshow? That's kinda creepy. You should talk to her, make sure she understands how serious this is. Those pretty moves won't help if our campus stalker makes an appearance."

Lyle turned away from the monitors. Was that a genuinely concerned expression? Maybe Dan hadn't been wasting his breath after all.

* * *

A crescendo of high-pitched notes marked the climax of the dance theme. Loudspeakers broadcast deafening music around the indoor sports hall. The accompanying drumbeats quickened in tempo as Cassie Simms started the final phase of her gymnastics routine.

Still in perfect synchronisation, she double-cartwheeled across the floor mat, coming dangerously close to the marked boundary. This composition was higher in difficulty than her previous attempts – almost international level – but Cassie had yet to falter. She finished with a handstand, which she held for eight seconds, then flipped into an upright stance with her arms spread out wide.

The music ended right on cue. It would have been a crowd-pleasing finale, except there was no audience to see it. Cassie thought of the United States colleges with vast arenas, giant scoreboards, and spectator seats. For British athletes, it was normally the floor space, equipment and little else.

"Just listen to that applause."

Bitter irony now, but one day, she'd do this for real in front of thousands. Awed onlookers would chant her name, drape their champion in the Union Jack, and cheer as she ascended the podium to receive Olympic gold.

Who was she kidding? Cassie was probably the best female gymnast at York University. If she was lucky, she *might* get noticed by national talent scouts. But the top Americans and Chinese were world class, in a different league altogether. These solo evening sessions had an ulterior purpose: drawing out the campus rapist. The trap was set, but he hadn't taken the bait.

You're doing good. Smile for the camera.

And she did, knowing at least one guy was keeping a close eye on her performance. Lyle had been supportive of the sting operation, even if Dan had done everything possible to discourage him. But the team joker would insist *The York Gazette* credit him if the plan worked.

Cassie checked her reflection in the portable tall mirror. A five foot three teenager with chestnut eyes glared back, unimpressive in stature but slim thanks to her diet. Her light brown, bun-tied hair was damp with sweat. The unremarkable red leotard had none of the glittery whirls or fancy design seen at televised events. A bitter reminder she was a long way from achieving her goal.

Enough moaning, Cassie. There were two pieces of

apparatus left. The beam was her strongest piece, so better to conclude with that and tackle the dreaded uneven bars first. She walked round the steel frame and wire supports, pausing to put on her hand grips.

"You won't beat me this time."

If talking to herself made her more competitive, who cared if she sounded stupid? Cassie needed the confidence boost. Only one attempt this week had ended without a fall, and that was the lowest difficulty sequence.

Nobody was on the sidelines to offer encouragement, but Cassie still had her secret weapon. She went to her laptop and played the edited footage of the Paris 2024 Olympic individual final, a snippet featuring the eventual bronze medallist. While gold was the ultimate dream, a podium finish was the first aim.

A fifteen second black screen buffer preceded the movie itself, ample time for Cassie to assume a ready position. Then came the countdown beeps she added to the soundtrack. At the third tone, she jumped onto the springboard and launched herself into the air.

The high fiberglass bar sank under her weight as she began with a straightforward mount, leading into a glide kip. After a swing to gain momentum, she rotated back, split her legs apart, and brought them together to complete the handstand. There was no audio commentary for the simple first element any elite gymnast would be expected to master.

Cassie swung round and released when she reached the highest point, launching herself backward. She cleared the bar but only just grabbed it on her way down.

"Starts with a huge Nabieva," the Olympics announcer said. "Straight into the Bhardwaj."

The complexity was ramping up and Cassie, still

recovering from her mistake, already lagged. She spun forward towards the low pole and performed a mid-air twist. After a near-perfect connection that shocked even herself, she maintained her focus to complete a second kip handstand.

"Back up to the high bar with the Van Leeuwen."

Now well out of sync with her video guide, the trailing gymnast let gravity bring her round and elevated her legs. When she had swung up into an upside down position, she released and twisted to face the other way.

For a fleeting moment, Cassie glimpsed a shadowy figure behind a viewing window. Loss of concentration proved costly, and she completely mistimed the high bar grab. She landed flat on her back, fortunate that the exercise mat cushioned her fall.

"...so perhaps a misconnection."

That was an understatement. Spotlights and girders danced around where they should be, and it took Cassie a few seconds to shake off the dizziness. Once her vision returned to normal, she checked the entry points to the hall, but saw nothing unusual.

"Huge Jaeger," the clip commentator said. "Connects this time into the Pak. Back up with the Maloney and straight into the Geinger. Wrapping up those. Tense there. Full turn. Just the dismount to go."

Cassie stood up and paused the recording. Applause stopped and the Olympic gymnast froze, arms out in celebration after she had finished her routine with only minor errors.

Had Lyle been watching? He wouldn't have heard the commentary in the security room since the camera feeds were video only. The constant references by the announcer to former gymnasts and their signature moves would have been unintelligible to him, but he would know Cassie had messed up.

No sign of the shadow. Perhaps she wanted a stalker to be there as an excuse for her failure. Ultimately, she hadn't been good enough.

Cassie must have stood silent in regret for a full minute before she removed her hand grips and snapped the laptop closed. Time to stop feeling sorry and redeem herself. The balance beam awaited her, the last test of agility and composure for this evening.

She forwent the music, chalked her hands and heels, and mounted the raised platform with a scissor jump. From a sitting position, she moved into a poised stance and began her acrobatic sequence. The beam was sixteen feet long and only four inches wide. Each move required precision and concentration.

On her favourite apparatus, Cassie grew in confidence with each element. She successfully executed a front walkover, a back somersault, a rotation on one foot, and consecutive split leaps. A minor stumble threatened to ruin those, but she soon regained her balance.

The penultimate move was a handstand with legs angled horizontal and parallel to the beam. Pressure built on Cassie's tired arms, but she held steady for five seconds. She was about to rotate her body upright and end with a backflip dismount when she spotted him behind the window.

A man dressed in a sports jacket and baseball cap. His clothes were dark, but that was probably the lack of illumination. The intruder was too distant to discern any facial features, but appeared to be wearing a mask of some kind. And he was looking straight at her.

Cassie instinctively screamed and dropped to the mat.

The awkward, ungraceful landing made her grunt. Her left ankle felt sore, though the injury didn't seem serious. The man had disappeared during her tumble, but the threat remained.

"You picked the wrong girl to mess with!"

She yelled the challenge out loud, mainly to calm her nerves. Cassie walked quickly to the exit and waved to attract attention. Lyle had better be watching this.

The corridor back to the changing rooms seemed twice as long as usual. The boxed-in, narrow passageway was well lit, but had almost no potential escape routes. Fire doors led to a dark, deserted campus where she would be easy prey. Most offices were locked or vacant, and the risk of getting trapped in a dead end room was too great. The overt cameras in the public areas weren't transmitting, but hopefully, they would deter the attacker.

Cassie had discussed her plan with Lyle many times, but that was all theory. Should she have done a practical run through? And what if the rapist did something unexpected?

A loud clang resonated around the corridor. Did a door just slam? The noise originated close by. Cassie quickened her pace, glancing over her shoulder to check the man wasn't following. Her sore ankle made every left step uncomfortable. The polished floor felt icy beneath her bare feet, and the chilly sensation crept up through her body. She might as well be naked, since her thin leotard afforded no protection.

The blast of warmth from the electric heaters was invigorating. Cassie had reached the presumed safety of the women's locker room. Air fresheners gave off a pleasant aroma of summery flowers, an artificial scent that did nothing to ease the tension. The layout was a veritable maze with tight spaces everywhere. Between the rows of steel storage units and wooden benches, there were plenty of spots to get cornered.

"I'm ready for you, creep."

A blatant lie, but Cassie needed to prepare herself mentally. She unzipped her leotard and removed the key lanyard from around her neck. That exposed her upper back, but bare skin was what that pervert wanted. A naked teenage girl in a steamy shower would be irresistible – and in plain view of the hidden camera.

Cassie opened her locker and reached for the towel. He was there in the mirror. The stocking-masked man was right behind her.

"I've been watching you."

She froze, rooted in fear. A sharp, cold metal object probed her back. A knife? She couldn't see it in the reflection.

This wasn't the plan! The sicko was supposed to watch her undress, then attack her. The assault was happening off camera, and Lyle would be blind to it.

"All those late night practices." His speech was slow and wheezy, piling on the creepiness. "You got great form, Cassie. Really like the way you split those legs of yours."

He knows my name. How long had this psycho been watching her? His heavy hand clamped her thigh, squeezing so hard she buckled under the pressure. The knife point dug deeper into her back.

"Will you split them for me?"

The sting operation was supposed to trap the stalker, but Cassie had somehow ended up his prisoner. Glancing down, she saw leather-gloved fingers press the leotard over her groin. Beads of sweat trickled down her cheek. Her instinct was to wipe them away, but she didn't dare move.

"Turn around so I can get a better look at you."

Cassie hesitated, then obeyed. The man released his grip

as she spun round.

The attacker was a few inches taller, his chin about level with her sight line. A brown stocking distorted his entire face except for roughly cut holes over the eyes and lips, but the white male was likely middle-aged. His sports jacket had university branding, but was weatherbeaten, a relic from the last century. Despite the shadow cast by his baseball cap, it was obviously black hair tucked under his ears.

He raised a razor sharp switchblade. Its metal end was short, about four or five inches, but still lethal. Cassie retreated, bumping into the lockers. Hers was directly behind, left open from earlier. She recalled the items she brought to the gym. Maybe there was something useful.

"You take a wrong turn?" she asked. "This is the girl's room."

Her jokey comment didn't fit the mood, but the attacker seemed put off by her brave outburst. Cassie reached back, searching between her rucksack and the towel.

The deodorant spray. She eased the lid off and placed her finger on the nozzle.

"My star student is a girl," the masked man said. "Show me what you can do, and I'll improve your technique."

He touched her breasts, leaving himself exposed. Cassie kneed the rapist in the groin, putting so much weight into the attack he actually yelled in pain. Before the fury-eyed lunatic could react, she thrust the aerosol in his face and sprayed.

"You goddamn bitch!"

The stunned attacker rubbed his eyes, dislodging the baseball cap from his head. He snarled in rage and lunged forward with the knife.

Cassie just about dodged aside. Seeing an opportunity,

she slammed the locker door in the guy's chest. And a second time, a powerful blow that knocked him back.

"Lyle!" she yelled. "Get your stupid ass in here now!"

The long corridor was a potential death trap, so she ducked towards the showers instead. Hopefully, her boyfriend had spotted her on the video feed, because the masked man had recovered and she was out of deodorant spray. Cassie threw the empty aerosol can, but he simply swatted it aside.

"You'll wish you hadn't done that, little girl."

He advanced toward the shower cubicles, knife held tight. Cassie's back was literally against the tiled wall. She had nowhere left to run. And then Lyle was there, heroically racing to her rescue.

"Get the hell away from her!"

The rapist spun around and brandished his blade, giving Lyle pause. The two men stared each other down, neither wanting to give ground.

Cassie looked about frantically. She threw open the nearest glass cubicle door, pulled the tubed shower nozzle from its holder, and turned the cold tap on full.

Doused in water, the attacker was thrown off balance. Lyle kicked away the switchblade, which skittered out of sight. He grappled with the masked man, struggling to hold him.

"Run for it!"

That had been Cassie's first instinct, but this was the moment they had planned for. Time to expose this bastard. She grabbed the stocking and pulled it from the maniac's head.

Lyle paused, seeming to recognise the attacker. That gave the unmasked black-haired man an advantage, enough to land a fierce punch to the jaw that knocked her gallant boyfriend out cold.

The psycho closed in. Now Cassie had a clearer view, the stubble-faced thug did look familiar, but even if she positively identified her assailant, solicitors would question a witness account. Had the video feed captured his face? This was all pointless otherwise. She glanced sideways at the ventilation grille where they concealed the spy camera.

The rapist followed her gaze. He gave Cassie a hateful stare, then grabbed the lens and pulled. The attached electric cable came out of the vent with it, glass cracking in his clenched fist.

"You were recording me this whole time!? I'll kill you!"

The man stooped to retrieve his knife, giving his victim the chance to sprint for the exit. She ignored her aching ankle and didn't dare look back as heavy footsteps thumped behind her. She split jumped over a bench to avoid the spilled water. Trainers squeaked as her pursuer skidded on wet tiles.

Cassie darted out into the corridor, ready to collapse from exertion, but she pressed on, fuelled by adrenaline. Her shadow on the wall was joined by a second. Her mild injury was enough to slow her running speed, and the attacker was within meters of catching up when Dan turned a corner ahead. Lyle, back on his feet, emerged from the changing room.

With numbers stacked against him, their quarry gave up the chase and made his getaway through a fire exit. Cassie cautiously opened the door to peek outside, but the man had fled into the night.

"Are you okay?" Dan asked her.

"What took you so long?"

"Wait until the guy attacks me. Be sure to get his face on camera. That was the plan, right? The one you insisted we follow?"

Those *had* been her instructions, but he must have known something was wrong. She looked to Lyle for support, but her boyfriend didn't back her up. Instead, he tapped his chin, then paused with one finger pointed at the ceiling.

"Earl Bennett."

How was Cassie supposed to respond to an unfamiliar name?

"Former star of the university rugby team?" Dan said. "Their old coach? He's the rapist? He played for England, for Christ's sake. Holy shit. You weren't kidding about this being a story."

Then she remembered a picture of the guy holding a trophy. In a publicly displayed yearbook, right here in York Sports Centre.

"Tell me we got the footage."

Dan nodded weakly in reply.

"*You* got it," Lyle said, zipping up her leotard. "But promise me you'll never do anything like this again."

"It worked, didn't it?"

"He's still out there, Cassie. And he knows about the camera. You made yourself a target."

"Good thing I have you to protect me, then."

She smiled, but Lyle looked away in disgust.

"Think your boyfriend's saying you almost got yourself killed," Dan said.

"We exposed a rapist. Probably saved an innocent girl from being assaulted. I call that a fantastic result. Why are we arguing? Don't we have the story of the year to run?"

Sirens wailed as an unseen emergency vehicle approached the campus.

"After we talk to the police," Dan said. "I called them

from the office. You *are* the victim of a violent crime. Or did you forget that?"

CHAPTER THREE

The Contract

He should have objected, and told Cassie how dangerous the plan to ensnare the campus rapist was. Lyle had watched his girlfriend risk her life to play heroine. He wanted to curse her naivety, but he never criticised the idea once. Her mother was a semi-famous TV reporter, a lot of pressure for a young woman studying an honours degree in media and communication. So breaking a major news story at nineteen was almost expected, and explained her death defying gamble.

Was this blind love in action? *Stop making excuses for her, Lyle.* The ill-conceived scheme was a disaster waiting to happen.

The students had moved back to the training hall while the police sealed off the crime scene. That's what the women's locker room had become, a reminder of Cassie's narrow escape. Had Lyle not reacted immediately when she appeared on the security monitor, or been half a minute slower in reaching her, she would be a rape victim. Not that sexual assault was a minor offence.

"So you recognised the man?" Detective Constable Moore asked.

The pony-tailed brunette was the less experienced of the two cops conducting the interview. She was the typical image of a plain-clothes officer, wearing a pressed white shirt with the collar button fastened, black jacket and matching trousers. The roundish faced woman couldn't be older than thirty, probably some hotshot on an accelerated promotion scheme.

"Earl Bennett?" Cassie said. "Only by reputation. I'm not in the habit of dating sex offenders."

"Just taking the law into your own hands."

"Hey!" Lyle intervened. "Are you here to take her statement or accuse her?"

He had remained mostly quiet so far, but the attacks were becoming increasingly personal, and the police were treating Cassie like an offender instead of the victim.

Moore typed on her tablet device, adding notes quickly with the autocomplete feature. "What you did took a great deal of courage, Miss Simms. But it was very dangerous."

"It was downright stupid!" Quinn boomed.

The Detective Inspector leading the investigation was much older than his colleague. He spoke with a thick Yorkshire accent, a stark contrast to the educated-sounding Moore. Wearing a ruffled lime shirt, loose tie, and slightly overlong jacket, the bearded, snow-haired man didn't seem bothered about his appearance.

"What kind of man uses some poor girl as bait?"

"It was my plan," Cassie said. "And we got the evidence. So maybe your poor girl did all right."

"Obtained without a warrant and an illegal surveillance camera. Good luck getting that past a barrister. You know what I think? You're just some spoiled teenager who fancied playing Nancy Drew. Perhaps you should leave detective work to the professionals."

"Three previous victims. All freshers on uni sport teams attacked on their way home from late evening training sessions. All the girls gave similar descriptions of a stocking masked offender. Plot the crimes on a campus map, and this building is right in the middle. How's that for detective work?"

Cassie had slipped a tracksuit top over her gymnast outfit, but that didn't shield her from the barrage of questions and insinuations. North Yorkshire's finest had made their patronising opinions clear, yet she had impressively held her own. Sat on the balance beam with her arms folded, the beleaguered teenager wasn't afraid to bite back.

"Seems our student reporters have been doing their own inquiry," Moore said.

Dan chose that moment to return with the uniformed officer he had volunteered to show round the sports centre.

"We checked the entire building. He's gone."

Neither detective paid much attention to the security guard's report. They were too busy grilling Cassie.

"Legal or not," she argued, "the video's enough to end Bennett's career. Expose him for the woman-hating bastard he is. His celebrity status won't protect him, not after the papers run the story."

"Hold off for now," Moore advised her. "We'll put together an official press release. That way, we can control the situation and keep your name out of it."

Cassie responded with a satisfied smile. Lyle suddenly

felt cold. Could she really have been so reckless? Had she listened to anything he told her in the corridor earlier?

Then Dan made the inference. "She already sent it to them. Looks like your girlfriend values attention over common sense."

"Wonderful," Quinn said. "Hexagon scandal's barely a week old, and you pull this crap. Welcome to York, the vigilante capital of England. Fancy making some cash, ladies? Get a guy to assault you. Easy money, no risk at all."

"Thought people should know a dangerous lunatic is out there," Cassie said. "Shouldn't you be looking for him? Instead of lecturing me?"

"After we've safeguarded the victim. Not so simple when she doesn't want to cooperate."

Lyle couldn't think of a counterargument. His girlfriend was determined to put herself in danger, to publish the Bennett story no matter what. She sure made it hard to support her.

"I'll speak to security," Moore said, "and advise them to increase patrols around campus."

Dan didn't hide his smirk. "A handful of guys armed with torches. That'll stop him."

"You believe Cassie's still in danger?" Lyle asked the detective.

"It's just a precaution. I'm sure there's nothing to worry about."

* * *

"All right, Ms Cole. Let's hear it."

That was Tamara's cue to address the Hexagon board. She found talking on her feet added more impact, and the option to circle around the conference table during her presentation ought to dissuade bored shareholders from checking e-mails.

"Oh, almost forgot. One more agenda item first."

Vince Harris had a smug expression as he leant forward. He wasn't even keeping his intent to undermine Tamara's position a secret. Wilson's premature death had left a power vacuum, and while members hadn't voted on a permanent replacement, the main candidates were already in campaign mode.

The acting director of Hexagon Sports had all the sleaze of his predecessor. His greasy, charcoal black hair was combed flat and his royal blue blazer tailored to fit perfectly. Wristwatches weren't so popular in the modern era, but he wore a fancy gold one just to show off. Still in his thirties, that hadn't damped Vince's ambition. This pathetic man would do anything to gain the advantage, but Tamara was a proven winner.

"By all means," she said. "Let's get the unimportant stuff out of the way first."

Vince ignored her jibe and pressed a button on the remote control. On the giant television screen, a high resolution photograph replaced Tamara's introduction slide. It showed a neatly cut piece of cardboard attached to the complex's chain-link fence with plastic clothes pegs. *HEXAGON SCUM* was crudely sprayed in silver, matching the style of the company logo.

"Fifth act of vandalism this year," Vince remarked. "It's become routine. The police have promised to look into it."

"At the previous meeting, we agreed to install shutters on all lower floor windows and doors. With the expensive armoured glass you insisted we purchase for the executive offices, I wouldn't consider a lone protestor a major security threat."

"Welcome to Fort Hexagon," a male exec said. He stopped chuckling once he realised nobody else found his comment funny.

Tamara took the remote from Vince and switched back to her presentation slide. He had made his power play – now it was her turn to assert authority.

The statuesque, powerfully built blonde didn't require high heels to boost her height. An ex-Olympic swimmer, she was naturally taller than most men around the table. Her laced flat sole shoes were practical, complementing her cream business suit. The other board members had resented Wilson for appointing an American consultant with little corporate experience, but they quickly learnt she was equally competitive out of the pool.

"Last month," Tamara began, "Hexagon suffered a setback."

"We're aiming for brutal honesty here," Vince said. "Lose the sugar coating."

She moved so everyone could see the screen and pressed the button to advance the slide deck. Analytical charts showed the company's performance, but fancy graphics couldn't camouflage the dire financial situation. The sudden nosedive in profit over the past four weeks was obvious.

"The revelations about the late director haven't helped our sales," she continued. "Revenue is down by a third, and still falling. Most major stores and online outlets are boycotting our products. Half our modelling staff have already left to sign with other companies."

"I'm aware of our problems. That's why we have analysts. Your job as head of marketing is to suggest a way out of this mess."

Tamara gestured to where Wilson's photo wall used to be. They had taken the framed pictures down out of respect, leaving small screw holes and discoloured rectangles between the brass lamps.

"The main issue is our image. With the Wilson files scandal, most people, women in particular, see us as out of touch. But Hexagon's share of the market was already in decline long before that."

Her doom and gloom message wasn't winning anybody over, but that was intentional. With the negative outlook established, she adopted a more upbeat tone for her big pitch.

"It's time to reinvent our brand."

After Tamara confidently spoke the last word, she launched her video with the remote. Epic music blared over the television speakers as the Hexagon logo appeared. The sudden shift in tempo roused most board members, but Vince remained stern faced.

"We need to show women we value their contribution to sport," Tamara said. "Their elegance."

A slim, delicate skater in a short-skirted pink outfit wasn't threatening to the macho psyche, so the shareholders were all smiles as they watched the auburn-haired female glide across an ice-rink. She sped up and kicked her long legs in rhythm with the background music. The routine ended with a rapid on-the-spot spin behind superimposed text. *Elena Savikova - Figure Skating*.

Tamara walked past the screen, keeping pace with the woman as she skated from right to left.

"Toughness."

She timed her comment to finish just before the switchover to the second athlete. Predictably, some male execs flinched when they saw a bronze-skinned Latina punch towards them. One even looked away when she followed up with a roundhouse kick.

The braid-haired fighter battled an imaginary opponent in a metal cage, fists blurring through the air. Then the image froze, and a name appeared in a semi-transparent overlay caption: *Raquel Valdez - Kickboxing*.

"Athleticism."

The third model needed no introduction. Everyone recognised the brunette who powered her motorcycle round the dirt track. This was a publicity video with no competing riders or safety gear. Some board members exchanged nervous glances as the text box appeared. *Monique Garneau - Motocross*.

"Very athletic," a man said. "Wilson went out with a bang."

It sounded like that idiot from before. His tasteless joke went without comment.

Tamara herself was next. She was much younger when they shot this footage, but still recognisable despite the hi-tech black swimsuit, cap, and goggles.

Vince pulled on his collar and readjusted his tie. So, watching his rival power to Olympic gold in the two hundred metres freestyle made him uncomfortable. *Get used to that feeling, you smug bastard.*

"And most important of all," the presenter concluded. "Success."

The promotional trailer ended with her on the podium. The name and sport were obvious, but she had included a caption for consistency. *Tamara Cole - Swimming*.

"Success is only judged after an athlete's performance, and that presentation hasn't won me over."

Quite a few ass lickers nodded at Vince's rebuttal. His negative reaction was no surprise, but it was disheartening to see the youngest female executive concur.

"You're turning down my proposal? This is the perfect

response to the Wilson situation."

"That's already being handled," Vince said. "We've promised to fully co-operate with the investigation into our former director's… activities."

One woman board member whispered to another. "Thought we weren't sugar coating."

"Co-operating isn't enough," Tamara said. "Wilson was sexually exploiting a model, using her to seduce our business partners."

"That's rather dramatic," Vince countered. "Miss Garneau blew the whistle on us. A man committed suicide as a direct result. She's hardly innocent in all this, and you want to reward her?"

Murmurs of approval suggested he still had the majority on his side. Not willing to concede, Tamara kept up the pressure.

"The public sees Monique as a hero. Keeping her on the team would go a long way towards rebuilding trust. It's not like anyone else wants to take a chance on her."

"And you do? I'll admit she has some appeal."

That remark earned a wolf whistle from that sexist jerk who persisted in interrupting. Tamara made a mental note to pension him off if she landed the director's job.

"But other than you," Vince said, "and Garneau, I've never heard of these women."

"In case you missed the news, A-listers aren't exactly queuing up to sign with Hexagon."

"Then there's demand. Despite the push for women's sports, they bring in a fraction of the male equivalent. Are you sure you want to take the risk?"

Vince practically threw down the gauntlet with that challenge, but Tamara had one last argument to make.

"What if we had a high-profile figurehead for this line?

Someone young, exciting, British. A local girl who everyone looks up to."

She pressed the remote button again, revealing a collage of front-page newspaper headlines. *RUGBY AND RAPE* was the bluntest, *PERFECT TEN FOR HEROISM* the smartest. *ANOTHER SCANDAL IN YORK* was the most predictable. Then there was the wordy *FEMALE STUDENT EXPOSES EX-ENGLAND STAR AS SEX OFFENDER*. Every broadsheet and tabloid featured the Earl Bennett bombshell as its lead story.

Tamara hadn't prepared a video for her final athlete, a trump card she received by pure chance this morning. For extra impact, she read the imaginary caption out loud.

"Cassie Simms. Gymnastics."

* * *

Cassie pushed against the hanging rings with all her strength. She had pumped iron in the gym and warmed up by jogging four laps round the sports hall. With her ankle healed, she was back to full speed.

But despite the preparation, her strained arms struggled to lift her body weight. She wasn't attempting a complex routine, just a pull up to raise her upper back to where the straps began.

That was the strategy, but male gymnasts made it look far easier than it was. Finally, Cassie succumbed to the pressure and dropped to the exercise mat. She stood hunched over, panting from exhaustion.

Lyle reacted with a dismayed head shake. A warning glare prevented an "I told you so" comment, but that didn't deter his smart-ass comedian friend.

"I'm new to the whole gymnastics thing," Dan said, "so I

could be wrong, but don't girls use the other equipment?"

He was definitely smirking behind that hand. Was everything a joke to him?

"The balance beam and uneven bars," Cassie clarified. "Yeah, but I like the extra challenge."

"And risking personal injury," Lyle said. "This is becoming a regular thing."

"Would it hurt to support me? We exposed a sexual predator who's been getting away with it for years."

"Think maybe the cops have a point? They're trained to deal with scum like Bennett, and have body armour, pepper spray, handcuffs. You had a deodorant and a death wish."

"You forgot to mention the positive result."

Dan finished his diet soda and tossed the empty can in a wastebin. "Well, I gotta go study. Those two exams won't retake themselves. Just one thing. Whatever you have planned for your next adventure, leave me out of it."

He walked off without looking back. Cassie turned to Lyle, who simply shrugged.

"Success doesn't happen because you want it," she said. "You have to push yourself."

Cassie performed a forward somersault across the mat, a simple acrobatic move to restore confidence after her latest mishap. She landed in flamboyant style and planted a kiss on Lyle's cheek.

"Which is why I need to finish my gym routine, and my handsome reporter boyfriend should finish his story. The media skimped on the details. It needs less Bennett, and more of us."

She waved at the press photographers behind the viewing window. The university legal team had requested some breathing space for their celebrity student, but the paparazzi excelled at finding loopholes.

Lyle stood there in grim silence, then turned and exited the hall.

"Be nice to display some enthusiasm," Cassie shouted after him. "And solidarity. Would that hurt?"

She took the vault as a challenge and sprinted along the run-up mat. Her heart pounded as she launched herself towards the platform and pushed off. In mid-air, she executed a full twist, and finished with a perfect landing.

"The heroine of the hour."

Cassie gasped out loud, taken by complete surprise. Her eyes met a tall, impeccably dressed blonde observer on the sideline. Actually, the height difference meant the much shorter gymnast was staring – somewhat rudely – at her visitor's breasts.

The woman was too classy to be a reporter and had no camera, crew, or microphone. Cassie spent a few seconds straining her neck before she recognised her admirer.

"Tamara Cole."

The gobsmacked teenager was so stunned that she flubbed the name. The American's record-breaking achievements in swimming transcended her sport. Since her high-profile emigration to the UK a few years back, she had become a figurehead for female athletes. Sadly, her company had made news recently for all the wrong reasons.

"I wanted to congratulate you in person," Tamara said. "What you did was inspirational."

"I'm inspirational? Ten Olympic golds. Would have been eleven if you'd won the relay in Rio."

Cassie took the water bottle from her gym bag and gulped down half the contents. It tasted like sweet ambrosia. She was sweating from her intense session and hadn't realised how overheated her body was.

"I prefer to focus on the positives," Tamara said. "I was

the fastest woman in the pool, three games running. World record holder in the two hundred metre freestyle. Sometimes it's your teammates who let you down."

"Or bosses."

That received a smile. An Olympic legend, and this felt like a normal conversation.

Cassie dropped her bottle and started a floor routine. She jazzed it up with some fancy moves, but nothing too difficult.

"One of the modern greats," she said between cartwheels. "Here to watch me?"

"Because I'm intrigued. Plenty of talent and determination in that young body, but you're still raw. If you want to achieve your maximum potential, you need someone to mould you into a champion."

"Are you auditioning to be my new coach?"

"More of a mentor role."

Cassie paused and observed Tamara from afar. This was just polite talk, often an ice breaker before important news. Dare she ask?

"Why are you here, Ms Cole?"

"I'd like to offer you a modelling contract with Hexagon Sports."

A good thing Cassie had swallowed the water, otherwise she would have spluttered it out in shock.

"I'm serious."

The star-struck gymnast didn't doubt it, but still couldn't figure out what to say. The watching reporters snapped photos as the women sat down on a bench, with ample space between them.

"Hexagon?" Cassie asked. "Hear their brand's toxic now."

"Which is why you're perfect. How better to ditch our

tarnished image than promote an athlete who exposed a sex offender?"

"What's the catch?"

Tamara shunted closer, her eyes sweeping, as if sizing Cassie up as a potential prize.

"This is a full-time commitment, not a scholarship. Eventually, you'll have to choose between modelling and further education. Not immediately, of course."

"A meaningful career without a degree? That's a huge ask, and my parents wouldn't exactly approve if I dropped media studies."

"This is your decision. You'll get hands on experience dealing with the press, and if your dream is to become a professional athlete…"

Tamara reached into her business suit and pulled out an invitation printed on a black card. Silver sportswomen silhouettes formed a border around the edges. Equally shiny banner text read MODERN WOMAN: *The next generation of female athletes.*

Cassie did a double take. The event was tonight, at Hexagon Sports headquarters in Poppleton. And it really was her name and sport written out under the title.

"I'm hosting a launch party for my new label," Tamara said. "I'd like you to be there. VIP guest list, but leave the evening dress at home. We're showcasing women of action, and I think we can upgrade the leotard to something more befitting."

"You're talking as if I've already signed."

Tamara pulled out another piece of paper and unfolded it. There were many paragraphs of baffling legal jargon, but the context was clear: a modelling contract worth half a million pounds over three years.

The document crinkled in Cassie's trembling hand.

"I'll need to discuss the terms with a solicitor."

A noncommittal answer, but she couldn't believe this was happening.

"You'll find the agreement is valid. Think of the extra exposure. The promotion opportunities. Is it that hard to say yes?"

CHAPTER FOUR

Modern Woman

Cassie Simms was in dreamland. She had never ridden in a chauffeur-driven limousine until this evening, when Tamara sent a courtesy car to collect her new model from the university campus. That raised eyebrows from other students, who were used to cheap taxis with dodgy-looking drivers. The journey to Poppleton took twenty minutes, but it felt like an eternity with the shaky nerves.

No Hexagon officials at the front gate, but the guard recognised Cassie from a Modern Woman flyer, and the security perimeter kept the trailing reporters from following the limo into the parking area. The awestruck teenager stepped out to pumping music, alive with dramatic beats and instrumental overtures. Loud enough to hear outside, and even more impactful beyond the propped open doors.

The lobby would be impressive without the booming

audio. Silver mannequins on hexagonal stands were monuments to past greats. Nearly every sport was represented: football, tennis, motor racing, golf, baseball. No gymnasts – were they reserving a spot for her? – or rugby players, understandably.

A burly security guard named Brad – according to his name badge – grunted as Cassie approached the reception. Dozens of guests packed the entrance hall, so he was a busy man tonight, but the guy could *pretend* to be pleasant.

"Cassie Simms. Sports model." She inhaled deep, reflecting on the gravity of her own words. "Did I just say that?"

Brad actually looked up from his men's magazine. He eyeballed the latest arrival, then soon lost interest.

Cassie had changed into the leotard delivered by the Hexagon rep. A noticeable upgrade on her own, the navy royal outfit fit perfectly. The embossed company logo over the stomach area connected the reflective lower section to the swirly patterned top and sleeves. This was competition standard gear, suitable for an Olympic performance.

Wealthy-looking women wearing fashionable evening dresses and far too much jewellery had dolled themselves up to mingle. All the men wore black bow ties and dinner jackets, so a teenage girl in sportswear must seem rather plain.

"Over there," Brad said.

He directed Cassie to a mannequin where a small, excited crowd had assembled. Tamara Cole was the centre of attention, both the silver statue and the genuine article. The two figures had almost identical clothing, except the real woman also wore a leather belt adorned with gold discs. When Cassie got closer, she recognised actual medals from the London, Rio, and Tokyo summer games. Six around the front and sides, and space for four behind. The perfect ten – symbols of a champion.

"Looks better than a business suit," Cassie said, inspecting the mannequin.

"Bit too flat, but our designer is a perfectionist. Every detail is correct, but where's the imagination? This is about selling a brand."

"Is this designer a male employee with no girlfriend?"

That raised another smile. Feminist jokes seemed to go down well with Tamara.

"You're slender and curvy," she said. "So maybe you can be our ideal woman."

After the American stepped away and drew the crowd, Cassie noticed the mannequin was part of a larger display. Five hexagonal stands with silvery mock ups posed on top, and plaques to identify the name and sport.

Elena Savikova, a figure skater at the far left, held her raised leg. Next was martial artist Raquel Valdez lifting a barbell on a bench press. The central likeness was Monique Garneau, stretched back on a motorbike seat. Then Tamara Cole in her beltless swimsuit, and finally an empty pedestal ready to add *CASSIE SIMMS - GYMNASTICS*.

"How does it feel to belong among the sporting greats?"

The Olympian had returned to place a hand on Cassie's shoulder. The grip was firm, yet reassuring.

"I'm hardly a great, Ms Cole."

"First, call me Tamara. We're on the same team now. Second, stop doubting yourself. You're destined for a podium spot with that talent. You need to be more focused and shed what's holding you back. Third, any woman can be great. She just has to do something unforgettable."

An announcement over the public address system interrupted the pep talk.

"Ladies and gentlemen, please proceed to the pool area for the opening speech."

That was Brad's voice, so it appeared they had given him tannoy duties. Cassie turned to continue her conversation, but Tamara was gone. Not knowing where to go, the gymnast followed excited guests through a side passage.

Chatter rose in frequency and pitch, echoing around a tunnel lined with posters advertising Hexagon Sports products. The teenager got swept along in the fast-walking crowd. Surrounded by strangers, the sickly smell of perfume and body lotions was overbearing. After a two-minute trek, they passed through double glass doors into a lavish poolside extension.

Hexagonal patterns were everywhere: black marble floor tiles, hive themed hanging lights, transparent roof broken into six-sided segments. The clouds overhead weren't the most picturesque complement to the Roman style pillars, but the relaxation bar had a healthy stock of alcoholic drinks and soda options to keep guests happy.

Feeling lost, Cassie was relieved to see three female models stood in a small group by themselves. They too had changed into sportswear. Raquel wore a tank top that left her ripped muscles exposed. Elena was in a flimsy-looking pink short-skirted dress and had to carry her ice skates. Monique's outfit was a partially unzipped leather jacket and skin-tight leggings. Most men – even some women – were enamoured with the alluring temptress.

The music died down as Cassie joined the others at the bar, and the audience gradually fell quiet in expectation. Lights dimmed except those above the diving boards. Tamara – who else could the tall figure be? – stepped forward to the upper platform edge.

"Athletic," she shouted.

Her voice carried without the aid of a microphone. She dived into the water, angling down with her arms outstretched.

Tamara made a large splash, but perhaps the ripples she created were symbolic. The fast swimmer remained underwater, crossing the entire pool length as lights came on to mark her progress. Retirement hadn't slowed the former champ down. She surfaced within a minute, climbed out, and tossed aside her cap, letting blonde hair drop onto her shoulders.

Dripping wet and gold medal belt glinting, Tamara commanded the attention of everyone present. Her publicity stunt had gone perfectly to plan.

"And beautiful," she said. "The two are not mutually exclusive."

A nerdy unshaven man in steamed up spectacles stepped from the crowd and knelt to take pictures with a digital camera. His shirt was untucked and his black pants creased everywhere. Not the greatest first impression, and some guests reacted with annoyed looks as the social misfit rushed about snapping photographs.

"In her opinion," a woman said.

The voice came from behind. Cassie peeked over her shoulder and saw the reception security guy beside Monique. She had his undivided attention as she lifted a cherry on a stick from a cocktail glass and sucked the fruit. After she finished, she pulled the juicy toothpick slowly through her lips. Brad looked ready to pounce at the suggestion. If they were alone, he probably would.

"Who do you think has the sexier ass?"

Such open bluntness and aggression. Her teasing bordered on mental torture, and Monique – judging from her malicious smile – enjoyed every second.

"Your boss wants you."

Brad jerked back, then hurriedly ran to Tamara to pass her a pair of low-heeled shoes. Their hostess returned to join the group, one very nervy guard trailing behind.

"With that in mind," she said. "I've hired these four lovely, accomplished ladies to promote our new brand."

Suddenly in everyone's gaze, Cassie smiled. An attempt at bravery, but it probably fell flat. Monique was a natural with crowds, and Raquel wasn't fazed by leering execs. Elena sipped a shot of vodka, unable to maintain eye contact.

A middle-aged man stepped to the front and clapped. He had the most stylish suit, so logic suggested he was someone important. Others joined in with the applause almost immediately, which confirmed his status. The black-haired executive exaggerated his movements, while Tamara looked on with disdain. A simmering corporate rivalry?

"Thank you, Mr Harris," she said.

Her compliment was cold and ungenuine, which validated Cassie's suspicions.

"Does that answer your question?" Brad whispered.

His hand was on Monique's buttock. If the guard considered this discreet, he had much to learn. But they were standing at the back, and everyone had eyes on Tamara. Clapping continued unabated, the VIPs all following Harris' lead. Finally, he stopped, and so did the rest.

The tall blonde walked through the crowd. Heads turned to follow her along the pool edge.

"We built this facility to bring Hexagon into the modern age. Our company designs modern clothes." Tamara raised her voice, ready to wind up the dramatic speech. "Produces modern equipment."

She beckoned Cassie and the models to join her. They did, two on either side. The local girl ended up with Elena, the shy couple opposite the aggressive Monique and Raquel.

"So let us embrace the modern woman."

Tamara lifted her arms high. More applause in response, this time without Harris' encouragement. He gave the speaker a forced smile, reluctant to concede he'd lost influence.

The nerdy guy returned to take photos of the women, capturing them from seemingly every angle.

"That concludes the launch," Harris said. "If you would make your way over to the recreation hall, our models will be through shortly, and pose for photographs."

He spoke with Tamara while the executives filed out, talking and typing messages on mobile phones. More publicity photos? How many did they need?

"Like dolls in shop window," Elena said, her broken English spoken in an Eastern European accent. "We just playthings to them."

"We're being well compensated," Cassie replied.

"By Tamara from America, land of capitalism. Where even dignity is for sale."

Elena looked towards Monique. Brad had remained behind after the others left, and was blatantly massaging the brunette's leather-clad thigh.

"And predator strikes."

"He's groping her in public. And you admire him for it?"

"Woman is predator. So many wealthy men to choose, and she goes for security guard."

"Most have wised up after she blackmailed the last boss," Raquel said. "Look, but don't touch. But Brad's an idiot with a big dick he can't keep tucked away. The worst kind of man."

The kickboxer's vicious rant suggested a dark past, but that would have to wait. Harris had gone on ahead with the remaining VIPs.

Tamara led the models around the pool to another pair of glass doors. The corridor was the same design as before, with more sports posters. Brad practically stalked Monique, staying within touching distance the whole time.

"Monitor things at reception," Tamara told him. "We've had a lot of haters recently, so make sure no uninvited guests sneak in."

An excuse to get rid of him, but a welcome one. Brad looked like an adrift sailor, alone in the corridor as the models walked on. Cassie didn't look over her shoulder, because that would only embolden his fantasies.

The athletics hall at Hexagon HQ was double the size of the campus gym, with actual spectator areas. Empty seats, but a grand arena to walk into. British flags hung from a pole, creating the illusion of a major competition venue.

Various sports "stations" were set up, all with designated zones for guests to watch from. Cassie's eyes went straight to the balance beam. The wood looked brand new, without chalk markings or scratches. Raquel had a kickboxing cage, and Monique sat on an elevated working motorcycle. She attracted the largest crowd, but a few executives waited eagerly for Cassie.

"I'll be in the pool area," Tamara said. "I know you won't let me down."

With high expectations set, the hostess left the gymnast alone with the guests.

At least it's not the uneven bars.

Eager to impress, Cassie mounted with a leap and performed a series of acrobatic turns, walkovers, and flips. Energised by the unexpected interest, she didn't put a foot wrong. Three onlookers became six, and then eight. Her near perfect attempt only faltered when that creepy photographer came over.

"Could you do the handstand where you split your legs?" he asked.

"What?"

Cassie glared angrily at him as she struggled to restore her balance. Respect and patience weren't words this weirdo understood.

"Your signature pose," he said. "From the newspapers. The article about your school gymnastics team."

That was four – maybe five – years ago. Had the nerd researched her whole life? She pictured him alone in a basement, leering at images of kids.

"It's just what we need for our promotional pack. The perfect combination of beauty and grace."

Saliva trickled from his lips. Freaked out, Cassie almost slipped from the beam.

"Hey!" Raquel shouted from her cage. "If you want kicks, I'll be happy to give you some."

She punched a training dummy. Twice for effect, then a powerful spinning kick that could have knocked the head off.

At the balance beam, a large crowd had assembled. Even Monique had been outdone for attention.

That high-ranking executive who had jousted with Tamara offered his opinion. "Don't worry about Justin, our chief technician. He might come across as strange, but he's very capable."

"His people skills need some work."

The nerd suddenly seemed hesitant with the exec there, but Cassie felt compelled to voice her concern.

"Vince Harris, acting managing director. Ms Cole speaks

highly of you. She says you could be our number one model."

That faint praise carried a veiled threat. Tamara's friend was his enemy by extension. A monologue was coming, so Cassie braced herself.

"But I'm not convinced. An employee who can't follow instructions isn't especially valuable. We've invested a lot of money in this Modern Woman venture. You were the star attraction, how Tamara swayed the board into backing her idea. It's time to deliver."

Vince waited expectantly as Justin peered through his camera viewfinder. Cassie, feeling apprehensive, gripped the beam and did a handstand. A simple move under normal circumstances, but that condition didn't apply here. She took a breath, ensured her posture was solid, then split her legs until they were nearly horizontal.

"Good enough?" she asked.

"It's a start."

Vince left, and a small entourage followed. Justin snapped several shots, mostly from a front angle.

"Hold still while I take your body measurements."

He strapped the camera around his neck and removed a tape measure from his trouser pocket.

"No need," Cassie said. "I can give you those."

"Estimates aren't good enough. When I prepare a mannequin, it has to be correct to the smallest detail. I'm a modelling expert myself. 3D design and graphics."

Justin took measurements of Cassie's thigh, then her waist. It was hard to hold position with the extra pressure. Handstands typically lasted fifteen seconds or less, but this had taken minutes.

"You finished?" she asked.

"One more reading."

The weirdo wrapped the crinkly metal strip around her neck and pulled tight. There was space to breathe, but only just. After what seemed an age, Justin stepped back and let the measure retract.

Cassie sat up straight on the beam. The technician – either oblivious or uncaring – grinned and walked over to Raquel's station.

"Try that move on me, and I'll show you a real chokehold."

She raised her fists in a protective stance and kicked high at the dummy. Justin snapped a picture from the cage opening, but kept his distance from the intimidating Latina. *Bet your estimates are good enough now.*

Cassie's rest break was short-lived. Lyle had gatecrashed the party, and approached from the entrance. He was underdressed for the occasion, wearing a red shirt and golden-yellow tie. Corporate types muttered among themselves as he strolled by.

"Glad to see you fitting in."

There was no warmth in his voice, only contempt. Cassie felt sweat trickle down her neck.

"How did you get an invitation?" she asked.

"Your new boss, Tamara, sent me one. She thought a story in *The York Gazette* would be good publicity. Turns out it was news to me."

"So I'm supposed to ask your permission now?"

Her loud tone got people looking, so she walked over to a seating area for some privacy.

"A discussion would have been nice," Lyle said. "People who care for each other talk about their problems."

"I was going to tell you. It's just… The offer came out of nowhere. This is a great opportunity for me."

"So that's why you ran the sting op. Money."

Lyle glanced at Monique. Men congregated to watch the sultry model rest her legs on the bike handlebars and lean back. She unzipped her top fully to expose her sweat-drenched chest and skimpy underwear. Justin couldn't wait to take photographs.

"You'll make a lot of that," Lyle said. "Sex is always a bestseller."

"It's not like that. Hexagon is marketing us as modern women."

Why was he being so negative? Didn't he understand how difficult it was to secure a modelling contract this prestigious?

"Modern women in tight swimsuits and leotards, or no clothes at all. You're talking soundbites, Cassie. This is the company with the pervert president."

"That was Wade Wilson. He's dead."

Everyone – even the females – had moved to Monique's station. Her boots and leather leggings were on the floor. Just underwear now, and exposed skin that Justin happily photographed.

"Doesn't seem like much has changed," Lyle said. "Are we still a thing?"

"Of course."

"We're reporters, remember? They know how to spot lies and half truths. I wonder which it is."

He stood up and walked off without even a goodbye.

"Lyle!"

Her part of the photoshoot was over, and she didn't want to watch executives fawn over Monique. Cassie needed a drink. She thought about returning to the poolside bar, then she spied another door opposite the corridor.

Her exploration yielded immediate benefits when she stepped out into the open air. This walled off extension housed a floodlit ice rink. Elena, forgotten by everyone except a female guest who probably wanted privacy, skated across the gleaming white surface. She danced with no music, a harmonious trail with jumps, spins, and one-legged skids. She swerved to a stop by the barrier.

"Nice routine," Cassie said, "but not much love in. Just us three?"

"You are fourth. There was man with camera. He asked me to do silly pose, took pictures, then go."

"At least you had the option to skate away. I was stuck on a beam, with Vince Harris insisting I put on a show."

"I wanted to take second option."

After that cryptic comment, Elena skated off. She gathered speed, then made a sudden turn and headed straight back towards Cassie. There was no hint of slowdown until she finished with a spinning move, one leg high. The razor-sharp blade glinted, leaving a thin silver trail as it whooshed through the air and stopped mere inches from Cassie's throat.

Somehow, the spectator remained calm. "But you thought better of it."

Elena let momentum take over and dropped her foot.

"Man was too far away."

"You clearly don't want to be here."

It was a harsh comment, but Cassie wanted to know more about the shy girl the guests had ignored.

"We do not always have choice," Elena said. "Want and need are different things. Hundred thousand is lot of money."

"One hundred thousand?"

Cassie blurted it out without thinking, and Elena's stern look made her immediately regret it.

"They are paying you more?" the skater asked.

"That accent. Georgian?"

A complete guess, but Cassie was eager to change the subject to a less awkward one.

"Ukrainian."

And suddenly the topic was even more sensitive.

Elena didn't have to add details. Her country had been at war with Russia for over two years. She was probably a refugee sent overseas for safety, with family back home. A brother or father in the army? Killed or missing in action? Maybe her relatives were struggling to survive in the country's west, away from the front lines.

"And you? What is your reason for being here?"

Elena's comment thawed the ice. A terrible pun, but it was easier to talk than ask painful questions.

"Chance for a better life, I guess."

"You wish to chase Tamara and her American dream."

Well done, Cassie. Way to put your foot in it again.

She took the initiative. Outside, the corporate influence felt weaker, and Elena was one person at Hexagon who seemed genuine.

"Your family. Are they…" She left the question hanging.

"Safe for now. But tomorrow, who knows? I do what I can, send what I make back home or to charity. When you experience war, all this seems hollow. If my skating saves lives, what is money?"

Elena's comment was sharper than her blades. Cassie suddenly felt materialistic, guilty at signing Tamara's contract. Had she done the right thing?

"Be careful around men and women in suits," Elena said. "I was only pretending before, but they… They are real cutthroats."

* * *

"Overall, I'd call that a success."

Unsurprisingly, Tamara gave her launch event the thumbs up. All the guests – and models – went home an hour ago, leaving only a skeleton crew of night shift workers at Hexagon. With the lights dimmed, the silver mannequins decorating the lobby were eerily lifelike.

Footsteps echoed as the executives headed for the main entrance. Vince Harris had only feigned support for the Modern Woman line, but it was better to keep tabs on his directorship rival.

Predictably, Tamara had made her idea an all-female endeavour. That might appeal to the public, but the toxic brand name would surely dent sales. He only needed to wait for disappointing figures, and then shift the blame. If, by some miracle, Tamara's enterprise was a success, there were other ways to discredit her.

"The jury's still out," Vince said. "Profit is the bottom line, Ms Cole. I'll admit you spoke well to the board, but it's our customers you need to convince."

Tamara stepped close enough for him to see her sweat glisten. She was wearing high heels, which made her a good four inches taller.

"See these medals?" She shook that arrogant belt of hers. "All gold. Not one silver or bronze, because when I compete in a race, I do everything it takes to win."

"I recall you coming second in a team relay."

"This time, I get to choose my partners. They won't let me down."

Vince looked up at his foe, resisting the urge to stand on his tiptoes. He wasn't afraid of the overconfident American and her girl band.

"At this company, you're not in first place. Something

you'd do well to remember. This competition, much like swimming, doesn't have a repechage. No safety net if you mess up, so perhaps you should be more careful."

On that sour note, they parted ways. Vince rode the elevator up to the director's floor. After crossing the assistant's area, he closed the office doors and took out his bug sweeper.

The fancy piece of gadgetry had cost a small fortune, but it was a necessary precaution. His business partner had proven to be an effective spy. Satisfied there were no listening devices or concealed cameras, Vince made the call on his scrambler phone.

"Well, that was more fun than I expected," Monique said. "An entire room full of hard dicks and jealous wives. Why are men so easy to manipulate?"

Was there a hidden threat? The ever-scheming woman was almost certainly recording the message, so better to keep the conversation cryptic.

"Our arrangement has worked well so far. I'd like to think I made a wise investment."

"Screwing Wilson had its benefits. For both of us. But if you're worried about me stabbing you in the back, maybe I could show you how committed I am."

Monique was less tactful with her word choice. She knew Vince had more to lose should the truth come out.

Wilson's arrogance had led him to believe he was untouchable, and his predatory attitude towards his models made an enticing temptress the perfect tool. A contractual bonus – and promise of an executive position – had persuaded her to record the video. But Monique was as ambitious as she was manipulative, and Vince wasn't keen to repeat his boss' mistake.

"Your last orgy ended up with a man killing himself

over stress," he said. "I'm thinking we should keep our relationship professional."

"Shame. You don't know what you're missing. Any suggestion who I should spend time with instead?"

"Not yet. But if this business venture of Tamara's fails, we'll need to persuade her to step down. She's a stubborn woman. If someone were to obtain leverage, I'd be indebted to them."

CHAPTER FIVE

The Illusion of Safety

Nobody understood the geek in the basement. He was the forgotten one, the computer nerd bosses came to whenever they needed "something technical" doing, but never invited to their exclusive award ceremonies. Hidden underground to protect the precious company image, Justin West had a gloomy office with overburdened shelves, spare parts, and obsolete equipment.

The thermostat had broken again, so it was even hotter than usual. His latest assignment was Modern Woman, and his task was to "Make models visually appealing while promoting their sporting talent for a contemporary audience." A garbled mouthful, but that's what Tamara Cole wrote verbatim in her e-mail. Buzz words, waffle, and business speak – the language of middle management.

Justin checked his computer screen clock. 09:32, only two minutes since the previous look. Why did time always pass so slowly in the morning? Still another eight hours to spend in this musty storage room without the proper tools. The inscription on the swinging glass door read *Technical Lab*, but there were no holographic panels, robot arms, or any of the flashy gizmos used by fictional TV characters. Just a cramped space, and one thankless job after the next.

"West!"

Justin sat upright. He'd been slouching in his cracked swivel chair, so lost in melancholy he hadn't noticed Vince Harris enter.

"What can I do for you, sir?"

A formal question that felt unnatural, but people with authority made him nervous. He cleared his throat and took off his glasses to rub them clean. Then he realised the acting director was frowning with impatience, so he stopped fidgeting.

"You get my e-mail?" Harris asked.

"The one about promotional material for Ms Cole's models?"

The request was only twenty minutes old, but Justin kept a regular watch on his inbox. Bosses got angry when their staff ignored them, and rumours of job cuts were circulating after the Wilson scandal. With two disciplinary warnings this month for poor timekeeping, this was an opportunity to show his worth.

"I've chosen the best shot for each girl. Some images had too much noise, or weak lighting. It's not as simple as adding photos and text. I have to adjust brightness, contrast, and exposure to get the balance just right."

Harris didn't seem impressed with the explanation. Why did these business types think post-processing meant pushing a button?

Justin replaced his spectacles and closed his internet

browser to free up the screen. The five model images were open in the design editor. Monique's photo occupied the main window, enlarged for viewing, with the others selectable by smaller thumbnails below.

Harris' hand clasped around the desk's edge, fingers scraping back. So, he was into the biker. Hardly surprising, since she was Hexagon's star model, and not because of motocross.

Justin was proud of that shot. A sex magnet, smooth body shadowed by the flaps of her unzipped jacket. The camera light had caught the dip between her well-rounded breasts, and moist underwear with nipple ridges promised more underneath. Her motorcycle leggings were skin-tight. What guy wouldn't want to get between those muscular thighs?

Sadly, Monique was out of Justin's league. He sighed and pushed his spectacles up his slippery nose.

"What do you think?" he asked.

Justin clicked on the four other images. Raquel lifting a barbell, Tamara with her arms up in celebration. Decent efforts, but Elena's graceful spin, with her leg held high, and Cassie's dynamic handstand split were far superior. Finding a suitable still pose for the camera shy gymnast had been challenging.

"Touch the photos up," the boss said. "This is going on our main website, so I want them looking sexy. Can you do that?"

"Girls this hot? I'll make them into sex goddesses."

"Good."

A less than enthusiastic endorsement. Had Justin overstepped the boundaries again? He wiped his stubbly chin, clearing the saliva.

"Mister West, take your time with this project."

"But the e-mail from Ms Cole…"

"Don't worry about that. I'm acting director, not Tamara. It's important to get this right, like you said."

Harris left with a spring in his step. More office politics, no doubt, but why did Justin always end up in the crossfire? He would either be blamed for failure or receive no recognition for success.

Cassie was on the monitor screen, body upside down as she balanced expertly on the wooden beam. The Hexagon Sports leotard gave the young model the appearance of a superhero. Justin's favourite comic books starred a female reporter who moonlighted as a crime fighter in blue spandex. Agile and capable, this champion in waiting was the real-life equivalent.

Her legs were split at an impossibly wide, almost hundred and eighty degree angle. Justin traced his mouse cursor along the upper surface, and the Y co-ordinate hardly varied. How could someone have such perfect form? His body would break attempting the move, but this flexible woman had no trouble.

The other four mannequins were complete, and only the gymnast remained. Justin loaded his 3D render of Cassie in the graphic designer and modified the wireframe mesh. Measurements were displayed in a second window for reference, but it required a few slider adjustments until her waist diameter and cup size matched.

"You're going to look absolutely beautiful," he promised.

The fiberglass moulds were stored on shelves at the very back, in the shadowy section where the lights flickered. Justin had to hold the torso piece close to ensure he selected the correct one, but it helped that he organised the storage system. The material was an ugly dull yellow, but the end product would be far more attractive.

Justin placed the mould in the vacuum forming machine, the three metre long open-topped box where designs became reality. Mannequins were important to Hexagon, so they had provided their chief technician with a fully automated setup. All he needed to do was load the clamps with a silver plastic sheet, alter a few settings, and press the start button.

Before completing the last step, he operated the computer and played his favourite piece of classical music: the *Blue Danube Waltz* by Johann Strauss II. Justin increased the volume to maximum. He'd already had one executive visit, and there wasn't likely to be another.

With the tune in full swing, Justin needed a dancing partner. He took Elena's rejected mannequin in his arms. This version had slightly short legs and bulky hips, but the limb parts moved fluidly. Dressed in a pink skirt, auburn wig, and ice skates, he could pretend she was the real thing.

The introductory section of the waltz concluded, leading to a lull in the orchestra. Justin checked the machine and saw the heated silver plastic had already taken on a liquid-like appearance.

"Elena, will you dance with me?"

It was a rhetorical question, because a genuine woman would reject him. As a computer boffin, he faced stigma throughout his childhood and student days. Endless bullying from less educated classmates and girls toying with his affections, only to make jokes at his expense. He was a social outcast at Hexagon too. The managers used his talents to increase promotion prospects while giving him strange looks in the cafeteria.

But this was Justin's world, where he had beautiful models all to himself. To him, the slim bodied mannequin *was* Elena. By the time the first waltz ended, he had completed several crossings of the floor space. The skater's skirt flapped against her upper thighs as Justin whirled her about. Despite sudden changes in direction, her wig stayed on throughout the entire dance.

The machine hummed as the floppy plastic lowered. Another quiet musical interlude allowed Justin to hear the softened sheet stretch over the fiberglass mould. Then the vacuum pump hissed as it sucked air from underneath. The moulded silver shell would soon be ready, but one last waltz remained.

Justin raised the mannequin's leg high, bringing the ice skate blade dangerously close to the ceiling. It was a risky routine, but she was worth it.

An energetic lead-in dance, two full spins with her skirt trailing behind, and the grand finale where he held her aloft. When the orchestra fell silent, Justin rested Elena's statue against the wall.

The cooled torso front rose from the trough. Its creator looked down with admiration, his face reflected in the shiny silver chest. Like a mirror, the smooth surface was flawless. The machine had enough space for a full mannequin, but he preferred to build his women one piece at a time.

Justin felt the contours of her perfectly shaped breasts. Cool and hard, the beginning of a masterpiece.

"Such a beautiful body," he said. "I can't wait to play with you, Cassie."

* * *

Earl Bennett was in all the morning papers again. Ever since the rape story broke, the press couldn't get enough of it. Three days on, the red tops still plastered his picture on their front pages. Combined with his celebrity status as a former rugby player, it was difficult to travel without being recognised.

Before the police could mobilise, Earl had withdrawn five hundred pounds from the nearest ATM. Limited funds, but sufficient to lie low for a few days. He had seen enough detective dramas to understand card payments left an electronic trail.

After ditching his car, he retreated to a rural Yorkshire village north of the city. The locals mostly kept to themselves, so *The Golden Lion* landlord asked no questions when a secretive customer paid in cash.

The cosy attic room, with its latticed windows and oak rafters, could serve as a film set for a historical period drama. Furnishings were antique, from the carved wooden headboard to the well-used dresser. The postman rode a pedal cycle on his daily delivery run, and the cottage shops were nearly all family owned. In this sleepy backwater, there were no CCTV cameras and few potential witnesses.

Earl had no personal connections in Stillington, and the reduced police presence made it the perfect place to hide. Friends had burned their bridges, and his closest relatives had disowned him publicly. But the cops would search his York apartment first, which gave him crucial breathing space to plan his next move.

"Enjoying the attention, you little bitch?"

The local Yorkshire newspaper featured a publicity picture of Cassie Simms and four other women. Hexagon Sports had offered her a professional modelling contract, and the reporter's mugshot looked like that guy she colluded with. These do-gooders pretended to be heroes, but it always boiled down to money and fame.

Earl took the pair of scissors from the drawer. Not wanting to risk a return to his home address, he had purchased supplies from a twenty-four-hour convenience store before leaving York. The duct tape and rubber gloves would be useful once he tracked that snotty little bitch down, and he still had his switchblade.

It was lonely out in the country, and Earl had considered hiring a prostitute to wear a gymnastics leotard, a practice session to satisfy his urges before the real thing. But there were no nightclubs, brothels, or escort agencies within five miles.

"You think you can ruin my life!?" he screamed. "What gives you that right?"

Someone thumped the wall. Another lodger? The old building lacked soundproofing, so he should be more careful, but the peaceful isolation was driving him crazy.

Earl cut out the publicity photo and added six solo images of Cassie from the broadsheets and tabloids. His paper tower was inches high. She escaped by sheer fortune the last time, but the national treasure would beg for mercy soon enough.

Today's women didn't appreciate the hard work needed to succeed. His father had educated him, with methods some would call barbaric. But after the beatings, Earl understood life wasn't supposed to be easy.

His classmates had ridiculed him in fake upper class accents, mocking his noble-titled name, but they stopped making jokes after he beat their ringleader in a schoolyard brawl. One punch had fractured the twit's jaw with a satisfying crack. Earl received a suspension from the headmaster for putting the lad in hospital, but nobody dared disrespect him again.

How many had thought themselves superior until he showed them who was stronger? Catherine – his unfaithful witch of a wife – slept with a well-off colleague. To punish her infidelity, he thumped her until she sobbed in regret.

The cops and courts supported the woman, of course, and weren't interested in Earl's side of the story.

The divorce settlement awarded her the house and ordered him to pay two hundred thousand in damages. Television networks dropped him from their punditry teams, but the dagger blow was the University of York taking away his dream coaching job. They made him a pariah, all because of that gold-digging bitch.

That happened ten months ago, but Earl had visited the campus many times since. Knowledge of security flaws and a spare key allowed easy access to the sports centre. The bastards had removed the Coach of the Year awards, but some old yearbook team photos remained on display. That explained how those student vigilantes recognised him.

Seeing all the pretty young blondes made Earl think of Catherine. He had represented his God damn country, so why should his lousy turncoat friends get the beautiful women?

York's streets were well policed, even at night, but the campus was his territory. The first girl quelled his sexual desire for a few weeks, but the compulsion returned. Two more satisfying conquests, and there would have been another if Cassie's boyfriend hadn't interfered.

Earl stabbed down and carved a cross through the reporter's face. Wooden splinters popped up through the slits.

"You're dead! You hear me? When I'm done, you and your pretty girl will be the story. How do you feel about that?"

More banging from next door, but Earl didn't care. He went through the news clippings, slashed female images with his blade, and dumped them in the trash. He saved individual Hexagon model shots, the group photo – the five bitches – and the gymnast's handstand for his target practice grid.

Nowadays, girls had it easy. All these positive action campaigns and women's sports scholarships had left them soft. Like the other deviants, Cassie needed to be taught a lesson.

A police siren wailed outside – still distant, but getting closer. They had found him.

"Damn it!"

Earl hurriedly shoved the important things into a carrier bag. Through the lattice window, he noticed a single blue flashing light. Just one patrol car approached along the country lane, but once they identified him, the Old Bill would swarm the village.

Loose paper and cutouts were everywhere, and there wasn't time to tidy up. With no alternative exit, he ran down the noisy staircase. The racket brought the burly redheaded landlord from the ground floor pub.

"Hey!" the snarling man said. "We've had complaints. You making a scene up there?"

The bumbling oaf wasn't a threat. Earl shoved him down and charged through the front door.

"You lousy bastard. You owe me for any damages!"

The fleeing fugitive wasn't about to stop. It was raining heavily, which should assist the getaway, but with the police alerted, he needed to avoid the main roads.

A dreary cross-country march lay ahead, but Earl knew where to resume his search for Cassie. Hexagon Sports.

* * *

Cassie's name was etched on the hexagonal glass plaque. In silver, below the company logo and silhouetted acrobatic gymnast. The commemorative ornament she'd received from Tamara was heavy. She held on tight, scared it would slip from her little fingers.

"Transparent," Elena said. "Just like woman who gave them to us."

Her trophy design was identical except for the athlete's details. The Ukrainian's long name was smaller in font size, awkwardly squeezed in at the bottom, and the engraved image depicted a figure skater with one leg raised.

"It's a gift," Cassie said. "To mark the launch of her new label. How many companies give employees a joining present?"

"Exactly my point. They want to buy soul, piece by piece. Pretend we are special. But we like mannequins."

Elena looked round at the array of statues that populated the lobby. The Modern Woman exhibit had displaced the sporting legends collection near reception. People would have to actually walk around Cassie's likeness to reach the lifts. Her pedestal was still vacant, but she would be a famous figure.

"To be moved about whenever needed," Elena said. "Today, we are star attraction. Tomorrow, maybe we are ones sidelined."

Her negative outlook suggested a story of upheaval. With families in Ukraine torn apart by loss and conflict, optimism was a luxury few could afford.

Elena had donned her coat, not the fancy fur stereotype associated with Eastern European cultures, but a simple hooded jacket. Black, like her perspective on life. One button was missing and there was a tear on the sleeve. She carried a cheap rucksack for her skates and outfit, and her thick winter boots were unsuitable for the season.

"You mentioned an older brother," Cassie said. "At the

launch party."

Elena needed a friend, even if she wouldn't admit it, and sharing stories might help. Their side booth was away from foot traffic, the perfect place to chat before they finished work.

"Not older. He is little one," she explained. "I take care of him. Before war even begin, I come to England to make money."

"See? We're not so different after all."

Was that the faintest of smiles? Elena's shell was cracking, then she went all stiff again.

"I share," she said harshly. "Not keep. Since father died, family struggle. Now brother in army and mother alone. It is not safe, but she will not leave home."

"I understand."

The standard response, but a white lie in reality. How could a sheltered Briton comprehend suffering on that scale?

"You brave woman. Way you exposed that man to world."

Elena's comment brought Earl Bennett into the conversation – and Cassie's thoughts. Was that sicko targeting other women? Waiting outside to ambush them on their journey home? Why had there been no daily update from the police?

Lights dimmed as the shift ended, and the clock chimed six times. The giant hexagonal face was integrated into the ceiling above, doubling as a window into the first floor admin office.

"You take risk for greater good," Elena said. "That is admirable."

"My boyfriend doesn't agree. He thinks it was reckless. We're not even talking anymore. You know what? To hell with him."

The skater put her gloved hand on Cassie's lap.

"He just concerned. Be grateful you have man like that."

"I guess. My parents thought the contract was a bad idea, too. They were angry I didn't consult them first. Don't they understand I'm an adult and make my own decisions? My mother always dreamt I would follow her into media, which pretty much decided what A-levels and degree I took. To her, gymnastics is a hobby, but to me..."

"You are woman of many talents, Cassie. I cannot say what path is best for you, but you will make right choice."

Elena's compliment lifted the tension a little. She stood up and exited the building, but not without an appreciative hug and smile. A wider one that suggested progress.

Cassie felt something dig into her upper leg as she stepped back. The sharp corner of a solid object.

Elena had left her Modern Woman plaque on the cushion. Face down on a blue background, the engraved text was almost impossible to read. Seen through thick glass, the blurry but motionless figure skater resembled a helpless fish out of water.

* * *

The storage unit lights flickered on, illuminating the row of five silver mannequins. Similar to those in the foyer exhibit, but produced by another company, they were ideal training dummies. The clothes and equipment were Hexagon Sports products, easy to purchase online without arousing suspicion.

Cassie's design hadn't been officially unveiled, but forward planning was essential. The mock gymnast was beside her fellow models, posed in her leg split handstand. Circular clamps around the wrists kept the figure stationary on the balance beam. People had praised the young woman for exposing Bennett, but her shiny leotard promoted the corrupt brand, and signing the contract had sealed her fate.

The black gloved occupant closed the sliding steel door. Poppleton Business Park was close to the Hexagon complex. Many items were covered by dark cloth to mitigate the risk of some passerby seeing incriminating evidence. Three years of patient prep work, but one careless mistake could undo everything.

Cold and damp inside, the unheated thirty square metre property was originally intended as a staging area. Until research exposed a back route into the tower. Those vain executives thought their offices were impregnable, but that was another company lie. Wilson's staged suicide had proved that.

Infiltrating the building was a crucial first step, but the top floor was protected by surveillance cameras. After making enquiries on the dark web, the killer bought a remote hacking module to splice into the video feeds. Fibre optic cables ran through a control hub in the sub-basement, and installing the device was shockingly simple.

The murderer pulled away a sheet to reveal the monitor screens. Brad wasn't the only one watching events at Hexagon. The predictable guard patrols had been easy to avoid. And Wilson was a weakling, no match for an assailant with extensive physical training on the barbells, treadmill and pull-up bar.

Every target had a dedicated section on the planning board. The killer had studied daily routines, building schematics, social habits, and potential entry routes. The false scheme to murder themself would confuse the police when they inevitably discovered the hideout.

Hexagon will pay for what they did to you.

The murderer inspected the glass fragments laid out before the charred mannequin. Meandering cracks across the reassembled plaque converged at the engraved female swimmer. Pulverised by a single punch, the company logo and inscribed name were unreadable. Over four years later, memories of that life-changing night in York remained vivid.

"Wilson was just the first. The others will die, too. The women who sold their bodies to Hexagon, and those who exploit them."

The killer opened the storage crate and removed their personalised outfit. It took a couple of minutes to change into the all-black disguise.

The mask clipped onto the hood, concealing the wearer's face and hair. A glance in the mirror showed visible eyes, but the thin-holed metallic gauze covered the mouth area, and theatrical paint would hide any telltale eyebrows or skin.

Protective rubber pads attached to the torso, limbs and crotch by nylon straps acted as armour. Any victims that fought back, or cops who interfered, would find the killer a tough opponent. Metal rings on the wrists and upper thighs were a recent addition, designed to work with the custom-made leather choker.

That was on the workbench with the electroshock weapon, dart gun, auto-injection ammunition, gas grenades, and combat knife. More dark web acquisitions to avoid leaving a trace. The spray paint, steel cables, and surgical gloves were already in the flat backpack.

The first model lived in the city, so that needed extra planning. A long coat and beanie hat would hide the incriminating outfit, and the mask wouldn't be required until the break-in.

The killer walked to the leftmost mannequin and brushed the auburn wig back to expose the silver face. Solid convex eyes reflected the masked person as they raised the choker and dropped it over the head.

They used the wrist rings to snare the metal hooks riveted to the buckled straps. A sharp separation of the arms and the collar tightened around the neck. The long hook arcs ensured the pulling loops wouldn't come free unintentionally.

Leather creaked as the murderer increased pressure. Hair caught under the noose pressed against the silver plastic underneath. After a fierce strangulation attack, the mannequin head came clean off, broken at the joint. It landed face up by the fallen decapitated torso.

"Time to die, Elena."

The voice was unrecognisable, muffled by the gauze. Creepy and intimidating, as intended. The hypocrite would be terrified, alone in her apartment. Then the choker would silence her screams.

CHAPTER SIX

A Coat of Silver

Elena Savikova was the only commuter standing on platform one. There were no numbered signs, and a single rail track ran in each direction. The only options were to travel towards Leeds or York.

Poppleton station dated back to the nineteenth century. Nearby buildings – including the old conductor house – were privately owned. The age of automation meant no staff or ticket booths, and facilities were basic at the small rural terminal. A glass enclosed waiting area and wooden benches provided comfort, and an electronic ticker displayed destinations and expected arrival times.

Wind whistled through trees by the white picket fence, developing into a fierce gust that made Elena's coat flutter. Bells clanged as barriers lowered at the nearby level crossing. The noise had startled her when she first started at Hexagon, but now she knew the chimes heralded a train's imminent arrival, they came as a relief.

Dusk was an hour away, so the floodlights were inactive. A woman travelling alone had to be careful, but compared to the war ravaged Ukraine, the Yorkshire Dales weren't so dangerous. In this country, backstabbing happened in boardrooms instead of combat zones.

Elena massaged her legs to ward off the early evening chill. Figure skating outfits weren't designed for prolonged exposure to cold, so this afternoon's training session had been unpleasant. Her casual sweater and knee-length practical coat were a marked improvement. The woollen scarf and thick hood shielded her face from the frosty breeze. Small comforts, but she had learnt to appreciate them, and would soon be in the warmth and relative safety of a railway carriage.

"Got the time?"

The impolite query made Elena jump. She turned to see a bushy bearded man with dirty brown hair and a deep, snaky scar below his right eye. He reeked of cheap booze – a horrid, repulsive stench.

"It is on board up there." She stifled a cough. "Do you need me to read?"

The electronic clock was in plain sight, but considering his drunken, bleary-eyed state…

"It is eighteen twenty-four. Almost half-past six. Do not worry. You have not missed train."

"Saying I can't read?" the bearded man sneered. "You a smart ass, eh? What's that funny accent of yours? Can't even talk proper English. You foreigners come here, take our jobs, and yer poke fun at us. So don't get coy with me."

His teeth were stained yellow with plaque, and his grimy overcoat and ripped jeans probably hadn't been cleaned for months. His opinion stemmed from a dislike of

Europeans, and this was an argument for the sake of having one.

"I only try to help. Not here to take job. Few men have correct balance for skating."

"Correct balance? As in bank balance? You one of them posh types, then?"

A poor choice of words, but would better phrasing have made any difference? The drunk was poorly educated and biased.

Mercifully, the train arrived before the conversation escalated into violence. It screeched to a halt beside the platform, and Elena dashed to the nearest door. The racist ruffian opted not to board, which was a relief.

It was evening rush hour, and the carriage was full of passengers. Which meant plenty of witnesses, so the man wouldn't dare try anything.

"Go back home!"

That outburst made commuters stop and look. Then the doors closed and stranded the bigot at Poppleton station. Prejudice and inaccurate assumptions about European workers were nothing new, but ill feelings weren't normally expressed so overtly.

Elena held onto a vertical metal pole, struggling to banish the incident from her mind. She intended no offence, not that the drunken lout cared. Since emigrating from Ukraine, she had transferred most earnings to her family. That left precious little money for the training a professional athlete needed, or English as a Foreign Language lessons.

Most British citizens had welcomed her, but there was a growing minority that valued nationalism above kindness. Elena sensed resentment from her neighbours whenever she mentioned her profession. They assumed sports models were rich, when in reality she was poorer than the average worker. While many employees owned cars, she depended on Northern Rail and its unreliable schedule.

The rest of the ten-minute journey was uneventful. Darkness had fallen when Elena arrived at York station, but the concourse under the curved wrought iron and glass roof was brightly lit. British Transport Police had officers on duty, there was extensive CCTV coverage, and the one-bedroom apartment she rented was within walking distance, along a pedestrianised route through a busy city centre.

So why was she apprehensive? The bigoted local who harassed her at Poppleton hadn't boarded the train, but Elena couldn't shake the feeling someone was following her.

She spied a tallish figure dressed in a black cloak and beanie cap standing outside the coffee shop. The mystery person looked at a nearby window instead of the framed menu, almost as if watching reflections of disembarking passengers.

It was surely paranoia, an overreaction after the nasty incident with the drunk. An automated service cancellation message played over the loudspeakers as Elena left the station. After crossing the River Ouse, she took a long detour south through The Shambles. She glanced over her shoulder several times, but didn't notice any black-coated men in the crowd.

Hemmed in by timber-framed medieval buildings with square muntin windows, the historic street was claustrophobic. There was no avoiding the pungent stink of raw fish from the market stalls. Shoppers stopped to sing along with a guitar duo act performing outside the Olde English Tavern, creating a bottleneck that Elena had to slot sideways through.

She quickened her pace and returned to her normal route, only slowing down once she reached the gloomy cobbled side street that led to *Minster View* apartments. The Victorian lanterns mounted on ornate brackets were stylish, but not the greatest light source. Flat soled boots didn't help traverse the uneven stones, but they were preferable to high heels.

Elena inputted the four-digit combination to open the electronic gate and rushed into the communal hall. To avoid the narrow, secluded stairs, she rode the lift to the fifth floor, grateful she wasn't the only resident using it this evening. It took a moment to find the key ring amongst the junk in her pocket, but she made it inside. Safe for another day.

Elena double checked she had bolted the door, then hung her cloak and rucksack on steel hooks by the maintenance closet. That faint hum was still coming from the junction box within, a technical problem the landlord hadn't fixed despite three phone calls. She regretted renting the apartment privately instead of through a letting agency, but low monthly overhead had been the priority.

This was no luxury abode. The furniture was a mix of battered second-hand cabinets and cheap catalogue store purchases. The bathroom sink had mould underneath it and the toilet bowl had a lingering smell of urine. Most light fixtures were only bulbs hanging on insulated cables. Paint had peeled off the radiators and the central heating was energy inefficient, so Elena usually left it switched off.

The kitchen and living area merged into a single, long room with varnished hardwood tiles and cream coloured walls. The fridge and oven had been surprisingly fault free over the two-year tenancy, and the unremarkable cupboards had plenty of storage capacity.

Decorations were limited to empty glass vases, abstract paintings, and tarnished brass ornaments. Those were present when Elena moved in and verified the inventory. The only cosmetic additions were steel framed photographs of her mother and older brother. They were her motivation whenever she felt guilty about working for Hexagon.

She prepared her evening meal, tipping a plate of pasta into a saucepan and putting the gas stove on medium heat. Blue flames roared through the hob, providing welcome warm air. Raised by wheat farmers in Berezivka near the Moldovan border, she appreciated a simple but healthy dinner. It would be ready in twenty minutes – enough time for a routine.

Elena drew the heavy chocolate brown curtains. More than once she had seen male voyeurs watching from the hotel opposite. Homes were private and, despite the apartment block's name, only one tower of York's iconic Minster was visible from the balcony. So much for the view.

Elena kicked off her boots and selected a music track to play on the sound system. Myroslav Skoryk composed *Melody in A Minor* during the Soviet regime. Known for embodying Ukrainian resilience, it was perhaps an obvious choice, but also a poignant reminder of why the figure skater tolerated her demeaning job, apathetic landlords, and racist louts.

In the weeks before Christmas, *Yorkshire's Winter Wonderland* offered ice skating at affordable prices, but attempting to perform a professional dance with fun-loving families was impossible. The living room space was obstruction free, giving Elena about six square metres to practise in. Much smaller than a purpose-built rink, but it didn't drain her bank account.

She skipped around and used her momentum to spin on one elevated foot. Then she raised her outstretched leg to waist height and completed two full revolutions before friction slowed her. Her quick turns suited the dramatic opening to *Melody*. Bubbles popped as the pan water boiled, spewing a faint cloud of steam into the clunky extractor fan.

The music's middle portion was much calmer. Elena closed her eyes and darted around the floor. Blotting out the visual world allowed her to reminisce about her beloved family.

Her mother knitted a sweater, the same garment she still wore. In the irrigated crop field, her brother reaped wheat, providing for the entire community. Elena imagined breathing sweet farmyard air instead of York's petrol fumes. Happy memories of teenage bliss, years before she left to seek a better future in England and the Russian invasion tore her country apart.

The music halted abruptly, and Elena opened her eyes. Everything in the flat was dark except the gas oven. Flickering blue light created moving shadows around her. The kitchen counter and cupboard were dim objects, identifiable by shiny metal handles and sharp edges.

"Durbelyk landlord."

A Ukrainian curse, but the gist would be obvious even to a non-native speaker.

"You expect me to fix panel? Why do I pay rent?"

Shouting wouldn't rectify the problem, but venting her anger was better than feeling depressed.

Bubbles were loud and frequent, but Elena needed the gaslight to see. She retrieved the electric torch from the cabinet under the sink. Fearful that would also break to compound her dreadful day, she was relieved when pressing the rubbery button generated a powerful, focused beam.

Everything was the right colour again. Elena hastened along the corridor to the maintenance closet. Behind her, water hissed and vaporised as the saucepan boiled over, but the overflow wasn't an immediate concern. She could switch off the oven once she restored power.

The dusty interior of the walk-in storage space could barely be considered a room. There was no wallpaper, only cracked concrete. Stainless steel shelves were bare except for a few miscellaneous items. The powerful torchlight revealed cobwebs around a packet of large cartridge fuses.

Elena grabbed them without a second thought and brushed the sticky threads from her fingers. Spiders were a minor inconvenience, nothing to be afraid of.

She opened the electrical junction box and shone the torch over the circuits to locate the damaged component. Except there wasn't one, and everything seemed normal. No scorch marks on the fuse casings, no smoke, and no exposed wires.

The main lever was in the downward "off" position, which made no sense unless an automatic safety mechanism had cut the power. But how? The system wasn't that sophisticated.

Loud, high-pitched beeping made Elena drop the spare part in fright. She spun round to check the closet, but saw only the half-open door and faint steam rising in the hallway. The boiling water must have triggered the kitchen smoke detector.

Elena exhaled with relief and turned back to the junction box. She was about to pull the lever when something flashed before her eyes. A blade pressed against her throat, held by a shadowy figure in black.

The weapon was a military style knife with a serrated edge and grip handle. Warm air blew against her neck as the intruder breathed.

"If you here for money, I do not have much."

No answer. What did this lunatic want? And how had he broken into her apartment with the door bolted?

A belt-like leathery loop dropped over Elena's head. The

mysterious attacker removed the knife and... Sheathed it? That's what the scraping noise suggested.

She instinctively reached up to remove the mystery object. Two faint metallic clinks, almost in sync, and the choker tightened around her throat.

Breathless, Elena flung the torch in panic. Light cast shadows on the wall: a slim female figure being throttled by a much bulkier person behind.

Elena's strangled gasps were barely audible over the smoke alarm, still beeping in the kitchen. The beam rotated, creating a lighthouse-like effect with periodic illumination. Briefly seen silhouettes showed broken action. The intruder pulled their arms apart. Straps tightened, hooked to wrists by rings.

The leather stretched as the attacker lifted Elena in the air. She kicked her legs, seeking a foothold. Even through her insulated socks, she felt cold, rough concrete under her toes.

One foot struck the power lever. The dull clang reverberated as lights switched on and *Melody* blurted from the living room speakers.

The masked intruder was visible in the hall mirror – an armoured assailant choking her to death. This was no ordinary break in. Someone wanted her dead.

The orchestra increased in tempo, reaching the climatic section as Elena struggled hopelessly. She thumped at the killer's wrists, but only injured her knuckles against the impervious protective rubber pads. An attempt to swing her foot into the intruder's face encountered the hard plastic mask.

Elena clawed at the choker, now tight as a hangman's noose. She grabbed one strap two handed, but it remained immovable. Her weak effort only twisted the leather. She kicked again, but her leg felt unnaturally heavy and barely moved.

Her family had presumed she would be safer in England, away from the war, but she was about to die in this supposedly peaceful land, thousands of miles from home.

Images of her Ukrainian childhood town flashed before her. Her mother berated her for some silly mistake. She hugged her brother and reassured him leaving was for the best.

As her sight faded and eternal night beckoned, Elena's final thoughts weren't about the identity of her murderer, but her family. How would they cope without her support?

* * *

The murderer switched off the stove and filled the saucepan with cold water. Dried pasta crumbled into hard tubular fragments that floated to the surface. To clear the steam, the killer opened the balcony doors, careful to stay behind the curtain. Black gloves might not seem suspicious to potential onlookers, but a masked intruder certainly would.

Almost everything had gone according to plan. Elena's train arrived at York on schedule, and deliberately being spotted by her instilled fear. The changed route enabled the fast moving killer to arrive at *Minster View* ten minutes before her and bypass the electronic keypad. Most residents didn't cover their fingers when they inputted the code, so it was easy to learn in advance.

As expected, the rooftop stairwell access was unlocked. The steel-lined door screeched as the intruder forced it open, but nobody came to investigate. It was risky tying the climbing rope to the railing, but the balconies were poorly lit. A black-clad, hooded figure was practically invisible.

It took a minute to descend, pick the simple lock, and hang the cable over a light fixture. That ensured the girl wouldn't see it should she peek outside. In these cold conditions, she was unlikely to venture onto the balcony.

Once inside the apartment, the maintenance closet was a perfect hiding place. The blueprints the killer had studied in advance were accurate. An eight-inch gap between the door and wall was wide enough to hide, mask up, and wait.

The Ukrainian was no fighter. Slightly built with twig-like limbs, she succumbed easily, and her tame physical resistance meant the armour was unnecessary. There were tougher tests ahead, but the choker, hooks and rings setup had proved effective and versatile.

The smoke alarm was unexpected. But fortunately, Elena switched the power back on, and music drowned out the constant beeps.

It was almost a costly mistake. After the extensive preparation, being thwarted by chance would have been disastrous, but the threat of discovery had passed, and the killer could prepare the murder scene as intended.

Modern Woman. Hexagon's promotional pack depicted these sellouts as heroines, but they were pawns of the corporate machine.

The intruder fetched the flat backpack from the closet, then the body. Elena was lighter than most women her age, and it required little exertion to drag her corpse to the kitchen counter.

The killer placed their tools beside the face down victim, then took off the black gloves to expose their rubber surgical equivalents.

First, Elena's clothes had to be removed. The sweater and leggings were easy to cut away with the combat knife. Naked except for a white bra and undergarments, her moist skin already reflected the spotlights above.

Her short-skirted pink dress and branded ice skates were ready, but before dressing the body, the killer would transform her into a symbol of exploitation.

They took the spray paint can, shook it, and wrote their eight letter message on the wall opposite the window. Seeing the silver angular styled word brought back memories of how this started. The connection with the past wouldn't be obvious to the police, but they would learn the full truth about Hexagon Sports and the person they sacrificed.

The first female to die was arguably the most innocent, but like the other models, she had sold her soul. The murderer sprayed silver paint over the victim's back and spread the coating until it formed a thin shiny layer.

Under the apartment lamps, the corpse looked better than intended. A reflective symbol of Hexagon's attitude towards women, Elena Savikova would be immortalised, posed for the world to see.

* * *

The School of Arts and Creative Technologies was suitably modern. Exterior walls were various shades of grey, though all of them appeared black at night. The two story building was accessible via a flashy glass panelled entrance fronted by a hedged lawn. Lecturers and students often worked into the late evening, and tall elongated office windows provided more illumination than the lamp posts.

The York Gazette editorial desks were in a single cramped room, sandwiched between a hi-tech media suite and a music recording studio. With the uproar around Earl Bennett and his university connections, the student reporters were extremely busy, and many had returned early from Easter break to cover the ongoing manhunt.

Lyle was more interested in Hexagon Sports. He had scanned his laptop browser for over an hour, searching every keyword he could think of. Opinion was divided on social media. Tamara Cole lauded her Modern Woman line as a new beginning, but while official channels supported her claim, independent commentary was far more scathing.

Cassie's sting operation had given the Wade Wilson scandal extra momentum, and the story wouldn't go away despite the company's efforts to bury it. Gutsy women accusing wealthy celebrities was the hot topic. Hexagon bashing had become a sport in itself, and the "breasts for business" controversy had even been debated in Parliament.

Predictably, the company website was censored. Wade Wilson had effectively been erased from existence, and the homepage showcased Tamara's launch event. The marquee image featured the five models in their signature poses, with metadata and a biography for each.

Cassie's leg split handstand had become an international symbol of a determined, non-sexualised woman. Lyle had found her now-famous photo championed across the Internet, and the gymnast's profile was the top trending BBC news article.

"Thought you and your girlfriend weren't on the same page," Dan said.

He normally worked on Thursdays, but the sports centre was closed indefinitely. A former employee with a history of domestic abuse had assaulted three women on campus, and nearly a fourth. That demanded an internal security review. The principal had taken personal charge, and damage limitation trumped budget concerns.

"Or should I say ex-girlfriend? Would you look at that? A national hero. Even your banker dad isn't in that league."

Lyle thought it best to humour his friend.

"Tamara Cole still wants me to run the story on her product label. It's a big story."

He glanced round the cork bulletin boards. Official notices and adverts competed with old headline clippings and award certificates. It was a messy collage, but Modern Woman model photos – and that leg split pose – were prominent recent additions.

"Well, your last great idea almost got me fired," Dan said. "And things don't seem to have panned out for you. It is okay to dump girls these days. No need to play the knight in shining armour."

"I told you…"

"It's all about Tamara Cole. Come on, admit it. It's not the Hexagon story that's hot."

Dan tapped the nearest photo of Cassie. Before Lyle could comment, an alarm siren drew his gaze to the laptop. A red bell icon flashed beside a superimposed caption box. *NEWS ALERT - ELENA SAVIKOVA.*

"Or maybe you found a new girlfriend? Guess that makes sense, though you might try a dating site."

Lyle ignored the sarcastic commentary. His hand tightened around the USB mouse as he scrolled through a pop-up window.

The barely readable text was full of acronyms and police lingo. *Major Incident Declared at Minster View Apts. CSI attending. Victim identified as Elena Savikova.*

"She's one of the models, right? I better not ask where you got that, or I'll be in trouble. Lyle, I realise this is a big scoop, but…"

Dan paused, mouth open as he read the latest line.

Murder enquiry launched. MIT to liaise with DI Quinn.

"Holy shit! We should leave this to the cops. We don't want to get involved…"

But Lyle was already on his way out. Ignoring Dan's vocal protest, he achieved record time and reached his parked car in under a minute. The roads from the campus to the urban centre were quiet, which gave him the opportunity to think.

A technically minded contact – a posh name for a hacker – had owed Lyle a favour. The *York Gazette*'s investigation into a stock trading scam last semester exonerated the software's author of wrongdoing and exposed corrupt insiders as the true culprits. At first, the indebted techie outright refused to scan intercepted police reports for Hexagon model related keywords. But the cleared debt and additional financial incentive – the "small" sum of five thousand pounds – prompted him to reconsider.

Now Lyle wondered if the information was worth the high price. What the hell was he doing? Cassie had made it clear the priority was her gymnastics career. But he couldn't leave this alone, not with Bennett on the loose. A violent rapist would have no problem hurting the woman who exposed him, or her equally attractive colleagues.

Lyle feared another sex attack might happen, but a murder… That news had left him so shaken he struggled to concentrate on driving. Should he have done more? Could he? Cassie refused to listen.

The cops had already established road blocks around *Minster View*. Officers dressed in hi-vis jackets directed intrigued pedestrians away from the apartment block. Lyle spotted patrol cars, two vans, and even some canine units. A student press ID wouldn't get him through that security net.

He opened his laptop on the passenger seat and accessed

the 3D mapping software, a farewell present from his contact. Science fiction music played as the camera passed over a blueprint style landscape of central York.

The pop-up information didn't list residents, only street address and postcode, but Lyle could tell Miss Savikova's place was on the fifth floor. The woman wearing the white lab coat must be forensics, which made that balcony – and apartment – a crime scene.

A few minutes of scanning revealed a vulnerability. The hotel opposite wasn't cordoned off, and its eastern entrance was away from police activity. Major chains usually had twenty-four-hour reception desks, so it should be accessible.

Lyle grabbed his professional camera and exited his vehicle. He dashed through the side alleyway, ignoring the idiot youths he passed. As he'd hoped, the hotel's main doors were unlocked. He nodded at the female receptionist, passing himself off as a guest.

Once out of her view, he picked up the pace. Five floors up, he headed to the corridor's far end and opened the window. Cold air blew in as he raised the camera and adjusted the zoom.

Elena's apartment came into focus. Someone had tied a rope to a roof guardrail, and used it to access the balcony. The forensics lady collected samples, and more lab coated investigators were inside, studying torn down curtains and a silver mannequin.

Those two detectives – Quinn and Moore – stared at it. The auburn wig was almost a replica of Elena's long hair, split across her shiny shoulder. With the pink dress and bladed ice skates, it was hard not to think of "her" as Miss Savikova.

It was the most bizarre scene Lyle had ever witnessed. A web of steel cables and rings held the statue's limbs in place, secured with locking bolts. A taut wire, attached to a light fixture, kept one leg elevated. Her outstretched wrists were bound to it with black plastic zip ties.

The pose – a figure skater clutching her ankle – was the same as the Hexagon photo. Even tiny details, such as the skirt draped over her raised left thigh, were identical.

But why were police so interested in…

Lyle adjusted the focus and almost vomited. He wasn't looking at a mannequin. It was *Elena Savikova* strung up in that apartment.

She was painted silver. Arms, legs, body. Every square millimetre of her face. A second skin that reflected blurry images of the crime scene investigators. Only the dead woman's eyes, staring vacantly ahead, were untouched.

A uniformed officer was called away, and Lyle saw writing behind the murder victim, sprayed on the wall in shiny paint.

ELEGANCE.

The same six-sided angular font design as the Hexagon Sports logo, but without background spokes.

Who could have done this to an innocent young woman? Lyle didn't have a name, but he could answer the question.

This was a perfectly staged death scene. The work of a cold-blooded killer.

CHAPTER SEVEN

Under Suspicion

"Eighteen years in this job. Thought I'd seen everything, but I gotta admit this is new."

Those were the first words Detective Inspector Quinn had spoken since entering Elena Savikova's apartment. In the lift, DC Moore had warned him about the shocking scene, but he dismissed her concerns as inexperience. She was young, and hadn't dealt with race riots, a high-profile kidnapping, or gang murders. Or stared down the twin barrels of a sawn-off shotgun during an armoured van robbery.

Those experiences hardened a person, made them cynical, but this crime scene was a whole other level of sadism.

"I said it was bad, boss."

Quinn would apologise back at the station. Right now, he had to deal with a deceased woman painted as a silver mannequin. The dressed-up figure skater was suspended by steel cables, hands fastened around her raised leg. The killer had treated the victim like a life-sized doll, a plaything in a pink dress.

Her family in Ukraine would have to be contacted. A sympathetic angle increased the stakes. How long before an opportunist politician blamed the police for an immigrant's murder?

Quinn directed his attention elsewhere, hard as that was. "So the killer cuts down the curtains and leaves the volume on full blast. He wanted us to find the body quickly."

The sound system was switched off, but the case began with a phone call from the resident below. A routine report of noise disturbance became concern for safety, then first degree murder. The Chief Constable would assign a Major Incident Team, but for the moment, Quinn was the lead investigator. Two months from retirement, a ritual killing was the last thing he needed.

Excited chatter came from the street. The press representatives were growing in number. Quinn wanted to shut the balcony doors and pretend those pests weren't there, but CSI hadn't finished with the forensic sweep.

"The girl was so young," Moore said. "What kind of monster does this? Somebody that doesn't like sports models? Who hates Hexagon?"

She studied the silver *ELEGANCE* message behind the dead model. The air nearby still reeked of fresh paint.

"That's a long suspect list, Moore. Too long."

His investigative partner looked round the room. It was the very definition of basic, a perfectly ordinary low budget flat. But this murder scene was anything but normal.

"We got no witnesses," she said. "No prints around the

body, and no real leads. Hardly any personal items. Only the essentials and two family photographs. What do we have exactly?"

"A damn headache."

A uniformed officer entered the living area, followed by a familiar student reporter. That annoying vigilante was wrapped in a thermal jacket, with a chrome laptop tucked under his arm. Quinn confronted the PC with a harsh glare, making his opinion clear.

"He said he had important information, sir. About Miss Savikova, the victim. And…"

The policeman gulped, his swallow loud enough to hear, and looked away from the body.

"You were saying?" Quinn prompted.

"Why the killer posed her like that."

"So he's an informant now. Wonderful. You'd best guard the door, son. Don't want to contaminate a crime scene with puke."

The officer nodded and left in a hurry. Quinn led the reporter to the rather uncomfortable sofa and beckoned Moore to join them.

"Lyle Norton, University Press and self-appointed media rep. Still chasing a scoop? All your brigade is here. BBC, Sky, Channel Five, Fox News from America. A murder in York is a novelty to them. And what the hell's your interest? It's not your gymnast girlfriend strung up."

That finally got through to him. Only a brief glance down at his computer, but it definitely resonated.

"I thought you could use some help," Norton said.

He opened the laptop. It was already booted up, with a browser window expanded to full screen. The URL was Hexagon's official website.

This kid was determined to interfere. Baiting a sex

offender was bad enough, but this was a murder investigation.

"I thought we agreed to leave police work to the professionals," Quinn said. "She worked for Hexagon, and so do about two hundred other people."

"Elena was a sports model. Just like Cassie."

Moore looked equally frustrated with Norton's nosy antics. "We gathered that. Do you have anything important to tell us? Or is this a dumb bluff to gain access to a crime scene?"

The reporter expanded a camera app window. He had images of the victim, taken from across the street.

"You out of your mind?" Moore asked. "Interfering with a murder enquiry?"

"*Helping* the enquiry."

The persistent Norton remained calm, moving his finger expertly over the mouse pad. He dragged Elena Savikova's Modern Woman image beside the crime scene photo.

Quinn did a double take and exchanged glances with Moore. The newer picture had a slightly different camera angle, silver painted skin, and less glamorous backdrop. But the poses were identical.

The website version had *ELEGANCE* superimposed below the skating model. In metallic blue, but the same character style as the killer's graffiti.

"You keep telling me I shouldn't interfere," Norton said. "But there's no way that's coincidence."

* * *

Lyle was waiting by reception when Cassie arrived at the Hexagon tower. She had barely walked in when he approached her. No hot-headed attitude today, just solemn silence.

"Come to apologise for the other night?" she asked.

"Cassie..."

He spoke gently and stepped forward with his arms wide, ready to embrace her. She recoiled as his fingertips brushed her jacket. Did Lyle think his transparent gesture made everything okay? That she'd forgive him for abandoning her at the Modern Woman launch, the most significant milestone of her gymnastics career?

"Cassie, Elena's dead."

"What?"

Events happened in slow motion as she looked round the foyer. A suited bald man – a detective? – interviewed the security chief Brad. By the windows, white-faced employees whispered to each other, one teenage girl in tears. Uniformed officers tapped on tablet computers as executives and admin assistants provided statements.

"They... found her... body at..."

Lyle's elaboration sounded like an audio track played at half speed. He talked about an intercepted police report, but Cassie wasn't able to process the information.

Her legs trembled as she battled the impulse to sit down. The lobby scene turned surreal. Mannequin displays and hexagonal light fixtures became blurry edged shapes, devoid of detail.

Except it was reality crumbling around her. Elena couldn't be dead. Cassie had spoken to her only yesterday evening, in this very room. She replayed the Ukrainian's story in her head.

"I share. Not keep. Since father died, family struggle. Now brother in army and mother alone."

Cassie wiped her wet eyes clear, took a breath, and walked round the reception desk. Twenty metres away,

Tamara and Vince stood by the Modern Woman mannequins, being questioned by two familiar detectives.

A fifth model had been added: a silver figure in a Hexagon Sports leotard, performing a leg split handstand on a shortened balance beam. The statue's hands and bare feet were stained with chalk residue, the same variety Cassie used during gymnastic routines. The wig perfectly recreated her bun-tied hair.

An eerily accurate likeness, and a tribute to Cassie's athletic prowess. But what did that matter? A woman was dead.

"Elena Savikova was one of our models." Vince spoke loudly to get his point across. "But I assure you, Inspector. The company had nothing to do with her death."

"You mean her murder."

DI Quinn was equally vocal. Lyle pulled Cassie behind a hexagonal poster stand. They were within earshot, but the solid object kept them concealed. She peeked around the side and watched the female detective who interviewed her – DC Moore? – study Elena's replica.

"Beautiful design. Saw one like it yesterday, in her apartment. The killer left the victim in that exact pose. Same skirt, same body shape, same skates. Even the same skin colour."

Cassie heard her stomach rumble. How could that woman describe a horrific scene so bluntly?

A moving image of Elena formed in the teenager's mind, except there was a silvery plastic replica in her friend's place.

"They want to buy soul," she said. "Pretend we are special. But we like mannequins."

Her convex mirrored eyes reflected an arrogant media student who wouldn't listen to reason.

"He thinks it was reckless," Cassie's double said. It was easier to imagine someone else was speaking. "You know what? To hell with him."

Lyle clamped his hand over her mouth, suppressing her squeal of terror. She was back in the lobby, the macabre vision of Elena gone.

"So?"

Cassie, feeling lightheaded, needed a moment to identify Vince Harris' voice.

"So, you might want to rethink your response," Quinn said.

"We posted a press article on our website," Tamara argued. "I'm sure you've seen the photo. Thousands of people have, and there's no love out there for Hexagon. Or women's sports. Somebody resented Miss Savikova's success and sent a message. Celebrity status comes with risk. We all know that. You're looking for a misogynist."

"Why does every amateur have an opinion? But now you mention it, the killer did leave a message."

Cassie peeped again and saw the inspector show Tamara a laptop. Vince stepped behind them and peered over their shoulders to view the screen.

"And where have we seen that copycat text style before? If only you'd investigated the vandalism more thoroughly..."

"Not sure we're looking for a hater," Moore said. "Murder is quite a few steps up from fan art."

Tamara spotted Cassie – who had remained in the open – behind the poster stand. The tall woman's body stiffened, accompanied by an angry stare that suggested a reprimand would follow later.

"We should continue this discussion upstairs. In private."

* * *

DI Quinn stood before his masters. That's how Vince Harris and Tamara Cole saw themselves. These corporate types always had over-inflated egos and delusions of grandeur.

The brass wall lamps sparkled, and he could smell furniture polish on the cabinets. Or was it the director's aftershave? The unpleasant truth covered up with layers of oil – how appropriate. Hexagon Sports had new managers at the helm, but despite a forced public apology for the sex scandal, Wilson's suicide had changed nothing.

"You come without a shred of proof," Harris said, "and make nasty, baseless accusations. You're treading on very thin ice."

"Interesting choice of words, considering we're discussing a figure skater."

The cocksure exec sat at the conference table's head, in a luxurious mahogany framed chair. His tailored suit was at least ten times more expensive than Quinn's, and that jewellery was actually gold. Wealth meant power to Harris, and the only surprise was he hadn't summoned a solicitor.

Quinn slapped his crime scene photos down hard. That made those two squirm, but was it the model's horrifying death or his defiance that unnerved them?

The crystal decanter vibrated and shifted on its silver tray, disrupting the perfect world. The board members would probably file a complaint, but so what? He would be claiming a good pension in two months' time.

"Your company stock's in freefall. It would take something pretty sensational to recover."

"Like killing our models?" Cole said. "You obviously understand nothing about marketing. It's not a viable strategy to destroy our key assets."

"*Your* key assets," Vince commented with a smirk.

"Don't feel so threatened. I know a worthy investment."

"Last quarter's dire sales figures suggest otherwise."

The tension was palpable. Ordinary folk usually needed buttering up before they volunteered information, but these two were using business terms to discuss a homicide and make power plays. Competitive instincts were second nature for corporate types, but money and influence were solid motives for murder.

A legal representative would advise their clients to stay silent. Their arrogance to be interviewed without counsel was an opportunity. Quinn had no evidence to confront them with, but some tough questions might loosen their tongues.

"To strangle a girl to death and arrange the body like that..."

He tapped the close shot of the victim's raised ankle pose, and a second photo that showed steel cables holding her in position. It seemed necessary to remind these bickering execs an employee was dead.

"Must have been a strong guy who did this. Or a strong woman, perhaps. A former Olympic athlete would have the muscle power."

He stared straight into Cole's deep blue eyes. Her response was ice cold, with no visual tells. With five years' experience at Hexagon, the former sports star had adapted to the corporate world.

"I had a look through your promotion pack," Quinn said.

The Major Crime Unit had enlarged the Modern Woman image. The detective placed his printout on the conference table and pointed to each model in sequence.

"Elegance, toughness, athleticism, success, courage. That's the tagline for your brand, isn't it? Your five champions. It's just that... someone with all those traits would make a very effective killer. One down leaves four to go. You should consider issuing a safety memo."

"Are we suspects, Inspector?"

Yes. That would be the obvious reply, but Quinn stayed quiet.

He spread two photographs and tapped them as he observed Cole's non-reaction. Could the self-styled "Modern Woman" be the murderer?

Nothing told him no. Her grey business suit didn't conceal her powerful arms, and that long blonde hair would tuck easily into a mask. A witness had reported seeing a black-clad figure rappel down to Savikova's balcony. Vague details, but any leads were precious.

"Persons of interest," Quinn said.

"So you have no idea who's responsible?" Cole asked. "You're fishing for red herrings, making baseless accusations. Vince and I finally agree on something."

A chuckle – did she think this was funny? Quinn placed his flat palms on the table and leant in her face, but she didn't flinch.

"You just confirmed you don't give a shit about Miss Savikova. I misspoke earlier. What I meant was... persons of significant interest."

* * *

The exterior ice rink wasn't in use. Why would it be, when the only figure skater at Hexagon Sports was dead?

Cassie stared down at the frozen white surface. Past the border fencing, she saw twin curved lines, about a hip-width apart. One spun into a spiral, while the other vanished during a single track segment, and re-appeared after a few metres. Without camera footage, the trails were the only physical record of Elena's daring raised leg spin twirl. How long before they were swept away?

"She was doing this to help her family. Elena didn't want to be a model. She hated it here."

Cassie tried to remain brave, but the shocking news had left her sobbing. She wanted to believe the company cared about its models, but there had been no official statement on Elena's murder. Just thinking those two words chilled her.

"But she took the money anyway," Lyle said.

"Trust a reporter to see everything in black and white."

"Sometimes the truth is simple. And you're a reporter too, unless you've quit your course?"

She swivelled to confront him head on, teeth chattering with icy rage.

"What do you care? I thought you broke our fling off. Tamara wanted you to cover Modern Woman, but writing an article about a dead model isn't what she had in mind. So neither of our big career moves went as expected. Let's leave it at that."

Cassie intended to stop after the first line, but anger fuelled her rant. Like opening a shaken soda bottle, her grief poured out.

Lyle angled his laptop sideways so she could view the screen and the photograph of Elena's body. Her mannequin pose. Silver painted skin with white, light reflecting streaks. Auburn hair partly raised in spots where the wind had presumably blown it off her back. Those eyes weren't the mirrors Cassie had imagined, but empty, soulless vessels.

She turned away in disgust. "Shut that thing off. It's sick."

Lyle placed a gentle hand on her shoulder. His patronising gesture enraged her further, but she lacked the energy or willpower to brush him off.

"Just because our relationship's in a rocky patch," he said, "that doesn't mean I've given up on us. I care about you, Cassie."

"I can look after myself."

"Elena probably thought so, too."

"Don't you dare—"

She ended in mid-sentence as Lyle scrolled to a second picture. A silver word written in the Hexagon logo font.

"Elegance," he read. "The killer copied Elena's promo image. This psycho's targeting the brand, not one woman, and there are four more models in Tamara Cole's line, including you. Sure exposing Earl Bennett was the smartest play?"

With the whirlwind of events – the contract signing, launch party, a shocking murder – Cassie had forgotten about her sting operation. But that bastard was still roaming free.

"You think Bennett did this? Why? Elena wasn't a student."

"But he knew one. The brave young lady who ruined his life."

Lyle finished with a smile. Was that criticism or a compliment?

"Exposing that creep to the world?" Cassie said. "Yeah, I'm really sorry about that. He didn't deserve to be reviled for assaulting three women."

She was back to neutral sarcasm, but not warm friendship.

"Or maybe it's your new boss you should be afraid of," Lyle said.

"Tamara?"

He rested the laptop on the upper fence pole and drew his finger across the touch-sensitive screen. The scrolling picture gallery had more distance shots of Elena's posed corpse that Cassie forced herself to watch.

Lyle sped through the morbid album and enlarged a photo of a baby-faced blonde girl wearing a Hexagon Sports swimsuit. She looked late teens, perhaps early twenties. Had she been on the news recently?

The young woman resembled a tamer version of Tamara. She had the same statuesque form, but her eyes were wide with fright. A deer caught in multiple spotlights from behind the camera.

The breeze picked up. Cassie clutched her overcoat and hastily fastened the zipper to prevent it from blowing away.

"Who's the girl?"

Lyle dragged the picture aside, and a broadsheet newspaper article replaced it. The front page had the photo in black and white, below the headline: *TRAGEDY OF A FALLEN CHAMPION*. Under that, in smaller but impactful print: *Disgraced Swimmer Commits Suicide During Olympics*.

"Gemma Bright."

Cassie didn't need to skim the text. The tragedy happened four years ago, ancient history in media circles, but she remembered the outrage and recriminations. Why had Lyle brought this up?

"I don't get it," she said. "What does a suicide have... Are you saying it was murder?"

"She was the European champion. The fastest swimmer in Olympic trials, tipped to break the world record at Tokyo. The bookies had her favourite to win the two hundred metres freestyle, Tamara's big event. What if the pool queen didn't like someone challenging her throne?"

Cassie regretted laughing under the circumstances, but this was utterly absurd.

"Excellent research, Lyle. Did you read that article? Bright was taking testosterone. She was a cheater, not a champion. They only used that headline out of respect."

"And the great British press fact-check what they print? The allegations were never proven. They found drugs at her house, but evidence can be planted. What if this was a cover up? We should go to Loughborough and find out what really happened four years ago."

"A romantic road trip to satisfy your curiosity? You're clutching at straws. What if some random nutter killed Elena? You don't know the rest of us are targets."

Lyle had no facts to support his wild claims, so why were Cassie's arguments so weak? Perhaps it was doubt creeping in. Elena's contract was a pittance, but her analogy about mannequins was chillingly on the money. To Hexagon, female models were products. And the "perfect ten" Olympic golds sounded better than nine in Tamara Cole's autobiography.

"Then there's Wade Wilson," Lyle said. "A company director dies, leaving an empty seat at the top table. Vince Harris might be the favourite to beat Tamara, but so was Gemma Bright."

* * *

"Do you enjoy playing with female bodies, Mister West?"

Detective Constable Moore had the crappy assignment again. New to the Major Crime Unit, she often received less desirable tasks. Her colleagues called it character building, but it was closer to bullying. As a direct entry recruit, the educated woman in the smart trouser suit had never truly gelled with old hands like Quinn.

She didn't envy him, though. The Superintendent had asked him to interview the executives. Despite being the university graduate on the team, boardrooms and plush carpeted corridors weren't Moore's scene, and questioning ordinary employees was a far less daunting prospect. Until she walked into the basement dungeon and saw Justin West caressing a female mannequin's torso.

"Being paid to create art," he said. "How could I not enjoy that?"

The unkemptly dressed weirdo stretched the blue gymnastics leotard and pressed the space between the breasts. Under pressure, the material tightened around the contours. The statue was an unfinished version of the exhibit upstairs, with no wig to cover the smooth domed head. But the silver likeness of Miss Simms was a faithful reproduction. Creepily so, to the point of religious devotion.

The hum of machinery – a computer and industrial mould forming press – didn't conceal the suspect's loud breathing. He walked along the line of five duplicate mannequins, inspecting each one. Away from public scrutiny, the technician was free to live out his sexist fantasy.

"We reviewed the security video," Moore said.

She stepped between the light and the model of Savikova. Deprived of their mirror-like shine, the skater's legs appeared dull.

"Got you checking out shortly after six. A lot of time unaccounted for, unless you can prove you were somewhere else last night."

The detective noticed a well-read comic book on a storage shelf between two cardboard boxes. She pulled it from the shadows. In the graphic panels, a busty woman in a tight blue catsuit battled knife-wielding thugs. Every drawing of the heroine was outlined in thin pencil – pinpoint accurate marks with signs of eraser smudges.

"A hobby of yours?"

Moore preferred to assume innocence, start easy with interviews, and build up to the important questions. But this place – with its choking dust, women's clothing racks, and plastic body parts – would unsettle her even *without* the grizzly faced technician.

"Where were you, Mister West?"

"Home."

He didn't take his eyes off the mannequin.

"Can anyone verify that? A friend? Relative?"

"You think I killed Elena."

Delivered in a pitiful monotone, the statement – at odds with West's socially oblivious behaviour thus far – caught Moore off guard.

"Did you?" she asked.

He lifted the mannequin's skirt, exposing underwear. Did this freak spend all day dressing his models?

"I could never hurt such a beautiful thing," he claimed.

"Are you referring to the mannequin or Miss Savikova?"

A ping from outside interrupted them. Heavy footsteps on concrete. Thankfully, it was Quinn who entered.

"No more questions for now," Moore said, "but don't leave town."

The Inspector grumbled as she joined him. That was an Americanism she had picked up from cop shows, a habit she couldn't seem to drop. West making her nervous hadn't helped either.

"Learn anything?" she asked, closing the door behind her.

"Just corporate buzz words. You?"

"Look up creep on the Internet, and there's probably a photo of Justin West, but that doesn't make him a killer. Then again, what do I know? I'm the new girl on the team."

Quinn didn't acknowledge her joke. Instead, he looked grumpier than usual.

"Boss wants us in Stillington," he said. "Apparently, Earl Bennett resurfaced yesterday, and those village idiots only just identified him."

"Where the bloody hell is Stillington?"

"Spoken like a true veteran, curse and all. Seems that character building paid off, eh?"

CHAPTER EIGHT

The Earl of York

Cassie's first visit to the director's office was under unpleasant circumstances. The acting head of Hexagon Sports, Vince Harris, chaired an emergency meeting to discuss Elena's murder. All the models – no, all but one – sat around the conference table.

"They think this Bennett guy killed her?" Raquel asked. "And is coming after us? It makes no sense. None of us know him."

"Except for me," Cassie said. "Maybe my expose sent him over the edge."

"You should have floored the bastard while you had the chance."

"He's a lot bigger than me. Okay?"

She was between Raquel and Monique, with Tamara opposite. The proverbial piggy in the middle. With the obtrusive curved table leg, there was little ankle room. Her chair was hard and uncomfortable, its rigid wooden bars an immovable cage behind her back.

Before the blame game started, Harris had outlined the facts. Based on new information not revealed to the public, the police had labelled Earl Bennett the prime suspect. Which made Cassie Hexagon's most unpopular model.

"I managed a kick in the balls," she said.

The usual etiquette had been abandoned, so humour might lighten the mood. She immediately felt guilty about belittling Elena's death, but Raquel mustered a smile.

"Those fancy gymnastics moves? He got off lightly. If a guy tried to rape my ass, I would make him squeal."

The Latina grabbed a nearby glass of water, held it up, and squeezed. The container cracked in multiple places, then shattered into pieces. Liquid spilled over the table. Shards clinked against the furniture, one leaving an ugly scratch on the polish.

Raquel shook her uninjured hand dry, grinning with no suggestion of embarrassment.

"Enough!" Tamara yelled.

She leapt to her feet, sending her chair skidding back across the carpet. There was a vibrating shudder, and nobody dared interrupt.

"This isn't a bragging contest. Do I have to remind you a model is dead?"

"So now you care about her," Cassie said. "Or is it lost revenue that's upset you?"

She hadn't forgotten Elena's low value contract, a fifth of her own compensation. Raquel and Monique – who had been quiet the entire meeting – simultaneously glanced at her. Tamara shifted back, just a fraction, but the accusation had struck a chord.

"I appreciate you're all on edge," Vince said. "This is a

scary situation for us all."

Empathy didn't suit the sleazeball one bit. His delivery was all style, no substance. He feigned sympathy and togetherness, but the victim was female, and the suspect a male sex offender. The models were the ones in danger.

"What did the cops say?" Raquel asked him.

"That we should be vigilant. Report anything suspicious, and stay in public spaces where possible."

"So they recited the rule book? Any helpful advice?"

"They don't need panic during an investigation," Tamara said. "Or people jumping to conclusions. It's frustrating, but I can understand their position."

Monique leaned forward, elbows shifting noiselessly on the smooth table. "Want to know *my* position? It's not the first time I've attracted attention from dirty old men. Wilson liked to fuck women, but I wasn't the soft touch he expected. Are you planning to screw me, Vince? A contract is between both parties. Remember that."

Her language was inappropriate, especially when discussing women's safety. Based on the executives' reaction, it might be the first time anyone had used the F-word in the boardroom.

Vince's lips trembled, and his knuckles cracked. What was going on between these two? There was definitely a hidden agenda, a veiled threat to Monique's comments.

"Not every woman wants to sell herself," Cassie said.

"Then why sign with Hexagon? You wanted the money, the fame, the rewards. For a female athlete, victory isn't enough. To be celebrated, she must be perfect in body and mind. Adapt to what society expects. That's a lesson I learnt long ago."

Cassie waited for someone to object, but nobody did. Monique had openly argued sex appeal mattered more than athletic ability. Was ethics an alien concept to these people?

Vince was a corporate vulture, and Tamara – despite her pretences – was of the same ilk. But surely Raquel didn't agree?

"What about Elena?" Cassie asked. "Are we just going to leave that… thing on show downstairs?"

She couldn't unsee the photos of the silver-coated body suspended in that deathly pose, or walk through the foyer without remembering her dead co-worker.

"That's a decision for the board." Vince turned towards Tamara. "We may have to pause Modern Woman as a mark of respect."

"There's no reason to remove the display. Elena was part of our brand. We should honour her memory. Unless you'd rather her death be for nothing?"

They were both manoeuvring for the director position, pretending the murder and company were unconnected. A crazy viewpoint considering the killer's spray painted message. Cassie understood Raquel's silence now. An argument based on morals was pointless when the other side had none.

Except for Tamara, the models barely spoke after that. After she had finished fencing with Vince, the other women were granted an early finish on police instructions, but Hexagon would no doubt deduct lost time from their monthly pay.

After Cassie returned to the lobby, she heard an engine start up outside. A helmeted motorcycle rider – surely Monique – drove at high speed through the gate and vanished from view.

"She would want you to stay strong."

Cassie had absentmindedly wandered to the Modern Woman exhibit and hadn't noticed Raquel join her.

When the sniffling teenager looked at Elena's mannequin, she imagined the Ukrainian skating on the ice rink, and recalled her sceptical observation about Hexagon's cutthroat executives. The keen observer had seen through their lies from the beginning. If only Cassie had listened.

"Tamara offered me money, and I didn't hesitate. I don't deserve to be called strong."

Raquel nodded, almost imperceptibly, and looked towards the lifts. A tall shadow fell across the mannequins.

"Cassie," Tamara said. "The police have advised us to review our employees' security. It's likely Bennett will come after you. Is there someone you can stay with?"

Was there more behind her sudden concern? Did she want to protect the company's reputation and avoid negative publicity? It could hardly get worse. Whatever the reason, Cassie didn't need charity. Not from this woman.

"I'm heading to my boxing club," Raquel said, defusing the tension a little. "She can come along. I'll teach her some moves, and hopefully self belief."

Thankful for the intervention, Cassie followed her out and never looked back.

* * *

It just had to rain. The excursion to the Yorkshire countryside was depressing even before the downpour. Black storm clouds blighted the sky. It was still mid-afternoon, but pitch dark outside the unmarked police vehicle.

"I don't buy it," Quinn said.

"So you've told me. Three times already."

Moore spoke louder than usual. She had to, with the endless patter of droplets against the windscreen.

The squeaky wipers cleared one layer of water, only for another to form straight away. Potholes were a constant hazard on the bumpy road to Stillington. Every few seconds, there was a slippery mud patch or ditch to navigate, then a rough landing that threatened to spin the car out of control.

"There was—"

"No evidence of sexual assault," Moore said, "which isn't consistent with Bennett's M.O. Four times you've said *that*. If he's not guilty, why send us all the way out here?"

The headlights shone through the thick drizzle, illuminating a green sign. Only two miles to go. They passed a quaint cottage with its lights on, then another on the opposite side. After all the empty rolling fields and electricity pylons, any hint of civilisation was progress.

"Murderer or not, he's still a threat," Quinn said. "We don't need a guy like Bennett roaming free."

"Now it's my turn to be sceptical. What's the real reason?"

Moore's face was wavy grey, ripples moving as water cascaded on the side windows and distorted the light. She had grown insightful, and the inspector was glad to have an understanding partner.

"The city's on edge. York is known for the Jorvik Viking Centre, its Minster, and shitty football team. We've had murders before, but that crime scene... Trust me. The force is under the spotlight."

"Even if Bennett's not our killer, arresting a sex attacker eases the pressure, and keeps cynics like you out of the way while the bosses take the credit."

"Us, Moore. Cynics like us."

A flash of lightning revealed the silhouette of a square-towered church, with houses further along the steep inclined road. After a loud rumble of thunder, raindrops became hail, icy pellets bouncing off the bonnet.

"Welcome to Stillington," Quinn said.

"What did you say the population was?"

"Three figures when I checked on Wikipedia. I don't remember the numbers."

There were dwellings on both sides now. Up ahead, the wind blew back a hanging metal sign, and the faded golden animal was difficult to make out. A figure in a raincoat hurried into a post office, the only person who ventured into the hailstorm.

Quinn parked near the pub, switched off the engine, and beeped the horn. He kept the button pressed until somebody threw open the door. The broad chested guy with red hair matched the description the landlord had provided over the phone.

The two detectives exited and raced inside. Their jackets were hopeless in this torrid weather, but it was only a short sprint to *The Golden Lion*.

The traditional English public house was cleaner than its urban counterparts. Locals chatted away in the bar, a constant murmur that came from the left. The warm, homely atmosphere might reassure Quinn if he wasn't hunting a dangerous psychopath.

"Nobody recognised Bennett?" he asked as they proceeded upstairs. "The guy in the news everyone's looking for? You get television out here, right?"

"Rarely poke into a man's business in these parts. Though it was peculiar mind, why he insisted on paying cash."

The landlord's accent was pure Yorkshireman. Unapologetic and clueless, he was a walking stereotype of a village idiot. A strong smell of manure surrounded him, and the creaky staircase and old banister rail didn't instil confidence. Did these yokels bother with maintenance?

"We'll take it from here," Quinn said.

With no further explanation, he closed the hotel room door. Closer to a log cabin in reality, as if they'd travelled back in time several centuries. Cabinets with exquisite brass handles, an antique bed, and a fenced-off fireplace. Quinn half-expected oil lanterns when he gazed up, but the electrical light fittings were modern.

"Why the hell didn't they call this in sooner?"

He walked to the desk. Someone – presumably Bennett – had laid out photograph clippings in a grid pattern. The gymnast was in the middle, surrounded by other models, all carved to pieces with crude cross cuts. That included Elena Savikova wearing the same pink outfit they found on the body.

"The original report was antisocial behaviour," Moore said. "The landlord insisted on a warrant to search the room."

"And they sent a pedal cycle cop to fetch the nearest judge."

A snide comment, but it wouldn't be a surprise if that actually happened.

Hailstone pelted the latticed window, even stronger now, and the howling wind was a constant distraction.

Moore watched Quinn reach down into the wicker wastebasket. He retrieved more shredded newspaper pages, X marks sliced across the faces of women. Every single female image had been mutilated in tabloids and broadsheets alike. Politicians, teenage girls, even an eighty-year-old grandmother.

"Suppose we were wrong," Moore said, "and we have found our guy."

"I think we need to."

* * *

After fleeing the isolated Yorkshire village on foot, Earl Bennett got a lucky break. Some moron had left an emerald green hatchback unattended near a scenic tourist spot, with the keys in the ignition. Perfect for reaching his destination, which took less than half an hour.

The owner would report the vehicle stolen eventually, but there were no traffic cameras around Poppleton Business Park, and the police presence was mostly inside the perimeter fence. He parked behind a broken stone wall further along the approach road, the perfect spot for a stakeout.

The six-pack of beer Earl found in the boot helped pass the time, but the long wait at Hexagon Sports dragged on. Until finally, late in the afternoon, it yielded a result. Cassie drove off with that boxer, a braided feminist who thought herself tough. Security was tight around the complex, but the women would be vulnerable in the city.

Earl followed a hundred metres behind in the car. He dipped the lights, inadvisable in poor visibility weather, but a low profile was essential now. The journey to York was short, and should take less than fifteen minutes despite congestion on the outer ring road.

The models were in a black company coupe with tinted windows. What gave them the right to an expensive benefits package? Society rewarded the undeserving, but he would teach these girls respect, just like those pitiful school bullies.

"You mislaid your butler, Lord Bennett?" the ringleader taunted him, evoking laughter in the playground of Saint

Luke's Comprehensive. "That's how we properly address an earl, lads."

The annoying background noise – pattering rain, the spray of water under the tires, and the booming radio in the van alongside – threatened to disrupt the flashback. Earl closed his eyes to concentrate, cruising the dual carriageway on autopilot. Distractions removed, he recalled the midsummer day he beat those smart ass punks into obedience.

"Who's in charge now?"

His blood-smeared fist connected with the leader's face. He followed up with a second, jaw-shattering punch, then a kick to the stomach. The lad's friends moved to stop the fight, but Earl warned them back with a threatening glare.

"Did I tell you to get up?"

Stamping on the kid knocked the resistance from him, and bold words had become girlish whimpers. Without a leader, the others were broken, one boy crying hard enough to soak his shirt. Spineless when faced with adversity – what a pathetic sight.

"You want me to stop? Then bow to the Earl of Saint Luke's. On your knees!"

A crowd of scared pupils watched the bullies sink to the ground, their authority destroyed. At Earl's insistence, they bowed repeatedly. All the way down, so their hands touched the gravel, then back to a kneeling position. He made them do it over and over until he was certain they respected him.

"That's right, you bitch," he said. "You're mine now."

Decades had passed. He was a full-grown adult wearing a stocking mask, and the blonde student cowered in fear before his switchblade. Her flowery patterned cellphone lit up, and a silly disco theme played. Earl snatched the device and threw it on the ground. The casing cracked open, revealing circuit boards which he crushed underfoot.

With the music interrupted, the University of York campus was silent except for the girl's rapid breathing. She didn't fight back as Earl pressed her against the wall and pulled down her leggings. Her thighs were tough, refreshingly warm to grope in the night air. Ignoring her timid screams, he unzipped his pants.

His other conquests conceded just as easily. The short-haired one with the black leather skirt, the studious girl with pigtails, and his treacherous wife Catherine. All the memories blended together into one uninterrupted sequence, accompanied by high-pitched shrieks of terror, pitiful sobs, and dampened cries for help. These women acted tough, but when challenged, they were weak.

Only Cassie had defied him. Earl pictured how it was supposed to be, admiring the gymnast from the exercise mat as she performed on the wooden plank apparatus. Graceful cartwheels, a perfect pivot on her foot, a double somersault. Then she finished with that sensational handstand. Her unclothed legs were wide open and inviting.

A horn beeped, and Earl found himself unwillingly yanked from his daydream. The van driver yelled some profanities and sped away.

He glanced at the dashboard, and the Hexagon promo photo stuck there with chewing gum. While waiting for Cassie to finish work, he'd listened to a radio news report where the police formally named Elena Savikova as a murder victim.

"You think I feel sorry for her!?" he shouted at the picture. "The bitch got what she deserved. They all will."

The company courtesy car turned a corner ahead. Even the heavy rain hadn't dampened its shine. Earl drove faster, relieved they were still in sight when he reached the junction.

The braided woman stopped outside a sleazy bar with a flickering pink *X-X* sign. The central neon bulb, where there should be another letter, was faulty. These were back streets, a dark bricked area the well-off usually avoided. Where were they going?

Earl shut off the engine and headlights, and watched the two models scurry down concrete steps. They had trapped themselves in a basement, and no heroic boyfriends were around to rescue them.

"I'm the Earl of York," he proclaimed aloud, "and you will bow to me."

He relaxed and returned to his perfect world. Her red leotard gleaming under the spotlight, the gymnast dismounted the beam with a backflip. She spun and dropped to one knee in a single flawless move.

"We are yours to command, Lord Bennett," she said.

The other Hexagon models appeared behind Cassie. Heads bowed, they knelt and pressed their bodies against the exercise mat in reverence.

* * *

Cracked plaster crumbled to dust, showering the training area with white powder. Rusty chains fastened to the ceiling clinked as Raquel struck the punching bag, landing a series of fierce blows that kept the cylindrical target at an angle. Her braids swung, unable to keep up with her fast-moving body. The kickboxer didn't need a weapon. A skilled martial artist, her hands and feet were dangerous enough.

"But I'm responsible," Cassie said. "If I hadn't been so cavalier, maybe Elena would still be alive."

"And if you hadn't run the sting, Bennett never would have been exposed. That asshole would be out there, taking advantage of women."

Raquel worked in a high kick that sent the heavy bag flying. Her eyes were unforgiving as she unleashed a flurry of attacks.

Where did this woman get her energy? Since starting her routine, she hadn't paused for breath. Were those boxing gloves to protect her hands, or the equipment?

The models were alone in the underground club. Unlike the state-of-the-art facilities at Hexagon, this was a low budget gym. Raquel had mentioned she knew the owner personally and trained under him as a teenager, which explained why she had a key. The boxer had changed the subject when questioned further, and Cassie got the impression the past was a thorny topic her co-worker didn't want to discuss.

With white brick walls, concrete floors, and no windows, this was a place for those who needed solitude. The central elevated boxing ring was bound by dirty ropes. Treadmills, bench presses, and rowing machines were arranged in rows on either side. Even without a proper inspection, Cassie spotted damaged conveyor belts, a handlebar missing its grip, and three dangling *Out of Order* signs.

Raquel ceased her assault and held the punching bag to steady it, showing a rare sign of restraint.

"If I beat myself up half as much as you," she said, "I'd be in a coma. Now, did you come here to complain... or train?"

Before Cassie could reply, the boxer reached into a box by the ring and tossed her a spare set of gloves. Not wanting to disappoint her self-appointed teacher, she slipped them on. The cloth interiors were rough and itchy.

"Let's see what you got."

In movies, martial arts masters always said that line before the novice student failed miserably, but Cassie was determined to succeed. She kicked the bag, a poorly aimed attack that barely touched the target.

"Those gloves are for punching," Raquel chastised her. "Start off easy, then the harder stuff. Yeah?"

Cassie followed the instructor's advice. Her blow connected as intended, but the hanging cylinder moved only a little. The impact had more effect on her throbbing arm. Her wrists already ached, and she had barely begun.

"You're hitting like a child. Put some weight into it."

Was the condescending tone meant to encourage her? Raquel watched her trainee's marginal improvement. The chains actually clinked after the third attempt.

Water hissed through pipes overhead, mixed with venting steam and metallic creaks. Neon lights hummed, hidden in the steel maze. There were so many twists, turns, and crossovers the utility network was more complex than a puzzle book challenge.

"You're doing well. Don't get distracted."

To emphasise her point, Raquel had sneaked behind. A foot tap to the ankle forced the student's legs apart.

"Fighting stance. Imagine Bennett's stood right in front of you, laughing in your face. He thinks you can't hurt him. Show him he's wrong."

Cassie screamed in anger, envisioning that bastard's facial features in the uneven rubber. She punched her imaginary enemy until her throat felt dry. Her knuckles must be red by now. She wanted to pull off the gloves to nurse her wound, but she fought on. Pain was a motivator, not a hindrance.

"Feel the fury build inside you," Raquel said. "Then unleash it."

A kick sent the bag swinging high. Cassie looked down at her leg. Had she managed that? She turned to see her mentor's admiring smile.

"What do you know? We got ourselves a fighter."

"You used Bennett to motivate me, but where does your anger come from?"

Raquel patted her on the back. "I'm going to freshen up. That was strong footwork. Be sure not to damage the bag."

The fighter left through the back exit. Why was she being so evasive?

Perhaps Cassie expected too much. They hardly qualified as friends, so why would they share secrets? There was a story behind the Latina teenager who took up kickboxing, and when Raquel was ready to talk, her trainee promised herself she would listen.

"Great moves."

Earl Bennett's voice.

Cassie turned to face her nemesis. No stocking mask – it was an exposed, snarling monster who stood inches before her. In the semi-obscured lighting, his switchblade was a criss-cross of dull grey and glinty steel.

"Stay away from me," she warned, but he simply snickered.

"Or what? What are you going to do, little girl?"

Bennett was preoccupied with insults and boasts. Cassie spotted a reel of adhesive tape sticking from his coat pocket. She needed to act before the psycho restrained her. She hopped to his unprotected side and kicked at his stomach. A powerful blow, but her leg bent out of shape.

The attacker grabbed Cassie's raised ankle with his free rubber gloved hand and twisted. A sharp pain, and she fell to the ground. The rapist knelt over her, clamped her throat to silence her scream, and squeezed. His dark-stained mouth stunk of cheap alcohol.

"Do you know what it's like to lose everything? To have your life taken away because some righteous bitch wanted a story? You think you can mess with me? I'm the Earl of York."

The nonsensical ramblings of an insane, drunken man. Cassie struggled, her neck pinned in his unyielding grip.

Bennett jabbed his switchblade between her breasts. Its sharp edge shined as he sliced her shirt down the middle, and parted the flaps to expose her underwear.

"Hey!"

Raquel launched a surprise assault and knocked the knife away with a well-placed kick. Faced with an additional threat, Bennett released his hold on Cassie. She coughed and spluttered as she breathed in stale but invigorating air.

"Bitch. You think—"

The enemy was still rising when Raquel kicked again. Fists raised, she threw her full body weight into an attack that sent the much heavier man reeling into the boxing ring ropes.

Cassie sat up to watch. Her model colleague had transformed into an instrument of vengeance. Bennett lunged at her, but she easily twisted to evade him. Then Raquel retaliated with a punch combination. The gloves had literally come off, and there was nothing to cushion the blows which pinned her opponent against the barrier.

Bones crunched, yelps of pain were immediately silenced, and teeth fell from Bennett's bloody mouth. The ropes creaked as he toppled over, legs pressed against the ring base. Sweat dripped down Raquel's lower back, but the muscular fighter was relentless, and showed no mercy.

"You like to beat up women?" she asked between two strikes. "So did my dad, but I taught him to respect me. You call yourself Earl? Think it makes you noble? You're vermin."

Bennett had all but given up. Raquel finished with a roundhouse kick, a knockout move any film action heroine would be proud of. Once again, a protector had come to Cassie's rescue. So much for toughening up.

"Thanks," was the best she could manage.

The kickboxer left her vanquished foe slumped in the ring. He had fallen back, upper body elevated by a rope on the verge of snapping.

"Seems we did the police's job. How about you call and give them the good news? I'll keep a watch on this jerk."

Had Raquel given her abusive father a similar beat down? Was that her reason for studying martial arts? Those questions could wait.

The female changing area was through a doorway and down a damp concrete passage with yellow cage lights. Steel pipes snaked through crude holes in the wall. Water leaked somewhere, regular drips echoing in the narrow tunnel, and a horrible stench emanated from the men's toilets. Cassie didn't want to think about what clientele used this underground gym, so she hurried past.

The women's room was in better overall shape, but that comparison wasn't flattering. Grimy metal sinks, a cracked wall mirror, and only three cubicles in service. Some battered lockers were missing actual locks.

Cassie took her bag from the nearest one that worked, unzipped it, and removed her cellphone. She punched in nine twice and was about to tap the third digit when she spotted the masked black figure.

The broken mirror only half reflected the armoured

intruder. A jagged diagonal line cropped the reversed image where the glass ended, but Cassie saw rubber pads covering his upper body, shoulders, and arms. Eyes watched through slits above a wiry gauze and gloved hands held a black metallic gun.

"Ra—"

Cassie managed one syllable before the mystery person fired a dart into her neck. A squish followed the thwack as an unknown substance was injected into her bloodstream. Her knees convulsed, teeth biting together as the anaesthetic took effect. Instinctively, she grabbed the sink basin but couldn't get a firm grip.

Her vision blurred, and everything shifted out of focus. She felt herself plummet groundward, completely off balance. The concrete rushed closer, but she fell unconscious before the impact.

Cassie awoke to searing pain down her left side. Had the attacker kidnapped her? She had a nasty splitting headache, and no idea how long the blackout had lasted. It took a minute to recover her bearings and sit up.

A locker door slammed shut as a drizzly breeze blew through the women's changing room. Rain fell in the alley outside the open square window, and dark buildings were just about visible. The wooden frame was snapped, and the forced locking catch hung by one screw.

"Raquel?"

Cassie stumbled to her feet, slipping on the damp floor. Battling drowsiness and leg cramp, she made her way through the noisy corridor to the training area, hugging the grimy tiles to avoid falling over. Eyes still blinking and unfocused, it took a moment to spot the pool of blood under Bennett's body.

A knife wound circled his throat. He was obviously

dead, in the same position as before. His neck and shirt were stained crimson red, as were the ropes and boxing ring around the corpse.

Cassie couldn't feel sorry for the bastard, but the killing was brutal, an execution style attack on a defenceless man. Too deep a cut for a switchblade, and his bloodless weapon was near the punching bag. Had Raquel done this?

No need to investigate further. She had to find her friend. And call the police. Was her phone still in the locker?

"Raquel!?"

Through the ropes, Cassie saw a silvery mannequin-like shape. With trepidation, she stepped around the boxing ring.

Screaming was associated with females in horror films, but she couldn't stop herself. A shrill cry, an unrestrained outpouring of grief and terror.

Raquel's body had been posed to match her Modern Woman photograph. Her skin painted silver, she lay flat on the bench press, one leg on either side and fingers closed around a barbell above her chest. Steel rings attached to pipes by thick cables supported the weighted pole, and zip ties secured her hands in place.

The killer had dressed Raquel in her Hexagon Sports tank top and shorts. Mixed with sweat, the reflective skin coating had a liquid sheen.

Cassie's face appeared squashed in the distorted reflection as she approached. A silver word in hexagonal font was sprayed on the wall.

TOUGHNESS.

Seeing photos of Elena was horrible enough, but this was a live crime scene. There were no stab wounds or blood. Had the murderer beaten Raquel, an expert martial artist, in a fight? Left her posed like this as some sick victory trophy?

Bennett's slit throat almost seemed routine by comparison.

The masked assailant in black was responsible, and the connection to Modern Woman undeniable. Cassie had many questions, but one stumped her in particular.

She had signed a modelling contract with Hexagon, was in the same website photo as Elena and Raquel, and had been at the killer's mercy.

Why would he leave her alive?

CHAPTER NINE

Fallen Champion

The paper cup shook in Cassie's hand. Fortunately, the plastic lid prevented coffee spilling out, but even with Detective Constable Moore's comforting arm, she struggled to hold on.

"Raquel was so strong," she said. "So brave. I never imagined…"

Emotion took over, and tears flowed. Her cheeks felt sticky. In a tall mirror beyond the forensics team, she saw a miserable teenage girl, dirty brown hair twisted out of shape and a deep purple bruise on her forehead.

Moore wiped Cassie's eyes with a disposable handkerchief. The rough, abrasive paper quickly became soggy, but the detective had plenty in reserve.

"There was nothing you could have done," she said.

"But that's it. I didn't do anything. I just… froze."

"It's okay to be scared."

Cassie sipped a large mouthful of coffee. The lubrication did little to ease the dry sensation in her throat that had been present since she called the police.

She placed the half-empty cup on the concrete floor and stood up. Without the boxing ring obstructing her view, both bodies were visible. Crime scene investigators took photographs of Bennett and Raquel. Some obtained blood samples from the deceased male, but there was far more activity around the silver-painted model and sprayed message. Two female murder victims with the same pattern had officially made this a serial killer case.

"What did I tell you? Bennett wasn't our guy."

It sounded like DI Quinn, but from her position, Cassie only saw a cheap suit behind the bench press.

"The mannequin killer. They actually proposed a name for this weirdo. How did the media get... Of course. Somebody talked. It's a big news story."

Cassie suspected his condescending opinion was directed her way.

It wasn't any easier to look at Raquel's body. Steel cables still held her in place under the barbell. In the twenty minutes forensics had worked the scene, they had scraped paint samples away to expose patches of smooth, unblemished bronze skin. A reminder the posed "mannequin" was once a living woman.

"She deserved better," Cassie said.

"Why do you think the killer chose Miss Valdez? And not you?"

"What are you saying? That I had something to do with this?"

She turned to Moore, hoping to find regret, but a neutral face greeted her. A detective assessing all the possibilities. As a media student, Cassie was familiar with interview techniques.

Except she was being questioned. A Hexagon Sports model, the last person – beside the killer – to see Raquel alive, and a suspect in her murder.

"You saw the attacker?" Quinn asked, coming over. "Yet you can't give us a description."

"He was wearing a mask and body armour. I only got a glimpse for about five seconds before the bastard knocked me out."

"Why not kill two birds with one stone? Or maybe I should say two models?"

Both detectives looked inquisitively at her, and the uniformed officers and forensics team paused their work. Suddenly, the underground club seemed very small, a windowless dungeon with squeaky steel pipes covering the ceiling.

Cassie squinted. There was a light flashing above. Not a long neon bulb, but a tiny red LED connected to a lens and electric cable. A spy camera, similar to the device they used during the sting operation.

"You must admit it's suspicious," Moore said. "Not that we think *you're* the killer, but…"

Following the wire was difficult with the confusing pipework. The thin black line often went hidden for whole stretches, and Cassie made a few wrong mental turns before she located the trail's end. More cables led to the same spot.

Quinn followed her around the boxing ring to the mirror. She felt the edges, searching for anything unusual.

"More amateur police work? Thought you'd learned your lesson."

Cassie ignored him, but smiled in satisfaction when she heard a click. The frame swung outward, and the secret door almost struck the sceptical inspector on the nose.

"Did you professionals find this?" she asked.

Lights turned on automatically in the room beyond. Surveillance footage showing the club appeared on monitor screens.

There were filing cabinets and an old-fashioned floor safe, but the hidden control area housed something far more important. Modern computers and hard drives, and possibly a recording of the murder.

"Look at this place," Moore said. "Was the owner a security freak?"

Cassie pointed at an image of Raquel's body filmed from a sixty degree front angle.

"Raquel mentioned there had been burglaries and assaults here. Perhaps the manager didn't trust the police." She turned for impact. "Why don't you check the footage? Once you've officially ruled little me out as a suspect, you can do your job and find this man."

Quinn responded with a malicious grin.

"You sure the killer's a man, Miss Simms? Thought you couldn't identify them."

Cassie wanted to argue, but in a world of powerful athletes, she had been sexist to assume the attacker's gender. That body armour could easily conceal a muscular woman like Raquel. Or Tamara Cole.

Quinn pulled a folded photograph from his pocket and opened it. The five models in a promotional shot, with black Xs drawn over the two victims.

"Something this case has taught me," he said. "Be careful with assumptions. The modern woman is quite capable of murder."

* * *

Raquel's dead. They think I was involved.

Cassie had said nothing else since Lyle found her standing outside in the rain, under a lamppost which provided no cover. The storm had subsided, but a persistent light drizzle lingered. Combined with the late evening chill, she could catch pneumonia.

"Here," he said, removing his cloak.

Cassie wore flimsy summer attire, trendy but already waterlogged. His thicker, thermal lined outfit offered better protection.

The girl still wouldn't talk to him, but he understood why. The memory of Elena Savikova's silver painted corpse was impossible to forget, and now there were two victims. Had the models been posed as an anti-exploitation message? It certainly seemed that way, but analysing this "mannequin killer" was a job for police psychologists. The priority was Cassie's safety.

"We should talk somewhere else. That building's full of reporters."

Wary of causing offence, Lyle gently placed his arm around her shoulder. His wrist brushed against her ice-cold neck and damp clumps of hair, but he couldn't let go when she needed reassurance.

As a media undergraduate, his argument was hypocritical, but *The York Gazette* hacks took after the British press. Facts were sketchy with the official police embargo, but Cassie was the key witness and a local celebrity, so insensitive journalists would hound her for details.

Lyle had already called Dan. That went as awkwardly as expected when he mentioned the reason, but the hard truth was preferable to a nasty rejection later. The part time guard was still bitter over losing extra income, but with the ongoing security review, they wouldn't be re-opening the university sports centre for a while.

"You don't want to help?" Lyle had argued. "Imagine if the cops find Cassie's body in that gym. This nut has already killed two women. Think it's bad now? Well, you'll be remembered as the guy who could have prevented a murder."

Despicable emotional blackmail – especially with Cassie in earshot – and irrational. What could an out-of-shape civilian do against a murderous psycho? But the pressure tactic persuaded Dan to agree to a fragile alliance.

The meeting place was across campus from the School of Arts and Creative Technologies, a good kilometre west. Fortunately, Lyle's wealthy parents had loaned him their second car. The compact SUV was a poor cousin to their convertible, and silver wasn't the best colour under the circumstances, but it kept Cassie dry.

She was too depressed to make conversation, so the only sounds were the moving vehicle and spitting rain. Powerful headlamps dispelled the misty drizzle, and they soon arrived at the sports centre.

Lyle retrieved his laptop from the rucksack under the dashboard. His rough case notes were missing crucial information, but hopefully Cassie would fill in some blanks.

Dan stood in the car park wearing a fluorescent yellow raincoat. He wasn't in a talkative mood either, so the group walked in silence as he escorted them to the rear entrance. Metal bolts clunked as the key turned in the lock, and the warm draught brought that familiar cleaning fluid smell outside.

Lyle hugged Cassie tight. They had returned to where this began, though it now appeared the Bennett sting was unconnected to the recent murders.

Dan had his electric torch and knew the light switch

locations, so they didn't spend long in darkness. His grumpiness and their echoing footsteps weren't reassuring, but mercifully, it was only a short trek to the security room.

With the cameras inactive, every monitor screen was dark. Lyle let Cassie use the wobbly chair as he started his laptop and navigated to the Hexagon Sports website. He placed the computer on the desk. Even with two models dead, the company was still promoting Modern Woman, but come morning, that would surely change.

"I can't believe Elena and Raquel are gone."

Cassie had been quiet so long Lyle jumped upon hearing her remark. Dan leant against the open door, arms folded.

"So, the dynamic duo are mixed up in a murder investigation. Don't tell me you're planning another crazy setup to lure the killer here."

"Nothing like that."

To Lyle's surprise, she summarised the harrowing details of the boxing club attack by Earl Bennett and subsequent double homicide. He considered asking her to stop, but keeping her gruesome experience bottled up would only make things worse.

Dan stepped away from the door, letting it slam shut. Cassie turned, fingers tight around the swivel chair arms. The off-duty guard raised his hands apologetically and looked at Raquel's photo.

"Someone strangled that hulk of a woman?"

Cassie's harsh stare gave him pause.

"Sorry," he said. "They murdered a kickboxer. And the police think a flimsy teenage girl did it?"

Cassie gritted her teeth, spun to face the laptop, and touched Raquel's picture. The screen flickered around her fingertips, then turned black until she removed her hand.

"They don't know what to think," she said. "Only that

someone's targeting Hexagon models."

"Whatever gave them that idea?"

Dan's comment was flat, with no trace of the usual humour.

Cassie typed in a web address and brought up the BBC website. Raquel Valdez – unofficially named as a victim – had a full profile. It was normally twenty-four hours before formal identification, but the mannequin killings were international news and live updates rife with media speculation.

"An abusive father," she said. "That's why she trained, to protect herself. She ended up exposing him and running away from home. There's a whole damn life history on here. Stats on domestic abuse, old school friends chipping in with comments."

Cassie stood up, paced over to the filing cabinet, and kicked out in frustration. Her foot stopped short of the lower drawer, but she only changed her mind at the last possible moment.

"Why did Raquel have to die before anyone cared?"

Lyle didn't have a suitable explanation. "The killer must be connected to the company somehow," he said, taking his girlfriend's place in the chair.

He clicked the back arrow to return to the Hexagon website. As he studied the models, the mouse cursor moved with his thoughts and hovered over Tamara, fourth in line between the biker and Cassie.

"The amazon?" Dan said. "That I can believe."

"You're as bad as the police," Cassie scolded him. "And those BBC reporters. Nothing but wild theories."

"Most of what we write is. But you have video evidence, right?"

"There were no cameras in... the women's changing

room."

"Ethics taken into consideration. Imagine that."

Dan hadn't missed the irony of her pause, or where she planted her own recording device to trap Bennett.

"We've got nothing," Cassie grumbled. "Except a four-year-old suicide that might have been murder."

"Two suicides," Lyle said. "Don't forget Wilson. What if Ms Cole has an ulterior motive?"

"Such as?"

"Running Hexagon. Think about it. Tamara kills her models to gain public sympathy. Finds a scapegoat, like the acting director. He takes the fall, she emerges a hero. Next thing you know, she's in charge of a world famous company."

Dan wolf-whistled and applauded mockingly. "That's one heck of a story. Complete shit, but great fiction."

"Maybe," Cassie said. "We won't find any answers here."

Lyle felt her grasp his shoulder. He turned to see an optimistic sparkle in her eyes.

"Perhaps we should take that research trip you mentioned."

He stood up and closed the laptop. They embraced, patting each other on the back.

"And all is forgiven," Dan proclaimed. "The gang's together again. Except the third stooge, who gets left out of the loop. I'm curious. You have the computer, so why involve me? Need a babysitter in case your girlfriend didn't come around? She *is* your girlfriend, right? Having trouble keeping up with the whole on-off thing."

"Appreciate the help," Lyle said. "I mean it. We can't trust anybody at Hexagon."

"Or the police, so I guess I'm the leftover."

"A friend."

"Who won't tell me where he's going."

"Loughborough," Cassie said. "To check up on Tamara Cole. She asked Lyle to write a story, and that should include all relevant background information."

* * *

The swimming pool at Loughborough University was a grand spectacle by British standards, though Tamara Cole would dismiss it as adequate. Olympic sized with multiple lanes, the layout resembled a London tube station with a concave white plastic wall opposite the entrance side. Instead of East End shows, giant posters celebrated former student swimmers who had achieved greatness. Gemma Bright was an unsurprising absentee.

Cassie hadn't slept all night despite a stopover at a motorway service station hotel. She and Lyle had shared the same room, though he insisted they sleep separately, with him taking the couch. A professional relationship with romantic promise, but they had bigger concerns. With a killer targeting Hexagon models, unearthing the long buried truth was a matter of survival.

Loughborough was known for its sporting links. Eight o'clock in the morning during Easter break, and hopeful athletes were busy training. Splashes were so frequent they became one continuous slosh, topless male swimmers half-hidden by white spray.

Cassie was happy to be behind a window, otherwise she would be drenched. Even in the observation room, there was a faint odour of chlorinated water, but that – plus the absolute need to remain alert – helped dispel her drowsiness.

"Think they bought our cover story?" she asked Lyle.

"We're about to find out."

A tall man entered from the pool area. Dressed in a blue tracksuit with *Loughborough Swimming* and a coat of arms embroidered on the lapel, he was obviously a coach. Mid-thirties, clean shaven, with blond hair in a crew cut and an assertive walk. Former military, most likely, a persona reinforced by an immaculately polished whistle and digital stopwatch on his ID lanyard.

"You the reporters?"

The guy crossed his hands behind his back and stood with his legs together. This no-nonsense ex-forces trainer would see through the ruse eventually, so they should keep the introductions brief.

"Lyle Norton, *The York Gazette*. Thanks for your time. I get that you're busy."

"All this flattery tosh." The coach's voice boomed like a drill instructor's. "I am indeed busy, so how about efficiency? Ask your questions."

Lyle had telephoned yesterday evening to arrange a short notice interview, giving the PR department a fake reason about Team GB's preparations for the next Olympic cycle. Without the materials or knowhow to create a false ID, he'd used his real name.

Cassie wore dark glasses and her hair tucked in a University of York baseball cap. She had to remain incognito, but that meant showing enthusiasm to avert suspicion. After a series of stock questions and uninformative replies, she changed tack.

"What about athletes who show real promise? Potential Olympic champions? That's a lot of pressure to heap on teenagers."

"The snowflake generation, eh? The kids of today need to

develop backbone. All this counselling and wellbeing drivel. What happened to good old-fashioned discipline?"

"You've had problems before, though," Lyle said. "When one of your top swimmers took performance-enhancing drugs."

"Gemma Bright," Cassie added. "I understand you were her coach."

A whining noise startled her. She glanced back at the source to see a bald, dark-skinned man in cream overalls. Seemingly oblivious to the racket, he swept the carpet with an upright vacuum.

"She was a waste!" The trainer's natural voice was loud enough to hear over the incessant cleaning. "All the talk of a Brit unseating the Yanks and Aussies. The underdog, sweet-faced darling of the nation. What poppycock! Bright was a fraud. Never seen any girl swim that fast."

"Yet she did." Unlike him, Cassie had to shout. "They reckon she would have beaten Tamara Cole at Tokyo and spoiled her perfect ten. That the defending champion would finish second in her big event, leaving her with only nine golds. Must have made her nervous. Convenient that Gemma got banned and took her own life."

The coach laughed. A bellowing, almost comical roar. Cassie wanted to berate him, but kept a straight face.

"You students and your conspiracy theories," he said. "She was using testosterone to boost her performance, simple as that."

"Then why didn't it show up in anti-doping tests?"

"Because she took something else to hide it. Spironolactone, water tablets. Research it on the Internet. Isn't that what you reporters do?"

"Got anything to back that claim up?" Cassie asked. "Maybe someone planted those drugs."

"You have this all figured out, so tell me. If Cole was behind this, why did she recommend Bright to her company board?"

"Tamara hired her?"

A spontaneous blurted reaction that didn't mask her surprise. The coach waved at the cleaner, gesticulating wildly until he shut off the vacuum.

Then the trainer knocked the baseball cap from Cassie's head and yanked away her sunglasses. As her hair dropped, he grinned in triumph.

"You're that gymnast. Another snowflake hero, and now a liar. You bring your problems from York down here to Loughborough. Looking for a non story, digging up dirt with your insulting questions."

He spat on the carpet. Behind him, the cleaner grimaced.

"We'd better leave," Lyle said.

Cassie took the hint, and they exited quickly.

"You students think you're so smart, but I saw right through you from the beginning!"

The coach's voice carried into the corridor. Cassie sprinted to the nearest T-junction, hid round the corner near a trophy cabinet, and waited to ensure the angry ex-serviceman hadn't followed them.

"Over here."

Lyle was further along the displays, looking at a tall glass case. Inside was a silver woman in a blue one-piece costume, her blonde hair gleaming like solid gold under an integrated circular light.

Cassie gasped, hand instinctively covering her mouth. But it was just a mannequin, a likeness of Gemma Bright wearing a Hexagon branded swimsuit. A European Championship winner's medal hung around her neck, next to a jewelled crucifix on a chain.

Were the silver and encrusted rubies real? The flat faces reflected the light too beautifully to be imitations. Dangerous to leave valuables on open display, but who would risk stealing from the dead? More importantly, why dedicate a holy epitaph to a disgraced former athlete?

"What do you think it means?" Lyle asked, looking down at the base.

A brass plaque was inscribed with Gemma's name, and her dates of birth and death. Under that text was a Bible quotation.

The Lord does not look at the things people look at. People look at the outward appearance, but the Lord looks at the heart. – Samuel 16:7.

"Was she religious?" Cassie pondered aloud.

"Her mother was."

An older and deeper voice than Lyle's. The display case reflected a faint male figure behind her. The cleaner from before had joined them. He stooped forward, hands resting on the vacuum stick.

"She was a devotee of God. I'm a believer myself, but Mrs Bright attended church services every day of the week. Her family has a lot of money and influence, so the fallen champion received a memorial. But not everybody approved."

"We should talk to the mother," Cassie said. "Wait... You said attended."

"Burying a daughter is a heavy burden. Sadly, too much of one, and her heart couldn't take the loss."

The vacuum rolled back and forth in the man's hands, revolving wheels scraping the linoleum floor. He hummed a tune that sounded vaguely like *Jerusalem.* No lyrics, just off-key notes.

Lyle gripped Cassie's hand tight. "We appreciate your

help, sir, but we should be going."

"That's not the original memorial." The cleaner had interrupted his song mid-verse. "Somebody vandalised the first. The night before Gemma left us."

"What happened?" Cassie asked.

"Arson. A student prank, the police said. They burned the swimming costume, like one of those effigies. The statue was scorched black, the colour of death."

A vivid description. She could almost picture it. "Did they ever catch the person responsible?"

"No, but that's not the worst part. They smashed in her…"

The cleaner trailed off and tapped his upper chest.

"Breasts? Someone smashed the mannequin's breasts?"

No living person was harmed in this historical retelling, but the symbolism was clear in Cassie's head. Two pitch black holes surrounded by burned plastic and a flaming swimsuit. A naked female body attacked and defaced in hatred.

"Any other clues?" Lyle queried. "Such as a message?"

"Yeah. How did you know? Love, or maybe grace. So long ago, I forget. In shiny writing, it was. And they were funny shaped letters, all with sharp corners. Like…"

"Hexagons," Cassie said.

The caretaker nodded in grim silence. She recalled Elena's corpse painted silver with *ELEGANCE* written behind, and then Raquel posed in the boxing club before *TOUGHNESS*. The vandalism fitted the pattern too well to be coincidence.

Gemma Bright hadn't committed suicide. The same killer murdered her four years ago.

Cassie and Lyle left, increasing their pace to leave the memorial and Christian cleaner behind. She felt her heartbeat slow as they turned into the main corridor. Then her pulse raced again when she saw DI Quinn waiting in the lobby, with DC Moore and the swimming coach.

"Miss Simms," the inspector said. "This interfering of yours is becoming a bad habit."

"Somebody has to do the legwork. How did you find us?"

Lyle stepped in front, like a human shield. "Dan told them. I shouldn't have trusted him."

"It was me," the trainer said. "Why would a reporter from York be so interested in an Olympics three years off? Then I heard about the mannequin killings on the evening news and it all clicked."

"Give him a gold star," Cassie mocked. "If you were already here, why wait?"

Quinn stepped forward from the group. "We thought you might turn up something interesting. You can tell us all about it on the way back to York."

CHAPTER TEN

Fort Hexagon

They viewed the video in complete silence. No audio accompanied the grainy footage of the underground club, and everything was out of focus. Boxing ring ropes had become fuzzy blue lines, and the mat's imprinted logo text was only readable because of the large character size. But it was clearly Raquel on camera.

The assailant took the kickboxer by complete surprise. After she secured the unconscious Earl Bennett to the rope, the black-clad masked intruder approached from behind and dropped a collar-like object over her head. The murderer leapt up, grabbed a pipe, and spread their legs. Metal rings on their thighs snagged the choker strap hooks and pulled the loop tight.

Cassie, the two other models, Lyle, and Vince Harris sat opposite the Hexagon boardroom screen, watching the surveillance recording. Edited footage, according to DI

Quinn, who stood to one side. The angle kept changing, swapping between distance shots and close-ups as it would in an action movie. But this wasn't make believe. They were witnessing the last moments of a real woman's life.

DC Moore was behind the director's chair, her expression solemn. During the initial assault, there had been a horrified gasp, an uncomfortable bum squeak, and a whispered comment, but now it was deathly quiet in the luxury office.

Without sound, Cassie had to imagine the fighter's gasps for air, her thumping retaliatory strikes, and straining leather. The killer had held Raquel in the bizarre thigh-ring stranglehold for over a minute, but despite her struggles, the attacker maintained a firm grip on the pipe.

"Come on," Cassie said. "Fight."

Lyle, to her right, warmly stroked her back. She realised history was permanent, but witnessing the horrible murder play out, knowing she couldn't alter the course of events, infuriated her. The other models gave her peculiar glances, but she remained focused on the video.

Raquel lifted her feet off the floor. Under the combined weight, the pipe broke, steam venting towards the screen. The image blacked out as both murderer and victim fell to the ground. Had the camera been destroyed?

A long-distance shot showed Bennett come around. Raquel struggled, head between the killer's spread legs. The bound male fought against his own bonds, yelling unheard profanities.

The kicking woman clawed at the choker, unable to get a grip. She grabbed the attacker's thighs, biceps bulging as she attempted – without success – to force them together and loosen the leather noose. She must have sweated profusely from the Herculean effort, but such details weren't visible from range.

Cassie surveyed the office. Tamara and Vince watched with hardened, indecipherable expressions. Monique sucked her lips. The faintest sound of swallowing saliva, but amplified in this environment. While Quinn didn't move except for the occasional blink, Moore kept shifting position, shoes rustling the carpet. Police officers dealt with violent criminals, but this lethally efficient killer had unnerved her.

Raquel – an experienced martial artist – was outmatched. Her elbows and fists did nothing against the protective rubber armour. She grabbed the crotch area, but that was also guarded by a hard shield.

A military-style knife, twice the length of Bennett's discarded switchblade, glinted as the trapped victim rolled onto her side. She spotted the weapon and pulled it from the killer's arm-mounted sheath. The murderer seized Raquel's wrist and twisted, forcing her to let go.

Deprived of a potential lifesaver, her struggles weakened and then ceased completely. Mouth and eyes wide open, she fell limp, head sinking between the assailant's legs.

The image suddenly jumped, time skipping as deadly events played out. The attacker held the pleading Bennett by the hair, pulled back to expose his throat, and slit it with the military blade. Blood spewed for a fraction of a second, then the picture showed a downward view of the bench press and Raquel's suspended corpse.

The masked assailant sprayed her body with paint, recolouring her buff stomach from Latina brown to reflective silver. Then the screen went black.

"Was that necessary?" Vince asked.

For once, Cassie agreed with the acting director, but Quinn displayed no sympathy.

"We wanted to make sure you understood the seriousness of the situation."

"Two women are dead. I think we get how serious this is."

The inspector gazed across at Cassie and Lyle, an intense probing stare. "Sometimes, I wonder."

The police had spent the return trip from Loughborough criticising the students for amateur sleuthing, and quickly dismissed the connection between Tamara and Gemma Bright as irrelevant. Apparently, the cops – with no leads of their own – were the experts.

"Which brings us to the response," Quinn said.

"We need to consider how best to protect the remaining models," Moore added. "While *we* locate the killer."

"Like a safe house?" Tamara asked. "Police escort? We're working to a tight schedule. There's another photo shoot next week."

Quinn looked aghast. Lyle simply stared. Cassie inhaled, her lips parted in shock. Vince smirked as he leant forward over the conference table, demanding attention.

"Which we'll cancel. Safety must come first." He ignored Tamara's cold-faced rebuttal. "I think stopping a murderer's more important than a failing product label. What course of action do you suggest, Inspector Quinn?"

Before he could answer, Tamara stood up, collected the remote control from the acting director's desk, and clicked buttons. The image changed to a snazzy 3D model of the Hexagon Sports complex. An animation played, with black lines and captions identifying key features. The epic fast-tempo music was designed for business presentations.

Quinn rolled his eyes in contempt. Tamara took the hint and muted the volume.

"We're already in a contained environment," she said.

"Only one entrance. All emergency exits are locked from the inside."

"What about windows?" Moore asked.

"Good thing I requested the steel shutters installed. Nobody's getting through those."

Monique tilted her chair back, looking past Cassie and the empty seat Tamara had vacated.

"Sending secret messages, Mister Director? If you want to arrange a date, I'm right here. But I expect you'll be leaving us in the company of these two fine officers."

Vince placed his mobile phone on the table and tapped the screen to select standby mode. "Since we're discussing employee safety, I thought we should bring in our man."

"Just one?" Lyle asked. "Not much protection. You saw what that psycho did to Raquel."

The office doors opened to reveal the receptionist – and apparent head of security – Brad. He entered slowly, looking alternately at Vince and Quinn as if unsure who to address. The three women may as well be invisible.

"We're in excellent hands," Monique said, crossing her legs.

The newcomer blushed. "The front desk has a dedicated phone line for emergencies. Any sign of trouble, and I call the cavalry."

"Except we'll be dead by the time they arrive," Cassie snapped. "This is a dumb idea."

Moore stepped up to the table. "Got a better one? It's not just the murderer. The media are clamouring to interview Hexagon models. We can't guarantee your safety in public, but here we can shield you, with a police presence on site."

"You two? What about the murder investigation? Who's handling that?"

"The Chief Con put in a request for mutual aid," Quinn

interjected bitterly. Seeing nonplussed frowns from his audience, he elaborated. "A special team from the Met will join us tomorrow and assist us with the enquiry."

"So we're prisoners?" Cassie said. "Shouldn't we be at the police station?"

Tamara got up, walked round the table, and joined Quinn by the screen. "That was why I suggested an alternative. Either you stay here, with all your comforts, or relocate to a safe house in the countryside. This building is secure. I'd stake my life on it."

"Good, because your models are doing just that. And where are we supposed to sleep? On the sofas?"

"We've set up temporary beds in the executive offices."

Brad reached into his pocket and pulled out a wad of white plastic cards. He distributed one to Cassie. The Hexagon corporate logo was smeared by dirty fingerprints, which she cleaned off with her sleeve.

The guard paused near Monique. She smiled seductively, eyeing his crotch as she took her passkey. "I assume you'll be checking in on us through the night."

"What about me?" Lyle asked. "I'm not leaving Cassie by herself."

"Seems she's got her own personal bodyguard as well." Monique added a wink. "But what about poor Tamara? Maybe Vince should keep her company."

"This is a police operation," Moore insisted. "We lock the complex down at seven. After that, the only people in the building will be myself, the Detective Inspector, models, and security. Clear?"

"Don't worry," Monique said. "I'm sure Brad will watch over us."

Cassie saw him fidget nervously behind his back. Brash sexual innuendo, corporate power games, and cops out of their depth. They'd fooled themselves into believing they were safe at the Hexagon complex, but she had seen the murderer up close, not in some censored cloudy video.

Nobody – except for Lyle – understood how dangerous the mannequin killer was.

* * *

The finished Modern Woman display was perfect, with the silver mannequins posed exactly as Ms Cole had requested. They were precise replicas of the five girls, the star attraction in the Hexagon lobby. Justin had spent days verifying the limb angles and body measurements were accurate, and now the boss wanted to shelve his masterpiece.

"Can't we leave Raquel on display?" he asked. "She's a work of art. Beauty and strength balanced in harmony."

Her left sports bra strap was on the shoulder curve, the elastic stretched out of shape. Justin repositioned it correctly, then felt her muscular chest and bulging muscles. Those were unusual features, and had required a custom mould to create, but chiselling a special design from clay was worth the effort. To diminish the kickboxer's strength would have been insulting.

"Showcasing dead models is bad for business," Vince Harris said. "Re-enacting crime scenes is catastrophic. Do you grasp the basics of PR? What a stupid question. Of course you don't."

It was just them in the reception area. Brad was off patrolling the building, and the women were to remain at Hexagon under police protection. They tried to keep secrets from lowly technicians, but Justin was the unnoticed nerd with a sharp ear. Information was a valuable commodity, so he had eavesdropped on the cops while they discussed security arrangements.

"Considering the current situation," Harris said, "the board has suspended the Modern Woman line indefinitely. A difficult decision, but absolutely the right thing to do."

He was playing the white knight – badly. Lying was commonplace in the corporate world, but he was shockingly inept.

The female cop exited the restrooms and walked around the foyer perimeter, heels clacking marble. Electric lights were dimmed to save energy, and the brunette was a distant silhouette. The executives had ordered Hexagon employees to leave early again, but they needed a low-paid technician available for mundane tasks.

"The project's been a disaster from day one."

Justin saw the boss' satisfied smile reflected on Elena's raised leg, mouth twisted by the curvature into a hideous grin. How could he call these beautiful creations a disaster? They were iconic.

"It's time we got back to basics," Harris said.

He paused before the leather-clad motorcyclist in the middle and unzipped her jacket to expose more of her sexy body. His alteration had ruined the look. Didn't he understand her clothes were supposed to match the promotional photo?

"To improve sales, we need models who catch the eye."

"Monique's a special woman," Justin said. "But Elena will always be my favourite."

He redistributed her long auburn hair, equalising the number of strands on each shoulder. Satisfied she had been restored to her true image, he reached under her pink skirt and found the boundary between the underwear and her smooth thigh. He moved his gentle fingertips along the upright leg, past the knee indentation, to the thinning ankle.

Justin stretched to reach the leather ice skates, but the sharp blade cut his finger. He recoiled, sucking the wound. Rivulets of fresh red blood dripped from the steel.

"Clean that mess up, West. And stop calling them names. They're just mannequins. Symbols of failure we no longer require, but keep… Monique on display. Put it behind reception while this blows over, but she has a future at this company."

"What about the others?"

Justin licked the cut dry, ignoring the sour taste. He expected an angry outburst for his poor hygiene, but Harris seemed more interested in Tamara. He stood on tiptoes to sneer directly at the tall swimmer's triumphal expression.

"Don't concern yourself with them. They won't be around much longer."

* * *

Monique Garneau zipped up her electric purple evening dress and viewed her reflection in the darkened glass window. She lowered the clasp, revealing her upper back. The parted silk skirt left her bare legs partially exposed, and the golden seashell earrings added extra class.

Official instructions were to bring one suitcase for an overnight stay, but Monique's associate had secretly messaged her. *Be ready to get some dirt on the competition.* That meant packing her fur skinned travel case with formal attire, perfume bottles, sex toys, and her trusty hidden camera.

To Vince, she was merely a tool, a hireling to record compromising footage. Ambitious and calculating, he would use every dirty tactic at his disposal to remove obstacles to the director's job.

Running Hexagon was his endgame, so he wanted Tamara out of the picture. To facilitate his scheme, he had guaranteed Monique board membership, but those were empty words, and she would become expendable should a more profitable option present itself. Therefore, she needed extra insurance, and that meant seducing that foolish security guard.

The women had been assigned temporary rooms on the upper floors. These top-tier offices had ornate bell-shaped lamps, genuine leather seating, oil paintings, and integrated bookshelves. There were two hardwood desks, but the secretary's had been shifted aside and replaced with a deluxe single bed that appeared downmarket by comparison.

Six-sided windows faced the green-carpeted corridor, tubular brass frames forming a tessellated hex pattern. The Venetian blinds were fully open, so anyone passing outside would see Monique. But that was the plan. She was the bait, ready to lure in her prey.

Brad arrived at three minutes past six, a little after schedule, and he was about to be delayed further. The guard stopped the moment he saw the occupant toss back her brunette hair. She beckoned him to enter with her finger, which he did without hesitation.

"It gets lonely after dark," Monique said, "when everyone has gone home. If you'd prefer some company…"

"I need to lock down the building. Make the final checks."

Devotion to duty? That wasn't like Brad. The police must have laid the law down hard.

Monique reached behind and switched on the desk fan. She had fixed the rotation angle, so the refreshingly cool air current flowing around her dress was continuous. She leant back against the overhanging wooden edge, trapping the rear flap of her skirt. The scent of lavender perfume dissipated, and Brad's mouth opened a fraction as he eyed her bared thigh and velvet frilled panties.

"All business," she said with a heavy sigh.

Monique applied another layer of glossy black lipstick and rolled her tongue in a full circle.

"Security guards don't get paid that well. No cameras in this office, so you should take advantage of the perks."

She pulled sharply on the zip, shuffled her body so the dress fell to reveal her pearly white bra, and knocked her high heels aside. Faced with a scantily clad barefoot woman, the sex-deprived guard would be desperate to fuck her. Water drooled from his mouth already.

"There's a murderer out there, Brad. I want to know a real man is protecting us."

Monique scrunched up her panties and tightened the material. That got him in the room.

As he approached, she tapped a control button that rotated the blinds, and another that dimmed the wall lights. The only source of illumination was the setting sun, low in the early evening sky, which gave the office an orange-yellow tint.

Brad unfastened his belt, tripping over his lowered trousers as his shoes caught on the polyester. While the smitten guard limped about in almost slapstick style, Monique removed an erotic strangulation device from her luggage. Entirely black leather except for raised steel pyramids around the goth collar, it would give any man an orgasm.

"The killer strangles women, but I'd rather choke you."

She gripped the attached strap tight and whirled the

ring in a circle. It whooshed, becoming a trailing motion blur.

"Excited yet? How hard is that dick of yours?"

Brad – breathing heavily – grabbed his briefs with both hands, ready to expose his privates. Monique whipped him with the choker, a loud smack that bloodied his lips.

"Let's make this a safe sex session. No intercourse, just desire. You'll have to imagine what it's like to impregnate me. Can you handle that?"

Monique slowed the rotation, snatched the leather ring from the air, and lowered it over Brad's head. She pulled the strap taut, closing the loop to cut off his oxygen supply. For all his bluster, Hexagon's security chief was pathetically weak, and it was easy dragging the stumbling puppet to a bookcase.

Once there, the model loosened her hold to allow Brad to breathe. She forced him against the shelves, knocking some business directories and leather bound textbooks onto the carpet.

Monique inserted her knees in the gaps, forcing her crotch against his. She could feel his hardened dick through the underwear. He wanted unprotected sex, but the collar gave her full control.

"You're not much of a man. All this time, you thought I was actually interested in you?"

She licked away the blood, feeling sharp unshaven whiskers brush her tongue. Then she tightened the choker again and squeezed his soft buttock with her free hand.

"Would you call this true love? I've experienced that, and this isn't remotely close, you sad bastard."

Brad's eyes bulged like inflated balloons. He was powerless, fists punching her exposed midriff in desperation, but he didn't leave a single mark.

"Careful. If you hurt me, you'll be billed for damages."

The idiot actually paused his attacks, so she took pity and released him. An intermittent wheezy squirt, and his briefs darkened around his erection. The ejaculated fluid left him wet and sticky.

Monique switched the lights on and picked up Brad's trousers.

"Don't you have a building to guard? Not that you'd be able to stop the killer. He wouldn't even bother turning you into a mannequin. Because who would glorify a man with such a tiny, limp dick?"

She tossed his clothes back. He staggered from the office without checking the coast was clear, struggling to put his pants back on.

Monique waited a moment after the door closed, then reached into her panties and removed the item she had palmed from his pocket. The guard's master keycard to Hexagon HQ.

Vince and Tamara – as board members – had unrestricted access. Now she did as well, and they would find their secrets weren't that safe.

Brad was the weak link in the security chain. Monique's methods were public knowledge, and he still allowed himself to be recorded by the camera she planted in her suitcase beforehand. It was unlikely she would need compromising footage of that bumbling idiot, but videoing intimate encounters had become habitual.

Sex with the "muscle" man was never on the agenda. He was a low-level employee, and there were far more important people to screw at this company.

* * *

The powerful blonde swam the length of the pool, generating white froth that erupted down, then rose to settle. Waves spread out from the half-submerged woman, rocking lane marker floats. Hive themed lights extended from the glass hex-pattern floor, reflected in the constantly shifting turquoise blue ceiling.

Everything was upside down from Cassie's perspective, but she had adapted to the disorientation early in her gymnastics career. In a sport where the horizon spun around competitors, it was essential to maintain a sense of direction and stave off dizziness.

She had held the handstand far longer than usual. Her wrists ached, but the thought of the sadistic killer displaying Elena and Raquel as mannequins gave her adrenaline to cling onto the stool.

The splashing rhythm was unbroken and regular. An elite athlete in a strict training regimen, every action optimised for maximum efficiency.

Tamara Cole completed another lap and stepped from the pool. The former Olympian approached the bar area, water trickling up her legs. Dry gaps appeared in the liquid film over her streamlined royal blue swimsuit. A well-conditioned body of incredible strength, and perhaps a diabolical mind.

"That's what I admire most about you, Cassie," Tamara said. "Your dedication. With everything that's been going on, a lesser woman would have surrendered to depression."

Cassie brought her legs together and flipped into an upright position. The swimmer towered above her, centimetres away. But it was time to display the courage her hostess claimed to admire.

After detaining the students at Loughborough, the detectives had escorted them directly to the complex and insisted they not return to their accommodation. With no chance to pack her own clothes, the gymnast had borrowed a Hexagon leotard the same colour as Tamara's costume. But that didn't make her company property.

"Your contract never mentioned I'd be risking my life, so maybe I am feeling depressed. But I don't intend to give in."

Tamara wiped the sweat from Cassie's brow. There was a firmness to the swimmer's touch, a noticeable lack of compassion.

"Ability and perseverance will only get an athlete so far," she said. "To reach the absolute pinnacle requires something more."

"A killer instinct? Heard an interesting story at Loughborough, about Gemma Bright modelling for Hexagon before her tragic suicide. You recruited her. They say friendly competition is healthy, but sometimes it's deadly."

Cassie studied Tamara's reaction. Her slowly moving eyes, and the faintest of wry smiles.

"Gemma took drugs," she said. "She brought it on herself. Anyway, it's good to have the brave Cassie Simms back. Yesterday, it was all doom, gloom, and tears."

"The murderer wants us to be afraid. I've been taken by surprise once, but don't worry. It won't happen again."

Tamara turned towards the pool. "This place is a fortress. No way the killer's getting in."

"What if he – or she – is already inside?"

CHAPTER ELEVEN

The Director's Chair

"I am *not* letting that bastard feel me up," Cassie had protested vehemently. "Or playing the sexy, distracting girl while *you* do all the investigation. And don't patronise me by saying how dangerous this is. I'd rather be proactive than wait for some psycho to bump me off."

Lyle had wisely stayed quiet during her aggressive rant. It had only been a suggestion to keep Brad occupied while he checked the lobby surveillance system, but she felt the need to establish some boundaries. Hexagon might be corrupt to the core, but seducing a chauvinistic neanderthal was Monique's area of expertise.

Cassie had backup arguments prepared about her superior knowledge of the complex and staff members, and an olive branch admission that her own recklessness had contributed to this dire situation. But Lyle, eager to mend bridges, had allowed her to decide the best course of action.

"Neat system you got there," he said.

Not the most convincing bluff, but it made Brad look up from the adult magazine he had concealed under the reception desk. Cassie stood on the opposite side from her boyfriend, near the entry flap. She had a clear view of the monitors and controls – and the lazy guard supposedly watching them.

"Yeah," he threatened. "You better not try anything."

"Whoa." Lyle put on an obviously fake placative grin. "It was just a compliment. Over a dozen cameras at strategic points. Good coverage of the lifts, stairwell, and all major corridors. Between you and the cops, I'd say the girls are safe."

Cassie watched the screens while Brad's attention was elsewhere. Most were static images, except for DC Moore patrolling the executive floor that now doubled as a hotel.

The detectives had shown the models their quarters before Cassie joined Lyle downstairs. The office carpet was a ghastly lime and dark green chequer pattern, and the walls varnished wood. From the trophies and sales charts on display, she guessed the room's usual occupant was an uptight male stockbroker obsessed with snooker and cricket.

Wait. Something was off about the camera images for the executive and uppermost floors. Not a person in sight, and that was the peculiar thing. There should be.

"You don't need to worry," Brad said. "I'll be watching them."

Thankful of being short with a desk between them, she buttoned up her tracksuit top to obscure her leotard.

"You ladies can relax. Nobody gets in this building without me noticing."

"Provided the security guard keeps his eyes on the

women he's supposed to."

His hasty scramble to hide the magazine under the guest register was almost pathetic. Lyle inclined his head, a silent signal to make excuses and leave, but Cassie wasn't through with this sexist pig.

"Did you and Monique have a good time?" she asked. "You've got lipstick on your chin."

Brad rubbed his mouth without thinking, checked his unmarked palm, then gave her an angry glare. It was a test, but his reaction – and the faint aroma of women's perfume – confirmed her suspicion about the thin, red impression on his throat.

"We're dealing with a murderer who strangles people, and you let her choke you? Why am I not reassured?"

She left him to contemplate his actions – not that he would – and reconvened with Lyle by the lift.

"Security's full of holes," he said. "Easy to avoid the cameras if you know their positions."

Cassie pressed the call panel. "As for the human element, the cops are complacent, and the guard's more interested in screwing the models than keeping them safe."

The doors opened with a ping that sounded deafeningly loud without the usual din of corporate activity. She followed Lyle inside, tapped the button for floor twenty-two, and watched the digital indicator increase.

"What are you thinking?"

He'd picked up on Cassie's foul mood and her general unease regarding the police strategy.

"You could be right about Tamara. She's taken a keen interest in me. At first I thought it was admiration, but it's closer to obsession."

"A wild theory." Her boyfriend let the paraphrased objection sink in. "Unless you have proof?"

"Let's find some."

Cassie pressed button number twenty-one. Lyle's eyes narrowed, and he gave her a curious sideways glance.

"The cameras for the top floor and director's office," she said. "They're on a playback loop."

"What makes you say that?"

"I watched DC Moore go upstairs, but she never arrived. So unless she magically became the invisible woman…"

"Someone's hacked the system. How is that possible?"

Cassie put her index finger to her lips and silently waved Lyle into the corridor. Lights were off, and the open lift doors appeared blinding white in the gloom. These offices lacked executive class, with ordinary rectangular windows and multiple names engraved on the door plaques.

"So we don't run into a wandering detective," she whispered.

Lyle hadn't questioned why they exited one level down, but her voluntary explanation should keep him quiet.

Cassie tiptoed to the stairwell access. That was unnecessary on the soft carpet, but the concrete steps required more stealth, so it was a slow climb. As a trained gymnast, she was naturally light-footed. Her companion did his best to emulate her sneakiness, but couldn't avoid the occasional scuffled boot scrape.

After the ascent, Cassie ducked under the door window and motioned Lyle to follow suit. Then she risked a peek. Moore stood with her back to the wall, on sentry duty by the lifts.

They were right about the lack of security, and anyone who knew the layout well enough could easily circumvent the cameras and patrols. The intrepid student reporters continued up the stairs. They had reached the top floor without being challenged.

Lyle grabbed her arm as they entered the assistant's room. "Sure about your theory?"

He glanced up at the security camera above the entrance. The green light flashed periodically, and there was no obvious damage to the lens or hardened metal case.

"Guess it's the moment of truth," Cassie said.

Lyle opened his mouth to protest, but she tugged her wrist free and walked past the unmanned desk to the electronic combination keypad. That protected the director's office, and her access card wouldn't have clearance. But it didn't matter, since the doors were ajar.

Cassie cautiously swung them open. The brass wall lights were on, which meant someone had been inside recently. She bent down to check underneath the conference table, but saw only wooden furniture legs.

"Only board members have access cards," Lyle said. "So it must have been Cole or Harris who left the door unlocked."

Sound logic, but his argument had a big flaw.

"Brad's in charge of security, so would have a master key. And he had a twisted sex game with Monique earlier."

"Two more suspects, and the police will have been given access." Lyle let out an exasperated sigh. "Which really narrows it down. But only execs have the code... right?"

His uncertain query invited another counterargument, and Cassie had one ready.

"A four-digit combination, so only twenty-four sequences if you know what buttons were pressed. When a number repeats, that drops to twelve."

Lyle checked the keypad and spotted the fingerprints on the zero, six, and seven. He still seemed puzzled, so she left him to the mental arithmetic.

"We're assuming the killer broke in here," she said. "When we... don't even know that."

Cassie stopped to view the picture wall. There were actual photos hung there now, only it was Vince Harris' life story chronicled. He somehow played the smug snake in every gold frame, whether he was the smarmy graduate or egotistical executive. She guessed Wade Wilson had a similar gallery before his supposed suicide.

"What if our theory is right," Cassie said, "but we've got the wrong board member? Vince had more to gain from Wilson's death than Tamara. He kills the Modern Woman models, leaves messages to paint a Hexagon hater cover story, and eliminates the competition."

"More theories?"

Cassie ran her fingertips along the surface of the conference table. Smooth, charming, and polished. The perfect complement to those who used it.

"The men and women sat around here decide whose lives to trade for profit. They chose me to represent their money making brand, and I accepted."

The director's chair was the focal point of the office, sought by corrupt and powerful executives. At the head of the board members' table, underneath the ceiling fan, with the commanding desk behind it.

Cassie entered a melancholy trance. She lifted the heavy mahogany framed seat, moved it back a tiny fraction, then sat down. The leather cushion sank under her weight, unseen springs adjusting for maximum comfort. Its curved black surface was bouncy and hard, like a gymnastics vault.

She felt the intricately carved arms, deceptively pleasant to view but with sharp ridges to catch the unwary.

"I was a greedy self serving woman who made a deal with the devil. Courage? I was weak and needed Elena and

Raquel for support. Now they're both dead."

"The mannequin killer's targeting Hexagon. It's not your fault."

Lyle placed his hand over hers, steadying the vibrations. Warmth circulated through her fingers. Reinvigorated and using the cushion as a launchpad, she sprang to her feet.

"When you've repented your sins," he said, "can you concentrate on what you do best? Ask those important questions. You check the desk."

While Cassie searched the drawers, finding only wealthy trinkets, Lyle switched on the presentation screen. A blue background with brighter lines projected across the table and carpet, appearing jagged at the boundary.

"A map of the complex?" she asked. "What good is that?"

"You never know."

Lyle removed a cellphone, connected a USB cable to the television, and downloaded the image. Then he stopped. Cassie followed his pointed finger to a clapperboard symbol labelled with a yellow triangle.

"Rick's Underdogs," he read aloud.

"That's the name of the club. Where Raquel was murdered."

"The cops erased the file. Why can't they be incompetent, like usual?"

Cassie's search had turned up nothing. She flicked through the appointment book, but Vince Harris had written diary entries in initials and shorthand.

"Good," she said. "Because I don't want to watch that video ever again. Unless the killer deleted it, which means it contained something important, a clue that could identify them. And we need one because this evil bastard – or bitch – is meticulous."

Cassie paused, spotting a fountain pen stand at a slight angle, which she lifted. Someone – Vince? – had cut a crude rectangular hole into the baize underneath. A flash drive was inserted so snugly she couldn't pry it loose by hand, and needed the pen to apply leverage.

"Does that phone have a USB port?"

Thinking ahead, Lyle had unplugged the cable from the television. He took the data storage device and slotted it into the adaptor socket. The contents loaded quickly, and the progress bar filled and vanished before the electronic beep sounded. A file explorer window opened, white space except for a single grey loudspeaker icon labelled *TC-Olympics*.

"Tamara Cole?" Cassie hypothesised.

Lyle tapped the screen to start the playback.

"You've shown great promise, but a true competitor doesn't need to bolster her chances. Have some belief in yourself. You're a natural."

The woman's voice was loud, so Cassie leant across and dragged the volume slider down. Although the words were different, the recorded conversation was uncannily like her own discussion with Tamara. And it was unmistakably the American swimmer speaking.

"You don't understand," another female argued. Her speech was high pitched with apprehension.

"You've been taking drugs, Gemma."

Cassie and Lyle looked at each other anxiously. No second name had been specified, but it was obvious who the woman was.

"It's no use hiding it," Tamara said. "You weren't yourself in the pool during this afternoon's photo shoot. Too aggressive, and none of the usual composure. There's something you need to understand. When I invest in a model with your potential, I monitor them closely."

"So I will succeed? We're competing for different countries, and that's not why…"

"It's nothing to be ashamed of. We all want to win, Miss Bright."

Confirmation of her identity. Lyle moved the phone closer. They couldn't see the two women on screen, only a ripply special effect that responded to the audio.

"All this hype about my perfect ten golds. There's a great deal of money in sports betting. If the results in Tokyo don't go as expected…"

"What are you saying?"

A short sentence, yet Gemma's voice rose and fell while uttering it – a nervous woman under pressure.

"To skip the drugs," Tamara said. "I'm a businesswoman now, and I know when to sacrifice for the team. Britain's golden girl would be worth a fortune to Hexagon, and Director Wilson agrees. But only a silver at the Olympics, or worse, a doping scandal. That would tarnish the brand."

The audio ended there. Lyle struggled to hold his phone steady, and Cassie's jaw had dropped.

"Tamara tried to rig the race," she said.

"Bright, Wilson, and Cole. Two conspirators conveniently commit suicide. She had a clear motive for murder, but how do the models fit in?"

"We need to talk to the police."

"They seem genuine. But with a story this huge, we can't take a chance. Quinn and Moore were awfully quick to dismiss our theory. What if one of them's an accomplice? Or been bought off?"

A ping from down the corridor. The lift – someone was coming.

Lyle shut off the mobile phone. He pulled out the USB

and thrust it into his pocket, removing his hand just as DC Moore entered the room.

"Interfering in police business again?" Blue lines across her face faded as she turned the lights on full. "It's almost seven. You'd better say goodbye."

Cassie feigned innocence and kissed Lyle's cheek. "You know I love you, right?"

"Think we can put the past behind us."

Moore led them from the office and closed the door. "Spotted you on the monitor. How did you sneak by the camera? Was the dumbbell of a guard paying attention? And what were you looking for, anyway?"

Either she was lying, or the intruder had removed their hack. How long had the killer planned this? Could they replace any surveillance feed with prerecorded footage whenever they wanted? That explained why Wilson's death was written off as suicide.

"Everything's connected to Hexagon," Cassie said. "But we didn't find anything useful."

* * *

"Fancy a swim, Monique?" Tamara called out.

She knew the identity of the noisy observer without looking. The distinctive clack of high heels against ceramic was unusual in the pool area, where athletes generally walked barefoot. Non-swimmers sometimes wore trainers or flat soles, but formal evening clothes were strictly for showcase events.

Tamara sipped her ice water, not bothering to turn as Monique sat beside her. The bar's aluminium spigots reflected the assured brunette. She could pass for a film noir femme fatale with that backless dress, long matching silk gloves, black eye shadow, and dark glossed lips. The steel studded leather choker and attached strap were modern and risque. Gender and sexuality weren't barriers to this scheming seductress.

"Swimming isn't my sport," Monique said, placing her spiral patterned purse on the counter. "But we motorcyclists do share something in common. Exceptional stamina."

The word games had already started. Had Vince put her up to this? Their manipulations were hopelessly shallow.

"One key difference. Swimmers remain cool during a race..."

Tamara placed her tall glass against Monique's exposed thigh, rolling it until sweat collected and condensed.

"...while cyclists wilt in the heat. We're both adults, so I think we can skip the foreplay."

The sultry model uncrossed her legs and reached out, flattening her palms against her companion's dry swimsuit. She caressed the slightly curved chest area and well-developed muscles. Under normal circumstances, a person in authority would vent her fury, but allowing this conniving, double dealing bitch to think she was in control was satisfying.

Tamara played along and licked the sweat vapour from her drinking glass. It tasted awful – worse than salty tap water – but she smiled the whole time, determined to appear relaxed.

Monique's eyes twinkled with excitement. "A woman of action."

"I thought you preferred to play with the director."

"With that body, you're more of a man than Vince could ever be."

A horrendously delivered pickup line. Why did male

execs fall for this nonsense?

Tamara lifted Monique's ankle off the circular stool rest and shifted it anti-clockwise to split her legs at a ninety-degree angle. Evening wear and humid, sauna-like poolside conditions didn't mix well, and her athletic body and black hair were drenched in runny sweat.

"And how much of a woman are you?"

Aroused by the question, the rapid-breathing model offered no resistance as Tamara pulled the damp dress from her breasts and reached underneath. Her skin was disgustingly clammy, but it only took a second to pull out the leather strap.

"Out of curiosity, what is Vince paying you for this?"

His henchwoman was about to deny any involvement when Tamara slammed her against the bar. One hand gripping Monique's throat, she pulled the thong with her other. The collar sections closed around the bitch's neck, dragging brunette locks together in clumps.

"How much?"

Her captive panted in response. Was she actually enjoying this?

Tamara tugged harder until the skin beneath the choker turned red. Hair strands swung like pendulums, midpoints fixed by the airtight loop. Gasps mixed with sexually excited panting.

"There are no cameras pointing at this end of the pool, so don't expect anyone to save your sorry ass."

Tamara let the strap slacken so Monique could breathe. The crazy woman, apparently unconcerned by her experience, tilted her head back and exhaled.

"A seven-figure contract," she said. "Four times what you're offering your top models, and you pretend to be a twenty-first century idealist. It's always been about money, and which employer pays more."

"And survival. There's a killer out there. Don't forget that."

Tamara turned the strap, closing the collar a little. Then she resumed her choking assault, pulling with all her might. With her arms fully stretched, the line from Monique's throat to the leather end was straight. The overdressed model writhed about, pinned flat on the counter.

"You seducing Wilson was Vince's idea. Do your call girl routine, make a kinky video, and collect a hefty pay cheque. That sound right?"

The biker was expectedly tough, but Tamara was stronger. Monique grabbed her attacker's arms, but couldn't break the stranglehold. Faced with death, the henchwoman's enjoyment morphed into terror, and pants of delight became desperate gasps. She kicked out violently with her high heels, but she was close to confessing.

"It was his plan. Wasn't it!?"

Finally, Monique nodded. Tamara released the strap and flicked it at her defeated foe's face.

"Yes," the accomplice coughed, catching her breath, "but Wilson killing himself wasn't. He was supposed to go to prison, or resign in disgrace."

"Weak men always choose the easy road, but thank you for confirming it on camera."

Monique followed Tamara's gaze to the purse. During the attack, she had re-angled it so the hidden device recorded their conversation. The side hole was well hidden, but not to someone familiar with the blackmailer's tactics.

"You came here for sensational footage, and you got some. Only, it will put me in the director's chair instead of your pimp. No Hexagon board membership for the sellout slut."

Tamara twirled the recorder in her hand, unable to resist a grin of triumph that outdid any of her Olympic celebrations. She buttoned the handbag and rammed its flat end hard into the recovering model's crotch. That made her squirm.

"You're very attractive, Monique, so it shouldn't be a surprise to get screwed."

The dejected woman took the purse and limped towards the corridor. After she left, Tamara pulled the camera's memory stick and stored it in her gym bag behind the counter.

The Olympic medal belt seemed appropriate, given her imminent victory, so the swimmer clipped it around her waist. She typed a message to Vince on her mobile phone.

Come see me by the pool. Urgent. About the footage you wanted.

That ought to get the duplicitous bastard's attention. Still twenty minutes until the curfew deadline, so he wouldn't have left the complex yet.

Tamara dropped the deactivated device in the drainage trough by the swimming pool and dived in. Though she despised Monique for allying with her rival, the traitor had put up a commendable struggle.

The refreshingly cool water soothed sore muscles and provided much needed hydration. After four end-to-end lengths, a familiar suited man entered through the main corridor doors.

"Come to gloat?" Tamara paddled to the side and rested her elbows on the wet tiles. "I may look like a minnow from up there, but they say appearances are deceptive."

Vince looked down with disdain. She ignored him, lifted herself from the water with her upper arms, and climbed out. Even barefoot, she had the height advantage.

"Things are exactly as they seem," he said. "A token

female who Wilson appointed for political reasons, acting above her station. I thought you'd mess up, but you surpassed all expectations."

Tamara moved closer, so her wet swimwear touched his suit. Water dripped from her overhanging hair onto his head. She felt the discarded camera beneath her foot and rolled it towards her.

"A slimy little man who got promoted by a male dominated board. Exactly what I expected."

"And about to get promoted again. Members voted this afternoon, and before you play the gender card, the decision was unanimous. They remember Modern Woman was your idea. Just like Gemma Bright, betting the company's future on inexperienced athletes backfired big time."

Vince smirked, braver than usual, but it was a hollow threat. With the other two conspirators dead – and no impartial witness – he couldn't prove a thing about their Olympics scheme, and he didn't have the guts to incriminate himself. He had always suspected she leveraged Wilson to gain board membership, but the former director's demise had removed any risk of exposure.

"It's about competence," Tamara said, "and you screwed up by hiring an amateur like Monique."

She stepped on the camera, shifting her weight. The crack of plastic made Vince look down. Sharp pieces of the broken lens cut her foot, but she shrugged off the pain and pressed down until she heard the crackle of electrical short circuits.

Her slimy opponent remained defiant, though he backed off a pace. "After the killer's caught, questions will be asked. Why didn't we review security sooner, and why did it take two murders before we regarded the threat seriously?"

Tamara dragged her injured foot, leaving a narrow trail

of blood as she swept the broken camera pieces into the pool.

"And I'm your fall girl. Remember, as managing director, you're the one at risk of repercussions."

She leapt backwards, spreading her arms and legs to increase the splash radius. White spray flooded the poolside as she submerged.

Tamara pulled her belt, displaying the row of gold medals to her bitter enemy. From underwater, she saw a blurry black attired man shake his trousers and storm off. She laughed, not caring when pool water filled her lungs.

He had underestimated her. Tamara had played the long game, but the end – and the victory she had sought for many years – was near. When the evidence implicated Vince in Wilson's death, the board would reverse their decision and elect her as director. Once she took charge, she could restructure Modern Woman – and Hexagon – in her image.

Monique was expendable. Cassie was Tamara's new champion, and she would either adapt or become another unfortunate victim like Gemma Bright.

CHAPTER TWELVE

Lockdown

DI Quinn had assumed his colleague's account of the technician's workshop was exaggerated, nothing more than the colourful imagination of a young officer settling into the Major Crime Unit. But her description of the "dark dungeon basement" was spot on.

Electrical circuits were faulty, leaving the computer terminal as the principal light source. A large industrial machine hummed in the corner, red warning indicators pulsing on the control panel. The contraption must have something to do with mannequins, like almost everything else.

Quinn equipped his electric pencil torch and directed the beam in a wide, sweeping arc. The wattage was woefully inadequate, and the bulb emitted a faint yellow glow that slightly pushed back the encroaching gloom. Disturbed dust was thick as smoke. Many unseen hazards awaited the unwary, and only the inspector's caution prevented a nasty fall over an unstable stack of storage crates. Alerted by sliding wood, he steadied the top container before the tower collapsed.

Silver gleams danced around a woman's outstretched leg, the glint brightest on her shiny curved foot. The still feminine figure was off balance, and would topple over without the supporting ankle vice and concrete cinderblocks. There were no rings or cables, but Quinn dragged the brown wig hair behind the left ear with his torch. Best to verify the leotard-clad gymnast was a mannequin and not a third murder victim.

A human shadow moved across the long rectangular bright patch cast by the doorway. Heavy breathing was audible between the machinery hums.

Quinn stepped forward, aiming the light beam at Justin West. The guy's chin hairs had grown to uneven lengths, greasy strands stuck together. His loose shirt hung from his scruffy trousers, and his spectacles reflected the torch glare.

"Cassie's beautiful, isn't she?" he said. "So lifelike. I'm not surprised you mistook her for the real thing."

"Most of us know the difference between a person and a toy."

Quinn kept his guard up as West approached. The weirdo felt the bodies of his stored mannequins. The closest had a twisted narrow leg, bladed figure skate tucked by its neck. A giant sculpture of Tamara Cole was impossible to miss, and the shadowy mannequin behind it must be the kickboxer based on the clothes and stance.

"You're missing one," Quinn said.

"Monique. Director Harris wants her kept on display."

That was the second time he'd used an actual name. This freak was in his own world, playing with women's body parts and dressing them up. The twisted obsession of a loner… or something more?

"But you've left space for her in your collection. Between Valdez and Cole."

Quinn nodded at the gap, then realised he too had started calling them names. He really needed to get away from this place. Senior joint force detectives would take over tomorrow, but he still had one night of insanity to survive.

"She's in danger, Inspector."

"With two girls dead, we kind of figured that."

West strode past, picking up speed as he cornered the shelf. He shifted the computer mouse to clear the screensaver. That image – the discontinued promotional shot of all five models – was displayed.

"Look at the order," he said. "First Elena, then Raquel."

The whispering oddball moved his index finger – the one with the badly wrapped, bloodstained plaster – across the women's necks.

"Now it's Monique's turn. Beautiful Monique."

"You should go home, Mister West. Stay here, and I might mistake you for a killer."

"They're not safe here!" he shouted, knocking the mouse into the keyboard so hard it overturned. "Somebody wants the models dead."

The laser beam shone dangerously close to his eyes. Foamy froth formed between his lips, bubbles popping to leave a whitish residue.

"Is that so?" Quinn asked. "An obsessed fan, perhaps?"

DC Moore walked in before he received an answer. The smartly attired woman with her neatly combed hair couldn't be a greater contrast to the babbling suspect.

"Brad's getting ready to lock down the complex," she said.

"Hear that?" Quinn patted West hard on the shoulder, and flakes of dandruff fell off. "You've got nothing to worry about. Unless you're the murderer?"

The technician seemed unsettled, panicked eyes enlarged by his spectacle lenses. Then he laughed. A deep, long-lasting chuckle that made both detectives shift uncomfortably.

The computer's screen flickered and the air conditioners ground to a halt. A few seconds passed before power was restored. West wandered about, zeroing in on a clump of insulated cables that disappeared through a floor grating. Was there an even deeper dungeon below?

"Another surge!" he exclaimed. "The previous one took out the lights, and they're becoming more regular. It's a pattern. Don't you see?"

"Hexagon are skint and didn't pay the electric bill this month," Quinn said jovially. "There you are. Mystery solved."

"He's in our system. The killer's here."

The inspector rested his arm on West's shoulder, careful to protect his hand with the sleeve. Those dandruff flakes had left him itchy.

"I think you might be on to something. Tell you what. DC Moore and I will do another sweep, but first, we need to get you safely home."

He pressed the computer's power switch to shut it down, ushered the blathering West into the corridor, and slammed the door. This loon was too erratic to be a plausible suspect in the methodical mannequin killings, but everyone was on edge. Allowing him to spread conspiracy theories wouldn't help.

Moore took the lead, and Quinn followed a few paces back. West's head was bowed in resignation, and he uttered no further prophecies of doom as they boarded the lift to the foyer.

"See Mister West out."

Quinn kept watch until they reached the entrance, then joined Brad behind the reception desk.

The guard perched forward as monitor images showed Tamara and Monique return to their rooms. The two women walked side by side, more interested in each other than where they stepped. A catfight seemed imminent until the swimmer broke off to enter her quarters.

"Give me a sitrep," Quinn said.

Brad was captivated by events on screen. Even on the small monitor, the model's flapping evening dress and bare legs were visible. She was in permanent seduction mode, swaying walk and curvy backside designed to draw attention.

"Who's still in the building? Sooner you answer, the sooner you can go back to girl watching."

"Just us, your partner, and the models."

Monique walked out of sight, and Brad finally turned his head. Moore re-entered the lobby and gave a confirmatory nod. The exterior camera showed a battered brown vehicle with a misaligned rear license plate – and the cursing technician driver – leave via the main gate.

A rumble of thunder followed, and raindrops struck the glass doors and windows. Another storm. This was England, after all, and the brief spell of sunny Yorkshire weather was over.

"Did the director check out yet?" Quinn asked.

"Five minutes ago. His clothes were soaking wet. Appears somebody dumped him."

Brad grinned, then remembered the telltale strangulation mark and gave it a quick rub.

"Garneau likes to leave an impression," the inspector noted. "What about the reporter?"

The guard fastened his collar to hide the bruises and nodded sheepishly.

"He say where he was going? You know what? Forget it. I'm just glad that nosy prick's out of my face. Lock the place down."

Brad's hand went straight to an enormous push button labelled *Emergency Lockdown*. The enthusiastic watchman paused, almost for dramatic effect, then pressed the switch.

Red lights flashed everywhere: the panel, swirling discs in glass shells, thin strips around the entrance threshold. Repeated shrill beeps broadcast over the tannoy, a warning noise similar to a reversing truck.

Motors whirred as roller shutters descended over the windows, and a thick, armour-plated steel barrier dropped beyond the front doors. The impact clang was unexpectedly muted. The rain was quieter with the security shields in place, and metallic clinks replaced spats.

When the commotion ended, the only red lights were locked door icons on the building layout terminal. The blueprints of Hexagon HQ cycled automatically, confirming sealed entry points across the complex. Green open padlock symbols overlaid the office doors, except the upper two floors where amber locks denoted restricted access.

Did sealing the exits violate fire safety regulations? Probably, but let the ethics team argue with Harris and Cole.

"Anything interesting?" Moore asked Quinn.

"This evening's entertainment. Watching videos and computer screens. Don't suppose there's any way to lock those annoying women up permanently? I understand the executive windows can be opened in emergencies, so the company's precious assets will be protected."

Brad pointed to the map screen. "From here, I can add or remove privileges. Say the word, and I'll turn their keycards into worthless bits of plastic."

"I was being ironic."

* * *

Cassie's latest brazen attempt had ended in another failure. Overconfident in her ability, she had overshot the high uneven bar during the backflip. She would normally have fallen onto the exercise mat and be suffering in pain for incompetence. Except there was no ground beneath her suspended silver painted self, only an impenetrable dark void.

She couldn't move a muscle, not even her neck. That was secure in a choker ring that restricted her movement, with the tiniest gap to let her breathe. Her entire body was effectively paralysed, including the motionless lock of hair at the upper frame of her vision.

"Help!" she wanted to scream, but only unintelligible moans came from her wide open mouth.

Her colleagues were behind the apparatus. The corpses of Elena, Raquel, Monique, and Tamara had been posed on their engraved hexagonal pedestals. Sportswomen in branded clothes, lives snuffed out and transformed into copies of their silver mannequins. Only the fifth model – Cassie Simms – was absent from the Modern Woman exhibit.

"You think you can do this? To me?" yelled the masked man. "I'm the Earl of York."

Bennett had returned from the dead to mock her. Powerless to even flinch, Cassie was forced to watch the sex attacker thrust his switchblade. Ice cold steel touched her skin as the sharp edge sliced her Hexagon Sports leotard down the middle.

It was about to come off and leave her naked when a black leather gloved figure grabbed Earl from behind. Their combat knife was enormous by comparison. A murder weapon that slit open the man's throat from ear to ear, cutting through flesh with ruthless precision.

Blood spewed from the wound. Cassie's whole body turned crimson, sticky liquid dripping onto her still tongue. A nauseating aftertaste, but she couldn't spit it out.

The dead man collapsed, leaving the armoured mannequin killer in his place. An anonymous masked figure in black, eyes obscured by shadow.

The murderer whispered through the metallic gauze. "Why should I spare you? You're like all the others."

A genderless voice that sounded vaguely familiar, but the assailant's identity remained a mystery.

Music played, a thumping tune that woke Cassie from her nightmare. The darkness disappeared, becoming the executive office with the horrid green carpet. Released from her imaginary shackles, she sat up and threw back the bedsheet.

She answered the cellphone on the bookshelf. "Lyle. Glad to hear your voice."

"Except I didn't say anything."

Cassie turned up the volume to counteract the rain noise. This high above ground, there were no trees or structures to dampen the breeze.

A storm was brewing over the fields of Yorkshire. Fluffy grey clouds flashed blue as a bolt of lightning struck. The thunderous boom that followed three seconds later was loud, even with the double-glazed window shut tight.

"Listen," Lyle said. "Me and Dan are heading to the boxing club to check the footage. Maybe we can identify this bastard."

"Not sure the killer's a guy. Tamara's either the murderer or involved somehow."

"You hang in there. We got this."

Dan's voice in the background, devoid of irony or dark humour. He was finally on their team and supportive, but his reassuring words offered little comfort.

"We both saw the footage," Cassie said. "Those rings that allow the killer to use lower body strength and keep their hands free. That psycho wants us all dead."

"But not you." Lyle speaking again. "At least, not yet."

"Seems I'm special, important to whatever big event this madness is building towards. Well, I don't feel like participating."

Cassie went to the window. The Hexagon Sports sign letters, bright spot lamps, and torrential rainstorm made it difficult to see the entrance gate far below. If those two blue emergency lights were police cars, there were – at most – four officers on duty. Plus Quinn and Moore inside. That wouldn't be enough.

Cassie tucked the phone between her shoulder and tilted head. She performed warm-up exercises – jump jacks and skips on the spot – to get her blood circulating. Sleeping in clothes had left her muscles stiff.

"Raquel put up one hell of a struggle," she said. "And the killer was ready for her. This crime spree was planned long ago, and the storm is perfect cover."

"Cassie, please…"

"You two need to figure out who's under that mask and the connection to Gemma Bright. Her alleged suicide is the root of this, when it all started."

"Solve a serial killer case all by ourselves? No pressure, then." Dan's serious streak hadn't lasted long. "You just relax in your nice cosy office, Miss Simms, and leave the rest to us."

***

They had all underestimated him. The police and Hexagon bosses thought their steel barriers would keep a lowly technician out. But he knew everything about their precious security system – and the weak points – since Ms Cole had consulted his department about the electrical installation.

The first problem was getting back inside the perimeter. Justin expected Brad and the cops would be watching through the surveillance network, so he had driven through the main gate to avert suspicion.

Exterior patrols were limited to three uniformed men and an attractive blonde, and they were far more interested in chatting and supping coffee than checking for intruders. The lashing rain was a great deterrent to legwork, which left two kilometres of chain-link fence unguarded.

Justin doubled back around Poppleton Business Park and looked for a suitable place to hide. His second-hand motor wasn't the flashiest model, but technicians were in a different financial league from models and executives. They had their sports cars and limousines, but he had the toolbox stored in the boot, and that contained all he needed to breach their corporate tower.

The narrow through road was unsheltered, and lights were off in the two neighbouring warehouses. No other vehicles meant no late shift workers to question who owned a suspicious parked car.

Justin stepped out into the whistling gale, feeling damp

hair whip his forehead. Rainwater flooded his spectacles and blurred his vision. Droplets arced in mid-flight, a misty sea of tiny stingers impossible to avoid. The pressure was constant, the conditions horrendous.

"Think you can stop me?" he shouted in defiance.

Fierce wind forced Justin to hug the vehicle, and he struggled to release the hatch lock with his numb hand. He collected the transparent raincoat and gratefully slid it on. That kept his body relatively dry, but his soggy trouser legs were unshielded. Rain found its way through his cracked trainers, and a squelch accompanied every step that squeezed water from his clingy socks.

Justin held his hood forward, creating a temporary covering for his glasses. He fetched only the wire cutters from the toolbox and made the short, but challenging, walk to the Hexagon Sports complex.

To sabotage the electric fence, he had removed a circuit box fuse before meeting Inspector Quinn in his lab. Without power, the bright yellow lightning bolt signs were empty threats. Justin's frozen hands were unresponsive, but humming the *Blue Danube Waltz* brought back happy memories of his dance with the silver beauty Elena Savikova.

Metal wires snapped under applied pressure, severed by his trusty tool. After a minute's hard work, he created an alternate route into the grounds.

Justin kicked the broken fence section out of shape and ducked through the gap. A loud rip, and he couldn't move.

Water seeped through his torn raincoat, drowning his shirt below the chest. He pulled the caught polythene, but it only became more entangled on the exposed, hook like protrusions.

Justin brandished the wire cutter handles and pointed

the open steel jaws at the illuminated office windows. Solitary bright lights in the sky marked the rooms where the girls were sleeping.

"I'm coming, Monique. Your hero is here to save you."

He didn't need the raincoat, so he pulled his arms free. The ripped plastic sheet blew in the wind. Fully exposed, he sneezed, a loud outburst that could have announced his presence, except nobody else was around.

A thin, vertical golden glow was a beacon in the oppressive night. That was the emergency exit from the gymnasium he had propped open with a wooden wedge earlier. In theory, that should have generated a security alert on Brad's monitor map, but Justin had disabled the electrical panel – and shutter – with a paperclip and soldering iron.

Once inside, he collected the triangular block and closed the door to cover his tracks. He wiped the water from his lenses. That only partially worked, since his fingers were also damp.

The gym area was dark, but there were no cameras between his entry point and the nearest stairwell. Unlike the police, the technician didn't need a map to find his way around Hexagon. He knew the little used closets and storerooms well enough, and most security measures protected public areas and upper level offices. The lower floors and sub-basement were his territory.

Justin reached his workshop without incident, switched on his portable battery powered light, and headed for the furthest storage shelf. The grey plastic case was free of dust, unlike the boxes surrounding it.

The technician discarded his wire cutters and released the two sliding locks. His backup implement had served its purpose. He now had access to his primary toolbox, where he kept the professional equipment.

Rubber gloves, steel cables, and a large serrated blade. Everything Justin required to complete his task.

* * *

DC Moore paused by the hexagonal windows outside Cassie's room. The young model sat on the bed, fingers interlocked and flexing her hands. Trouble sleeping? That was only natural in this situation.

The upper corridors of power were luxurious, with faux antique light fittings and plush, vacuumed carpets without a single patch of dirt. A false image the company wished to present.

The trainee detective had resented interviewing the creepy Justin West during the initial investigation, but his flaws were on the surface. This was Hexagon Sports, where women were commodities and sex objects, and well-manicured businessmen would betray their closest friends to advance up the corporate ladder.

"Everything okay, Moore?"

The male voice crackled through her radio. A worse connection than the previous hourly check, with static hisses between the words. It was likely interference because of the storm.

"No sign of trouble," she reported. "All clear, as usual."

"Don't sound too enthusiastic. You're... cosy, and we're stuck... this crappy weather."

"If you prefer, there are rich bitches in here to babysit. Just be grateful for the time and a half, Benson."

She had recognised the Liverpudlian accent. A recent transfer, and another "senior" copper who resented her promotion.

"Moore out."

She twisted the dial to stop transmission and stowed her radio in its belt holder. Sensing someone close by, she checked the corridor, finger poised to press the panic button. But she saw only shadows and office furniture. Irregular rumbles of thunder were constantly in the background, a reminder of the remote location.

Moore stepped into the gymnast's room. Cassie, ready to respond to any intrusion, was partway through standing when she acknowledged her visitor with a shy wave.

"Don't know why I'm so nervous," she said. "Should be used to it by now. Being the bait, I mean."

"The building's secure. There's nothing to worry about."

"You told me that before. At the sports centre, when we talked about Bennett. How did that work out?"

A fair point – nobody was safe with a model-slaying psycho out there.

"I'll be right outside if you need anything."

Moore closed the door gently and walked towards the lift. The corridor seemed darker than before. Or was it her fickle imagination? No, the stairwell light was out.

Supposedly, this building was better protected than a police safe house, but countryside farmyard smells and rickety cottage windows would be a less haunting experience.

The detective opened the door to check. A metal grille with narrow spaced slats rested against the corner wall – a vent cover unscrewed to expose a rectangular duct at eye level. Someone had taped a clear cellophane sheet across the hole, and the space behind was full of dense green smoke. Plastic crinkled under pressure.

As the detective reached down to sound her personal alarm, a gloved hand clamped her mouth, and she tasted rubber between her lips. She grabbed the radio as a strong unseen attacker lifted her chin.

Something extremely sharp cut her neck, all the way across. The assailant thrust her forward. She staggered, covering her wet throat as blood gushed over her fingers.

Dizzy from the attack, Moore spun and fell backwards down the steps. Concrete edges banged her back as she slid down a half level, unable to slow her descent. Her head collided with the floor, leaving her skull sticky at the contact point.

Vision fading, she saw a silhouetted figure in the doorway. They twisted a gleaming bloodstained knife in a white surgical gloved hand. The person wasn't bulky enough to be wearing the body armour seen in the murder footage. Who was it? Moore couldn't even discern the basics: height, race, or gender.

"Anything happening up there?"

Quinn. She had to warn him.

Moore lifted her weak hands to her belt, but felt only an empty holder. The shadowy figure held up the stolen transmitter, and another object beside it.

"All clear… Moore out."

It wasn't her that spoke, but a voice recording. She wanted to scream for help, but the punishing fall had sapped her energy.

The mannequin killer – it surely must be them – closed the door, leaving Moore in near total darkness. They knew she was close to death. As life slipped away, she realised Cassie and her boyfriend had been right.

The police hadn't protected the models by locking down the building. They had trapped them inside with the murderer.

CHAPTER THIRTEEN

Unsafe and Insecure

You are in a twisty maze of passageways, all alike.

A quote from the 1970s, the bygone era of bedroom programmers, but any genuine geek would know the terse room description from the classic text-based adventure game *Colossal Cave*. Every time Justin ventured into the depths of the Hexagon complex, he recalled that line.

The sub-basement corridors were a labyrinth of T-Junctions, crossroads, and dead ends. Nobody – not even the humblest worker – had an office down here. Plaster flakes had disintegrated, leaving exposed concrete and a lingering mouldy smell. Arrow signs at intersections were supposed to provide direction, but the dirt caked words were unreadable.

Strip lights were flush with the ceiling. Protected by rough opaque plastic, they hummed like refrigerators. Appropriate, since it was deathly cold without the luxury of central heating. Still wet from the thunderstorm, Justin's hair had turned ice hard.

It was an endurance testing slog, and every tired footstep created an echo. The sliding steel doors and dust clogged vents were ancient by Hexagon standards. Ignored in the recent renovation, these areas housed essential equipment the bosses took for granted. The technician kept the maintenance key in his workshop toolbox, away from prying eyes. That, and the sub-level access lift, were trade secrets.

Justin held his breath to block out the garbage stench as he passed the recycling dump, knife clutched tight in his gloved hand. Trouble could lurk around any blind corner.

"I'll save you, Monique."

A promise to comfort himself. The communications relay was two floors beneath the lobby, and Justin smiled when he saw the well-oiled hinges. Polished and clear of rust, they stood out from their counterparts, which meant somebody had cleaned them recently. That never happened on this floor without a work order, and the next checkup wasn't scheduled for another six months.

The technician reached into the indented handle and slid open the door. It moved far too quietly, a further sign of unauthorised use.

He flipped the light switch and waited a full minute. Nowhere to hide inside the cubical room, since shelves were too close to the walls. Silence except for clicking from the control panel, and the long approach corridor was surprisingly well lit, without a turn for twenty metres.

Satisfied he was alone, Justin walked to the central relay box. Insulated grey cables, fed through humped brackets, converged at the covered audiovisual processor. Technical terms those bumbling detectives wouldn't comprehend, but he was an electronics expert, and knew the power surges weren't coincidence.

Justin used his army knife to remove the six flathead screws. It wasn't the most suitable tool, but safety was the priority, and against a murderer, a screwdriver would be a useless makeshift weapon. One by one, bolts popped from the holes. Then the steel cover came free.

"I knew it," he said.

As expected, the intruder had spliced into the primary cable. The inner workings of the hi-tech black plastic cylinder were invisible, but the foreign object was a top-tier hacking device.

Multicoloured wires connected to a mini tablet computer with a digital timer readout. Every few seconds, five red indicator lights flashed in quick succession. If the police had discovered this, they would have called the bomb squad, but the casing was too small to house an effective quantity of explosive.

Justin tapped the screen, and multiple surveillance videos appeared. Thumbnail size, real-time camera images combined into one large picture. That butch guard was stationed in the lobby, unaware his setup had been rendered useless.

A wave segment pattern icon blinked beside the last digit, the universal symbol for Wi-Fi. The hacker could access the splicer remotely, perhaps through a specialised cellphone app, and substitute misleading camera feeds whenever they needed to move about undetected. Otherwise, the security system would function normally, which explained why nobody had discovered the intrusion.

Though the tech whiz could theorise the setup, he didn't know how to disable it, so he adopted a crude solution. He pulled out the wires in one big clump and sliced them with his knife.

LED indicators flashed, and a red error message appeared over the broadcast images. *Video Feed Interrupted.*

"Yes!" Justin fist pumped the air. "I've done it."

The door slammed shut, and the lights went out, almost at the same time.

Justin squinted, but the room was pitch dark. He backed away from where he presumed the entrance was, knife pointed forward.

Metal clanged as his foot collided with something hard. Was that a shelf leg? He listened for any sign of the intruder, but only heard his own heightened breathing.

Another red light blinked above, revealing a curved plastic surface and a white box. He had tripped a motion sensor and foolishly trapped himself.

A hairless shadow moved. In front, very close. Justin stared ahead, still adjusting to the gloom.

Lightning flashed before him, arcing between two contact points. The dark figure thrust the stun gun at his neck.

Electrified, he bit his tongue and tasted blood. The discarded knife clattered to the floor before he could raise it in defence.

The sudden shock left Justin vibrating on the spot, somehow still standing as high voltage numbed his senses. A metal gauze over the attacker's lower face flashed blue. Intermittent light revealed body armour and tools on the black-clad intruder's belt.

Justin felt he recognised the unblinking eyes surrounded by shiny hard plastic, but his scrambled brain wouldn't process the visual information. The shadow split, dividing into several that fleshed out as reality shifted to a nightmarish hallucination. Vince Harris, Tamara Cole and

DI Quinn laughed at his ineptitude.

All three drew a polished black gun, then his tormentors merged into a single, faceless humanoid figure. A brief hiss of air, followed by a sharp pain in his central neck area.

Justin wanted to remove the needle, but couldn't lift his tired hands. The feeble technician, stupid to believe he was a hero, stumbled backward. He crashed into the shelf and lost consciousness.

* * *

Lyle opened the driver's side door, exposing himself to the torrid weather. He had kept the engine running to keep warm while he psyched himself up. The false comfort his parked vehicle provided made the storm and unfolding horrors at Hexagon seem distant, but the sudden inrush of chilly air roused him from his moody contemplation.

"You sure about this?" Dan asked.

"Wasn't that supposed to be my question?"

Lyle exited before his friend reconsidered helping. He'd parked close to *Rick's Underdogs*, so the steps to the underground club were only a few metres away.

After dark in this miserable rainstorm, it was unsurprising the lesser travelled alleys of York were deserted. Which was good, since they were about to commit a criminal offence.

"No speech?" Lyle queried. "About this being against the law, and me not giving a shit?"

"From what you told me, we can't trust the police. And I don't either, so I got your back."

Dan was a wretched sight, hooded sports jacket and baseball cap only slightly reducing the rainfall on his dripping wet face. His jeans were a darker shade of blue from the ankles down. Hands stuffed in his pockets, he was tightlipped and fierce eyed. This was a situation even the perennial joker couldn't make light of.

Lyle looked down the staircase and saw a door beyond the flooded lowermost step. Almost certainly locked with crime scene tape across the frame.

"They're holed up in their Poppleton fortress," he said, "thinking it will keep the killer out."

Dan slapped his electric torch in Lyle's hand. "Then they talk even more rubbish than you."

They descended the slippery steps to the club entrance. Lyle stood to one side and aimed the light beam at the tumbler lock. His coat was thick and thermal lined, but this narrow passage trapped the rain, and neither man avoided soaking their shoes in the three-inch deep puddle.

Dan pulled out a cloth wrapped set of curved metal probes. Probably picking tools, but Lyle didn't ask for specific details. His reformed gang member friend was taking an enormous risk, so it wasn't appropriate to dredge up his criminal past.

"Thought the owner was security conscious," Dan said between two metallic scrapes. "This lock is child's play."

"Concealed cameras inside, and a secret control room. A seemingly easy target, with CCTV to record criminals in the act." Lyle reassured his companion with a shoulder pat. "But don't worry. If they're still switched on, we'll delete the footage."

"This all sounds very familiar. Can't believe you've talked me into this shit… again."

Unseen cog wheels spun inside the mechanism and a bolt slid back. The door was stiff and required a hefty push, but there was no burglar alarm siren.

Lyle sighed with relief and ducked through the crime tape. He found the light switch, operated it, and waited for Dan to close up behind them before returning the electric torch. There were no signs they had tripped a sensor, but nerves were evident from his constant looking around.

"You know, we could have asked the club owner nicely for the key," Dan said.

"I don't want to involve third parties. What if we can't trust him? I'm trying to save Cassie's life here."

"Just be careful not to wreck your own in the process. I'm with you, but we're crossing a black line."

The overhead pipes creaked as the heating system kicked in. Police had removed the two bodies and evidence, but a dried bloodstain remained in the boxing ring where Earl Bennett was murdered, and cleaners hadn't yet wiped away the silver *TOUGHNESS* message behind the bench press.

Yellow folding tags marked key locations of the crime scene where the mannequin killer had claimed their victims. Five murders altogether, if the "suicides" of Wade Wilson and Gemma Bright were cleverly staged killings.

From Cassie's description, Lyle had a good idea where the owner's secret spy room was, but the numbered sticky note made it obvious. The mirrored door was slightly ajar, and neon strip lights switched on as he entered.

Two minutes later, they had settled in – as best they could – and booted up the surveillance system. Manipulating video files was more in Lyle's comfort zone, and he fiddled with the controls until the screens displayed the unedited recordings of the double murder.

Unlike the footage shown by police in the Hexagon boardroom, these were uncensored. Multiple camera shots played together, synchronised and time stamped.

Dan gulped and turned away, unable to watch the killer choke the kickboxer. Various angles showed the strong Latina's struggle against her masked attacker, and her thwarted attacks against a heavily armoured opponent. All those pictures, and no clear front view of the murderer. Identification seemed impossible, but they had to try.

"You think that's the blonde under the mask?" Dan still refused to watch.

With the evidence implicating Tamara, she was a suspect for sure. But so was Vince Harris, and the killer could be someone else entirely. Lyle would rather avoid assumptions.

He put the videos on fast forward. The assault blurred by as time sped up.

Raquel fell limp in the chokehold. After slitting Bennett's throat, the masked attacker dragged the model's body to the bench press. They spray painted her chest and arms, although her silver skin appeared light grey on the grainy video. To pose the corpse, the assailant secured the victim's limbs with steel cables. Then they added the message to the wall.

Dan had partially overcome his fear, though he looked ready to puke. "You want to go through *that* in slow motion? What exactly are we hoping to find?"

"Whatever we can."

* * *

Justin's wrists and ankles were tightly bound by a hard edged material that dug into his skin, causing sharp pain every time he attempted to move. The thin strips felt like plastic, possibly zip ties.

His attacker hadn't blindfolded him, so this must be a

dark room. The surface beneath him was rough, with tiny holes at regular intervals. Sideways shifts had revealed hard surfaces in both directions. When he tried shuffling forward, his bare feet encountered a similar obstacle, and pushing back had left him with a nasty head bump. He was alone in a coffin-like box, waiting to die.

Justin heard a whirr outside the container. A fan – not a powerful air conditioner, but a smaller scale version. And some illumination at last, a faint green glow that revealed a rectangular object above him, slightly narrower than the trough's outer rim.

Classical music played – the unmistakable *Blue Danube Waltz* – and the technician knew where he was. The vacuum forming machine in his own lab.

"Hey! Who's there?"

No answer, but Justin suspected he wouldn't like the killer's response.

He had created many silver mannequins in this contraption and watched countless body sections form around fiberglass moulds. Was he destined for a similar fate?

A partial human shadow fell across Justin's bare, hairy chest. The captive realised his buttocks and testicles were as cold as everything else. While he was unconscious, the murderer must have stripped him completely naked.

A sequence of electronic beeps, not part of the orchestra. The flat plastic sheet above glowed orange, shimmering as heat spread. Warmth diffused down through the mould press. Justin wished the chill would return, but the temperature continued rising.

"I don't know anything!" he bellowed at the gap. "Please!"

Through the opening, he saw the assailant's armoured

chest. Black cloth and protective rubber pads appeared golden yellow, their outlines distorted by shifting air currents.

Behind the murderer, Justin spotted the steel crisscross cage of a transportation cart. Large enough to hold several bulky crates, or wheel an unconscious man along the basement corridors. The killer must have stolen his key and operated the maintenance platform.

"Let me go!"

The assailant ignored his pleas and reached down. For a fleeting moment, Justin saw the killer's unforgiving eyes through oval holes in the black mask. When the unknown person stood back up, they held a radio – a bulky police transmitter with a keypad and oversized antenna – and a digital audio recorder.

"I found something in the basement," a woman's voice said. "Meet me downstairs."

Constable Moore? No, she sounded different. A close resemblance, but without the normal fluidity. The killer must have synthesised her speech with sound processing software or artificial intelligence tools.

"It's not her!" Justin shouted. "Don't listen!"

"That music in the background. You in the workshop?"

Inspector Quinn was walking into the murderer's trap. The *Blue Danube Waltz* continued to play, building to its finale.

"Stay away! It's a trick. A fake voice."

"Hold tight," the unaware cop said over the radio. "I'm coming."

"No!"

The killer must have switched the two-way to receive only. Which meant the warnings went unheeded.

The black-clad figure retreated from the vacuum press,

leaving Justin to sweat under the hot plastic. After what seemed an eternity, he heard approaching footsteps.

"Watch out!"

"West? What the hell's happening here? ... Here?"

A distorted repeat at the end. Quinn's natural voice, followed by a radio transmission.

The scruffy dressed detective turned beside the vacuum machine, jacket back visible under the heated plastic. A whoosh, then a squish. The sound pattern repeated three more times.

Justin remained quiet and watched Quinn's hands disappear from view. He clutched his chest area, gasping weakly. Then he collapsed.

The black garbed killer stood in the detective's place, holding a blood-smeared knife. They must have stabbed him to death. Lured by a cleverly plotted ruse, Quinn never had a chance.

The murderer reached for the control that lowered the rig. Justin screamed as the ripply orange-red rectangle descended towards him.

He heaved himself up, only to be pushed back down when the searing hot plastic pressed against his naked skin. There was no escape from the inferno. Without clothes to protect him, Justin's entire body felt on fire.

He writhed about, generating creaky noises as the floppy material bent out of shape. His spectacles spared his eyes from being boiled in their sockets. But that only magnified the agony everywhere else.

Constant hissing came from below as the vacuum system activated. Molten plastic sunk into his open mouth, surrounding his burnt tongue and silencing his screams.

As Justin suffocated, the pressure increased, trapping his bound legs at an awkward ankle. Mercifully, he passed out within seconds.

* * *

Reflective silver plastic cooled around the technician's body, his twisted death pose frozen into the hardened sheet. Powerful vacuum suction had captured minor details, such as his terrified final scream and dislodged spectacles. Justin had enjoyed moulding his mannequins, so it was fitting he become one.

After the murderer had gassed the models unconscious, they used the secret sub-basement route to the business park hideout. There, they changed into their black protective outfit and mask. On the way back to the Hexagon complex, Justin triggered the silent alarm. The killer's quick intervention hadn't stopped him from destroying the hacking device beyond repair.

Even with employee building access, it had been difficult finding somewhere the splicer wouldn't be found by routine maintenance checks. Had the nerd interfered sooner, he could have ruined everything, but with the two detectives taken care of, only the incompetent security guard and civilians remained.

The technician's maintenance lift key made it easy to transport the body upstairs, more efficient than pushing the cart up the service ramp. Eliminating Justin wasn't part of the original plan. He was a low paid employee, not an executive or model sellout, but his meddling warranted a painful death.

The killer stored the police radio and audio recorder with their equipment. Those AI generated speech patterns had proven useful in distracting DI Quinn, and would be invaluable later.

The backpack contained the steel cables, locking rings, and spray paint. For weapons, the choker, electrical stunner, ketamine dart gun, and cleaned combat knife should be sufficient.

With the hack disabled, the cameras were active again, but the few between the workshop and reception area were easy to avoid. Even if the dumb guard was alert, he would only glimpse a masked figure.

The killer took the stairs to the ground floor. The lift, with its noisy arrival ping, might have alerted Brad – had he been attentive. But the moron, absorbed in his adult magazine, wasn't watching the reception desk monitors.

He remained oblivious as the murderer edged closer, gently lowering their boots to make almost no sound on the marble tiles. They unhooked the choker from its holder, widened the circle, and dropped the leather loop around the guard's neck.

Unlike Elena and Raquel, the dim-witted sentry reacted slowly. The killer snagged the hooks with their thigh rings and spread their legs to tighten the straps.

Brad tossed his magazine and clawed at the constricting noose. He attempted to pry the attacker's armoured limbs apart. As if such a puny man could. The kickboxer was a far stronger opponent. Compared to her, this guy was unfit and poorly trained.

Strangled gasps became more violent, and the chair shook, almost toppling as the guard wheeled about. He reached for the alarm switch on the desk, but the killer stepped back, pulling him away. His trainers squeaked along the floor.

Fingers shaking, Brad punched at the assailant's face, but only bruised his knuckles on the mask. He had no skill or strategy, only desperation.

The murderer grabbed his shoulders to steady him, then twisted their thighs. There was a loud crunch as his neck snapped in the vice like hold. After the assailant unhooked the choker and removed it, the deceased man slipped off the swivel chair onto the floor.

Now to disable the security systems. The killer unsheathed the combat knife, accessed the panel, and chopped the wires until they sparked.

The masked murderer typed commands on the computer, deactivating all the issued keycards except their own. That should trap the sleeping models in their rooms, where they would be easy prey. Because of the armoured corridor glass, the only potential escape routes were through the emergency window release system. Twenty-two stories above ground with no ladder, that drop wasn't survivable.

What next? That cursed Modern Woman exhibit had been moved behind reception. Four inscribed pedestals were empty, and only the biker's mannequin remained.

You need a makeover, Monique.

An unspoken promise to set the mood. The intruder searched for a suitable weapon and settled on a baseball bat taken from the statue of the Major League player.

Hand clenched around the wooden handle, the killer marched up to the mannequin and kicked it off the motorcycle seat. The brunette wig fell off, leaving a bald silver figure sprawled on the floor.

The murderer knelt down, unzipped the leather jacket, and cut away the underwear with the knife. That exposed the round breasts Justin had insisted on perfectly measuring.

A mental image of another likeness – the mutilated recreation in the display case at Loughborough University –

was the inspiration.

The killer swung down with the bat. At first, the hardened plastic deflected the blows. Wooden clunks became more intense as they attacked with greater speed and increased force. The left dome split down the middle, and another hit smashed it in.

The right breast proved more resilient, but a couple of heavy boot stamps knocked the curved shards into the hole. Mirrored jagged edges reflected the black-clad vandal.

HEXAGON SCUM.

The attacker spray painted that message over the engraved stands and surrounding floor. The company leeches were learning the price of their betrayal four years ago.

Cassie Simms was the nation's idol. How fitting that her iconic pose would make international news – a fallen silver heroine for the world to mourn. But first, she would watch Monique die.

CHAPTER FOURTEEN

High Difficulty

Cassie awoke to a loud thump. Bed springs creaked as she sat up. The last things she remembered were speaking to DC Moore, stretching her body to stay awake, and…

A green mist coming from the vent.

Had that made her doze off? The air was clear now.

Still drowsy, Cassie reached for her mobile phone on the coffee table, only to feel flat glass. She spat on her finger and rubbed her sticky eyelids, blinking to focus her vision. Black floaters hovered in her view, aftereffects of the change in brightness.

Her cellphone had disappeared. She checked the carpet, then leaned over to peer underneath the bed, but it wasn't there either.

Had the killer been inside her room? Nothing else was missing, so perhaps the endless worrying had made her paranoid, and she had simply misplaced it. The storm still raged outside, so she must have heard a thunderclap or a heavy burst of rain.

Something struck the exterior window, so hard the glass vibrated. No marks or fractures, but Cassie hadn't imagined the missile. A grey marble cuboid – taken from a trophy? – spun after the impact, then dropped as gravity took over. There was a metallic clang, likely a secondary collision with the Hexagon Sports sign.

"Cassie!"

A faint female voice, but she couldn't pinpoint the source.

"Are you awake?"

It sounded like Monique, or maybe Tamara. Too quiet to tell for sure.

Cassie launched herself off the springy bed and landed on the carpet, switching to a ready stance in mid-flight. The move was fluid and effortless, befitting a gymnast.

She pressed her head against the window. The reflective blue rods that formed the company sign were far brighter than they appeared from the ground. She cupped her curved hand across her forehead to block the disorientating glare.

Cassie flinched as another object struck the sign frame. It flew by quickly, but looked like a high-heeled shoe. Even with her temple squashed against the cold windowpane, she couldn't see the impatient woman. How could someone have thrown items outside? The window had no handles, and didn't open.

Then she noticed the lever on the ceiling, inside a green painted metal border labelled with the emergency exit symbol. Difficult to reach for a short person, but Cassie jumped, utilised the pane as an unorthodox springboard, and grabbed the thick rod with both hands.

The handle dropped thirty degrees, and the glass swung

outwards on a seamless hinge built into the frame. An escape route, but little use without a very long ladder to climb down.

"About damn time," Monique said. "I've been screaming my head off. We're locked in."

Cassie recognised the motorcyclist's voice now, but the ungrateful rant made it difficult to empathise.

With the howling wind, the sleepy eyed gymnast couldn't think clearly. The sign's frames were spread out to make the letters distinguishable from afar, but provided minimal protection from the chilly rainstorm.

Monique's room was next door, above the bottom of the T, so the length of these executive offices put that about eight metres away. Both windows had opened to the right. The brunette model's blue-lit face kept altering shape, distorted by the rain-streaked glass.

"What do you mean?" Cassie shouted over rumbling thunder. "We were told about the lockdown."

"Not downstairs, you imbecile. Check the door!"

The keypad scanner's green rim light had been replaced by ominous red. It was obvious the card Tamara provided would no longer work, but Cassie snatched it from the coffee table, and tried regardless. As expected, there was a prolonged buzz. The exit remained shut tight, and smashing her clenched fist on the release bumper did nothing.

Inspired by Monique's antics, she grabbed a snooker competition trophy – a sculpture of a golden ball mounted on a miniature cue – and threw it against a hexagonal corridor window. Instead of smashing the glass as she hoped, it bounced harmlessly off.

The killer had trapped her in the office, with no way out. She kicked the armoured pane in frustration, a senseless act of violence that gave her a throbbing foot ache.

"Why the hell did they install this unbreakable shit?"

"Protection," Monique said as Cassie popped her head back outside. "Hexagon's a high-profile company, which makes the VIPs a target for activists. The glass is bulletproof, so if we're attacked, security can seal staff inside."

"Yeah, and so can the fucking mannequin killer."

Cassie thumped the window in anger, ignoring her achy palm. This wasn't like her, using expletives in every sentence, but Monique had also shed her assured persona. Sexual manipulation and seduction were her principal weapons, useless in this scenario. From this height, they could scream all they wanted, and the police posted by the entrance gate wouldn't hear.

"That bitch took my phone while I was asleep," the soaked brunette said. "When she comes back, I'm ready for her."

The strong-armed woman snapped a leather strap taut, generating a crack louder than the thunder. She held a gothic choker, an erotic variant of the device the murderer strangled Raquel with.

"You think Tamara's doing this?" Cassie surmised. "Why?"

"Who else could it be? All the others are—"

Monique shrieked without warning as a gloved person grabbed her hair from behind. The unseen assailant pulled the stunned model away from the window. Pottery smashed amidst sounds of a struggle.

"Monique!"

Cassie's cry was answered by choking. The strangulation noises became quieter, drowned out by rain.

A ringtone made her jump. It wasn't her own. The sound originated from the bookcases near the bed, where a green glow illuminated two business directories. Wedged apart, with a smartphone lodged in the tight gap.

Cassie rushed over and pulled the device free. She pressed the receiver button to answer the incoming call.

Monique's face appeared on the screen. A clump of damp black hair covered one eye, but her other moved about constantly as the unseen attacker throttled her with the gothic choker. The leather strap was taut, pulled offscreen to the right.

The gasping woman turned her head and clawed at the loop. Sharp fingernails cut her own neck, leaving parallel bloody lines. The gloved murderer grabbed Monique's throat below the noose, a strong grip that pinned her against the flowery bed quilt.

Her tongue stuck out between parted ruby red lips as she gasped for air. Strangled gurgles and thuds played over the phone's speaker. Through all this, the camera remained fixed, too steady to be handheld. Had the psycho set up a stand to record this?

Cassie stabbed the end call button to switch the snuff video off. It continued to play, and pressing digits didn't stop the transmission. The killer had disabled the keypad's usual functions.

Of course. Why give her the means to contact the police?

"Get off her, you sicko!"

Snarling in frustration, she threw the cellphone at the window. It skidded on the glass, then dropped into the darkness. A clang resonated as it struck something metallic below.

The sign.

Cassie sprinted round the bed to the opening. Horizontal struts supported the hexagonal frames, with diameters narrow enough for a person to grasp. Those spotlights would be too hot to touch safely, but not the reflective blue and light-absorbing black rods. A framework of metal poles and an aluminium grating platform beneath them. The path to Monique's room was dangerous, but it existed.

"The uneven bars," Cassie muttered. "It had to be."

All those falls in the university gym came flooding back, but she pushed those thoughts – and the recent nightmare – from her mind. She was a gymnast. Staying trapped in here wasn't an option.

She leant backwards through the window to check the roof. A maintenance gondola hung from a yellow painted crane. Workers would use the cage lift to clean the facade or repair the sign's electrics, but it was two floors up. Which left those dreaded bars.

"Never mind. You got this."

Self-reassuring pep talk done, Cassie opened her bag and removed the leotard. Although it wasn't her own red favourite, the lightweight, flexible fabric was designed for arduous tests, and this certainly qualified.

She discarded her trainer shoes, socks and everything except her undergarments, and slipped into the smooth royal blue costume. Hexagon sportswear was of elite quality, custom made and tailored to fit. She was ready for the challenge.

The barefooted Cassie surveyed the sign struts a second time.

Damn it. The rain had created a slippery coating. Her little fingers would come right off just from hanging, let alone a momentum building swing or handstand. The route suddenly seemed far more treacherous.

How to even the odds? Travelling to Poppleton under police escort had left her unprepared, with no personal effects except for her casual clothes. She needed to improvise. The Venetian window blinds were rail mounted, with no cords to fashion a safety rope from. Was there anything else? Cassie checked the desk, bookshelves, and cabinets.

Chalk. Snooker memorabilia, but a godsend in this predicament. She took the paper wrapped cube, placed it on the coffee table, and bashed it with a sports trophy. A few strikes, and the block crumbled to white dust.

She rubbed her hands in powder until both palms were covered, then spread some on her bare soles. That would provide additional grip for the tricky acrobatics ahead, but would it be enough?

Cassie held her hand outside. Spitting rain, a brief respite from the downpour. A lull in the storm. And an opportunity.

What about grips? She didn't have those either. A search of the desk and shelves revealed nothing useful, but there were stationery supplies in the top drawer, including a pair of scissors.

Cassie cut up her socks, shearing the tough cotton until she had four loose pieces of fabric. She wrapped them around her hands and feet, overlapping the material to form weak knots. Not very secure, but they should hold long enough.

"You got this," she repeated, taking a breath.

With the wind intensity drop, it had gone quiet. No more sounds from Monique's room, so she must be dead or knocked out. It didn't matter right now. Morbid thoughts wouldn't help. The priority was escaping this locked office before the murderer came back.

Cassie stepped down onto the narrow aluminium platform, and immediately felt a chilly sensation spread through her foot. She was beside the letter P in Sports, and the first move was a simple climb to the central strut.

Her hand squeaked along the wet metal pole, fingers slipping. She quickly split her bare legs between the lower hexagonal frame and window ledge. Narrowly averting a fatal fall at step one, that highlighted just how difficult this would be.

Far below, blue lights flashed on the police cars. Even if the officers glanced up, the gymnast would appear a tiny figure – a mirage – to them.

Cassie climbed to the pole and planned a sequence of moves past the letters O and R. *Keep it simple. You're trying to survive, not win a gold medal.*

"You won't beat me this time," she said.

The phrase she always used in training before her attempt inevitably ended in failure, but this time was different. Lives were at stake, and there was no exercise mat to break her fall.

A gust of wind blew through the P, shaking her hair. But she – and the tied bun – held firm until the breeze subsided.

Cassie started her routine. She swung back and forth to gather speed. Then she kipped to a handstand, her heels coming within millimetres of a pole above. That could have been catastrophic, but she avoided a collision and propelled herself forward. After a high release, she twisted through the air, passing through two struts to grab a third.

She overshot slightly and caught the bar under her elbows instead of her hands. The leotard slipped on the watery surface.

Cassie shuffled towards the sign and regained her footing on the frame of the O. The drizzle was a distraction and crosswinds hazardous. Her unprotected legs were numb, but she persevered and reached the summit of the reflective blue hexagon.

Her right foot grip unwrapped under stress and came off. Rain had washed away most of the chalk, and high difficulty had become extreme.

No time to rest, since the longer she was exposed to this weather, the more that could go wrong. Her soaked hair bashed her neck, hard as a human slap. Water flooded her eyelids. But she wouldn't be stopped.

Cassie heaved her tired body onto the O's upper pole. Crossing her thighs under it to hold a sitting position, she rubbed her face dry with her leotard sleeves.

If she made it to the top of the R – a metre away – she could leap over Monique's window and get inside the building. The wind dipped in intensity.

Now, Cassie.

She vaulted on the thin rod and rose into an upright stance, arms outstretched to keep her balance. This was a beam skill – her strongest discipline – but with a curved wet surface.

Cassie drew on her experience, all those training sessions in the warmer sports centre, and took a literal leap of faith. A forward somersault from one letter to the next, a near-perfect execution under pressure. She felt cold metal underfoot, but that meant a successful flip.

She jumped to the window. A strong breeze blew it away from her towards the tower, almost beyond reach. Cassie's fingers grabbed the top of the glass. One makeshift grip caught on the edge while the other came loose and flew off in the storm.

That improvisation had been vital. Because chalk alone would have sent her plummeting to her doom.

She grasped the window's side, struggling to maintain

any sort of hold as freezing water dispersed over her palms, an unwelcome lubricant that swept away the last trace of powder. The window swung outward as her extra weight shifted its momentum, sending her back towards the T.

Cassie shunted her hand along the top and pivoted round the glass pane moments before it struck the sign. She had escaped being crushed, but her stretched wrist was at breaking point.

Almost there. She summoned what energy remained for the last move.

She lifted her feet above her waist, coiling up to increase the tension. Then she back flipped off the window, over the ledge, and into Monique's room.

One relieved – and soaking wet – girl brushed her hair behind her ears. For a moment, she sat crouched in her landing position to recover from her insane ordeal. Then she remembered why she had done all this.

"Monique."

Cassie spun and rose to her feet. She was the only person present, but everywhere she looked, there were signs of a struggle.

The unmade bed. A porcelain vase shattered by the bookcase. An overturned table. An upside down suitcase with expensive formal dresses, sexy underwear and assorted cosmetics littering the surrounding carpet.

And an open door with a green keycard reader. Cassie checked the corridor was clear before she discarded the remaining wraps and searched the office.

The high heel shoe – Monique had thrown the other to attract attention – would be impractical in a chase, but the black tights were usable. They were ridiculously long, so had to be rolled above the kneecaps with the suspender clips left dangling.

Cassie felt like a prostitute, but it was safer than walking about the building barefoot. Was Tamara in her room? A telltale green light surrounded the keycard reader.

Beyond the unlocked door was an undamaged office. No smashed vases, a closed holdall, and a freshly made bed with a depression where someone had sat.

A strong chemical smell drew Cassie back to Monique's room. An oily black stain, a couple of centimetres thick and straight except for the occasional wobble, led to the lift. The digital indicator displayed twenty-three, the floor above.

Cassie reached for the call button, then withdrew her fingers. The staircase was a better option than a box trap. She cautiously opened the access door and entered the shaft. Her borrowed stockings stuck to the concrete.

A blood trail down the steps ended at DC Moore's twisted body. The lifeless detective lay slumped in the corner, slit throat and shirt stained crimson red.

It was Earl Bennett all over again, except for a young and far more sympathetic victim. Cassie suppressed a scream, reducing her reaction to a sniffle, and swallowed vomit that left an acrid taste.

A ventilation grille had been removed, and there was a cylindrical black object in the air duct. Out of reach, resting against a pulled metal pin. *A gas grenade.*

So, Cassie hadn't imagined the green smoke, or unwillingly falling asleep. The killer was acting brazenly, carrying out their twisted plan without fear of capture.

Perhaps the dead woman had a police radio or a mobile phone. Her belt holder was empty, as were her inside pockets. A warrant card hung around her shirt collar, but the plastic wallet felt thicker than it should.

A keycard was stowed behind the photo ID. Something important the murderer missed when searching the body.

Issued to a police detective, it might be encoded with full access privileges.

"I'm sorry."

Cassie took the pass and closed Moore's eyelids. How many more innocent people had to die?

She tiptoed up the concrete steps to floor twenty-three, holding her breath, and only exhaled after a wide angle glance through the narrow window.

The assistant's office beyond the threshold was quiet, and the camera was motionless. Its indicator light wasn't flashing. The killer had deactivated the surveillance system, which meant the reception guard was probably dead, too.

Another black, oily trail led to the locked double doors. The psycho could be waiting in the boardroom, so Cassie checked the desk and tables for a weapon. In the digital age, finding a letter opener was out of the question, and the only documents on display were Hexagon promotional leaflets.

Was there anything... *The assistant's lamp.*

Cassie unplugged the cord from the wall socket and wrapped the wire around the brass stand. The lightbulb unscrewed easily and the pink plastic shade was surprisingly easy to remove. A glorified candlestick would be ineffective against the armoured assailant who defeated Raquel, but it was better than bare hands.

Cassie held the club with the wide end pointed up and swiped the security card against the reader. The light turned green, but the keypad lock required a four-digit code to grant entry.

Those fingerprints were still on the numbered buttons. On her last visit, she bragged to her boyfriend about the small number of possible combinations. Now she had to guess the correct sequence.

Cassie completed the lengthy keycard swipe and digital

input process three times before she typed 0676. The numbers flashed green and the electronic lock released with a click. Possibly a month and year of birth, but who cared about the logic?

She stored the plastic card in her stocking, gripped the lamp, and pushed the nearest door inward with her foot.

The antique wall lights were switched off. Monique sat cross-legged on the director's desk in her sexy promotional pose, brunette locks blowing under the spinning fan. Dressed in her unzipped leather jacket, tight fitting leggings and motorcycle boots, her face and exposed stomach were spray painted silver.

A cellphone was mounted on a tripod, with the rear side facing Cassie. Its screen light shone on Monique's still body, hair shadowed face, and the erotic choker she had been strangled with. Steel cables connected her stretched motionless arms to furniture. The same method as Elena and Raquel, and a now-familiar Modern Woman reference was sprayed on the darkened window backdrop.

ATHLETICISM.

The masked killer stood behind their latest victim, next to a wheeled industrial cart. They pulled the leather strap tight.

"No!" Cassie yelled, unable to stop herself.

The murderer released the noose, stepped around the desk, and unsheathed the combat knife. Sharpened steel flashed as they passed through the phone light.

Cassie pulled the doors shut. Hurriedly unwrapping the wire cord, she fed it through the handles several times and tied a knot. One door opened, jamming on the obstruction.

The killer stabbed their blade through the narrow gap and sawed through the cables. Plastic insulation pieces fell onto the carpet.

Cassie turned and ran. She pressed the call pad and entered the lift already on this floor. The descent to ground level seemed to take forever, lasting through many nervy foot taps and heavy breaths, before the doors finally opened.

After exiting, the exhausted teenager reached in and thumped a button at random. She didn't know which, but hopefully, her misdirection would confuse the killer. Against a strong and well-armed tracker, any advantage was crucial.

"Brad," she called out. Quietly, because she wasn't expecting a reply.

Monique's mannequin – the only Modern Woman left on display – had been knocked over, and both breasts smashed into fragments. A further connection to Gemma Bright. What was the murderer's obsession with her?

Cassie ignored the wreckage and stepped round to the reception area. She spotted the security chief's motionless body beside the swivel chair. Mentally prepared for the sight of yet another murder victim, she still gasped.

There were two strangulation marks around Brad's throat. The second red patch was thicker and more indented than the wound Monique had inflicted with her rough sex games.

Computer panels were pried open, and their innards pulled apart. Wires sparked and circuit boards smouldered. Screen messages broadcast a *Full Emergency Lockdown* and *System Failure*.

Cassie lifted the cordless desk phone, but heard no dialling tone. She typed on the keyboard, to no avail. The killer had sabotaged all the systems, and those steel shutters over the doors and windows cut off any route to the outside world.

The surveillance monitors displayed intermittent video

feeds. Which meant the murderer could be anywhere in the complex.

Was it Tamara behind the mask? Monique's argument made sense. So far, the killer had left Cassie alive. At the boxing club, then her room here at Hexagon. Had they spared her for some twisted finale?

A sudden whirr from above decreased in pitch and volume, then faded to silence. All the lights went out, leaving Cassie in complete darkness.

CHAPTER FIFTEEN

Mannequins in the Dark

Everything was pitch black. With the shutters down, and computer and surveillance monitors disabled, there was no ambient light whatsoever. Was the killer in here, waiting for Cassie to give herself away? She listened intently, but heard nothing.

She doubted the power cut was accidental. This was some twisted plan to terrify her into making a mistake. Did that mean electricity was off throughout the complex? Perhaps the police would notice the enormous Hexagon Sports sign wasn't lit up and race to the rescue.

No chance. You're on your own, Cassie.

Mustering the courage to move, she swept the air with her arms and stepped slowly forward. Her left hip bumped into a rigid surface. Wheels spun – the swivel chair? – and something heavy slammed on the floor. The seat had toppled, coasters turning until the rattle died away.

Cassie had only sound to paint a mental picture, but she was behind the reception and almost tripped over Brad's corpse.

"Sorry," she said. He'd been a sexist asshole, but everyone deserved a chance to atone for their mistakes.

Cassie dragged her feet across the marble tiles, probing for the furniture. She found the desk corner, felt down, and located the drawers.

The top one was full of glossy magazines, but at least she didn't have to look at pornographic photos of nude women with breast implants. Paper rustled, but there was nothing else except a long plastic object with a tapered end. A ballpoint pen?

More "not safe for work" material cluttered the bottom drawer. How much did this guy have? Cassie's fingers touched a foil wrapped box with squashy stick-shaped things inside, and flaky ash. She sniffed her hand and coughed to clear her throat. The disgusting odour of tobacco.

If Brad had cigarettes secreted away, maybe there were matches or… *A lighter!*

The metal was worn, with scratches everywhere. Cassie wasn't a smoker, but had seen them used enough to know the ignition procedure. She soon identified the fuel release button – or whatever it was called – and the pointy edged wheel.

Her first two attempts produced only sparks, but the third gave her the flame she so desperately wanted. Wavy orange fire danced above her thumb.

The flickering glow didn't extend very far, and the hands of the giant ceiling-mounted clock were faint glimmers. A quarter past three. Before the knockout gas attack happened, it was shortly after midnight. Hours wasted asleep while the killer roamed unhindered.

A ping from behind the divider. Cassie stopped the fuel injection and extinguished the lighter. The silver mannequin of a bare chested male boxer reflected the lifts, where a blurry figure stepped through a white aperture that closed after them.

"I know you're in here."

The killer spoke in a creepy whisper. Had they noticed the orange glow? Or was it a bluff?

Cassie flattened her back against the reception wall, feeling the protruding company logo letters. In the short time the flame was alight, she had seen the overturned chair and Brad's body. Some mental navigation markers, but one misstep would be costly.

A click from her left, and a focused white beam illuminated that side. Multiple bright points appeared in the silvery athlete replicas around the lobby as the masked killer activated a mobile phone light. From the reflections, Cassie theorised it was belt mounted, which left two deadly hands to strangle her with.

The unarmed gymnast shuffled right and kicked until her stockinged foot touched Brad's corpse. She stepped over the obstacle and cornered the divider just as the spotlight turned towards her. Half the wall ahead changed to white, abruptly becoming black where the partition's shadow fell.

The beam moved away. Cassie peeked round the narrow edge and saw the killer's rubber padded back. Brass rings twinkled on their gloved wrists. The upper knife edge glinted above the sheath, and the strapped leather choker swung on a thigh holder. The psycho had an arsenal of murder weapons for their deadly vendetta.

Cassie stowed the lighter in her stocking next to the keycard. Those tights were proving quite adaptable, but she needed a weapon, like the baseball bat by the smashed mannequin of Monique. Could she reach it without being spotted?

The gymnast darted – quicker than her fastest ever vault runup – and snatched the wooden club. She felt a sharp prick below her big toe.

Her instinctive foot swing knocked a shattered plastic fragment into a nearby pedestal. The mirrored piece bounced off and alerted the killer.

Cassie ran for her life and took cover behind the divider. The phone beam illuminated only a fleeing shadow, but that was enough to reveal her presence.

"Not quick enough."

That whispered taunt was slightly higher pitched than before. A woman's voice?

Reflections of the masked murderer appeared in the broken convex shards. They unhooked the choker and stretched the straps.

Cassie gripped the baseball bat, holding it to her chest. Nowhere to hide between her current location and the lifts, and moving along the partition was too obvious.

She watched the shadow angles shift as footsteps grew louder, waiting until the black patch behind the dividing wall had all but disappeared. Then Cassie swivelled on her toes and swung at the murderer's head.

The blow struck their gloved hands instead, padded rubber absorbing the impact. This close, their plastic masked face – black except for the eyes and metal gauze – was perfectly framed by the raised choker.

The killer tilted the collar horizontally, ready to attack. Cassie kicked the phone side footed, the powerful blow Raquel showed her. The device flew from its holder and clattered upside down a few metres away. Bright light faded to a narrow circle.

Cassie threw the bat and cartwheeled sideways. She heard a wooden clunk as it made contact and felt the dropped choker bounce harmlessly off her knee.

While the murderer retrieved their phone, the darting gymnast hid behind the nearest sports star mannequin: the female tennis player. As she hoped, the killer shone the beam on the divider first.

That gave Cassie the chance to align her arms and legs along the statue, knees and elbows bent to match the ball serving pose. Her form fitting leotard made her figure slim, and years of training had imprinted the discipline necessary to hold the stance.

Light swept the room, moving with the murderer. Cassie used it to judge her stalker's position, holding her breath as the beam focused on the tennis star's statue. The shadow cast before her was a single woman that grew in size and intensity. The killer headed straight for her.

Then the searchlight shifted away, directed towards the lifts. Three metres of space separated hunter and prey, at most.

The teenager reached up and pried the ball from the mannequin's curved hand. She hurled it across the foyer, retracting her arm before the first bounce.

The murderer fell for the distraction and checked another statue by the doors. Cassie ran to the dividing wall and climbed the Hexagon Sports logo. Much easier than her daring antics on the giant sign in a rainstorm, but she couldn't afford a mistake.

She pulled herself on top and flattened her prone body against the surface. A ball smacked against the floor, thrown hard. The murderer had realised the deception.

Cassie had chosen the best hiding spot available, but it was only a matter of time before the searcher found her. She kept still as the white light swung back. The beam was low, but if the killer looked up now…

A mobile phone rang with a catchy adventure theme, horribly inappropriate in these circumstances. Then it stopped.

The murderer conducted another sweep, feet pacing as the spotlight moved quickly. They checked everywhere except the partition. The marble divider was damp beneath Cassie's sweaty palms.

After a hasty patrol, the masked figure called a lift and stepped inside. Cassie saw a grid like shadow – the transport cart? – before the doors closed and darkness descended once more.

She was safe for now, but who had telephoned the killer? And what was so important they abandoned the search?

* * *

"Replay it."

Lyle wanted to see the footage again. Because he was convinced there was a sensational hidden clue that would solve the mannequin killer murders and make them national heroes. Or not.

"How many times are we gonna watch this girl die?" Dan asked.

"As many as it takes."

The designated assistant checked his wristwatch, a cheap digital model that had lasted years. Kids of today used mobile phones instead, but Dan's inner city background made him wary of pickpockets and pedal cycle snatches.

He chuckled at the irony. *They* were the criminals

trespassing and tampering with evidence. He had sworn never to re-offend after his last juvenile conviction, but this was an extreme situation.

Lyle reached across Dan, gave the uncooperative helper a disgruntled glance, and pressed the loop track button. The kickboxer came back to life. Two minutes and eleven seconds until she died again. The tied up rapist had an extra half minute before the psycho in body armour slit his throat.

"That thing the killer's wearing," Dan said. "It's called a mask."

"It doesn't cover the eyes."

"We already checked. Paused, stepped frame by frame, zoomed in. When will you accept the video is too blurry?"

Dan's vomiting had ceased now he'd grown used to death and reviewed the gory surveillance recordings a dozen times. But more than once, he had glanced over his shoulder at the secret room entrance.

Raquel Valdez was a powerhouse who could have beaten the average man in a fair fight. But the murderer – protected from head to toe, and decked out with custom-made gear – was playing *unfair*. The tough woman's attacks bounced off like striking solid steel.

"What about height?" Lyle asked. "Body shape?"

He was desperate to help Cassie. Dan understood that, but this escapade had become the definition of a wild goose chase, and he was repeating the same questions.

"Nothing conclusive. Camera angles make it impossible to tell. I'm sorry, man. With the padded armour, we're not even sure if that's a dude or girl under the mask. What do we know? This nut enjoys strangling models and painting them silver. They don't like Hexagon or Modern Woman much, either."

Lyle buried his face in his hands, eyes peering through

fingers as the footage reached the user defined end point: the two bodies as the killer left them. Later surveillance would show Cassie enter the room, but one play through of that segment had been traumatising enough.

"I wish there was more." Dan disliked his pessimistic opinion, but it needed saying. "We should get out of here."

"She's counting on us. You keep looking while I do some research."

"On what?"

Lyle stood up and took out his cellphone. A laptop would be more useful, but they had wisely travelled light.

"Hexagon," he said. "Harris. Cole. Anything that's a lead."

Yesterday, those names would have meant nothing to Dan, but his reporter friend had briefed him on the major players. And the recording he and Cassie discovered in the director's office.

"Still think we should go to the cops, Lyle. We got evidence a superstar swimmer fixed a race."

"Would have done until Bright pulled out of the Olympics. It's hypothetical, and the audio file isn't specific enough. A good lawyer would get her off. We're looking for a murderer, not a cheat."

"Unless they're both the same person."

Dan leant back in the creaky chair. They hadn't even started another replay. It was pointless, and lover boy knew it.

Lyle scrolled through an old news article. *Hexagon Backs Team GB Star for Pool Glory*. Gemma Bright was pictured in her sleek swimming costume, with the serious-faced Tamara Cole behind.

Tall, muscular, and dangerous. With those biceps, either girl could snap Dan's neck like a twig. Super strong women, victims posed to match their promotional photos, a mannequin with its tits smashed in, corporate intrigue... This case was plain out weird, and they were stuck in the middle of it.

"So Cole moved from fraud to murder?" Dan speculated, though a motive for bumping off her cash generating models eluded him. "Or does Harris want to eliminate his competition for the director job? Who knows? Maybe your girlfriend's doing this and is playing us for suckers."

That was in poor taste and ridiculous. They couldn't be certain of the height, but it must be a tallish woman or man behind the mask. And the lithe gymnast had the alibi of appearing a minute after the killer left the club, in a completely different outfit.

"Look at this," Lyle said, presenting his phone.

"Who am I looking at? Wait. Isn't that..."

It took Dan a few seconds to recognise the blonde in an evening dress. She almost looked attractive out of her swimwear.

"Check out the person talking to her."

Before he figured out who the mystery companion was, a skinhead appeared at the door, holding a gun. Aimed straight at them.

"We need to warn Cassie," his oblivious friend said. "Now."

"Lyle. We got a problem."

The pistol was a high calibre weapon. At this range, it would blow a hole in their faces. The middle-aged guy wore a sleeveless leather jacket, ripped jeans, and had black snakes and skulls tattooed on his bare arms. Steel piercings through his nose and ears complemented the thuggish look.

Lyle finally spotted the newcomer. Threatened at gunpoint, he lowered the phone and stepped back to the surveillance screens.

"Hi there," the bald man said without a hint of friendliness. "The name's Rick. What the hell are you doing in my club?"

* * *

An age passed before Cassie dared pull the cigarette lighter from her stocking. How long had she waited to convince herself this wasn't a trick? Five minutes? Ten?

Fingers warmed by the freshly lit orange flame, she could see again. The ceiling clock's metal hands now read half past three. Only a quarter hour for the close encounter with the killer and the nerve shredding apprehension that followed. But unless some giant battery drove the unseen gears, the power cut couldn't be building-wide. Which meant the lights were on upstairs, and all would appear normal from outside.

Cassie jumped down from the partition, bending her knees to soften the impact and landing noise. Stealth had become a habit, and gymnastics an essential survival skill. The boring media lectures she used to hate didn't seem so bad in context.

According to the – still working – lift floor indicator, the murderer had gone to the basement. While pursuing them was an obvious risk, so was being ambushed in the dark.

Cassie held the lighter high and searched the reception area. The baseball bat had proven unwieldy, but pieces of silvery curved plastic glinted around the wrecked exhibit. Those fragments looked extremely sharp. She chose a four-inch segment with a spiky point and sides blunt enough to hold without cutting herself.

A broken mannequin breast for a knife? This is insane.

The office stairwell only led up, so Cassie took a chance on the lift. After a speedy descent, she stepped out with purpose. No sign of the black-clad killer, but neon strip lamps were on along the corridor.

She switched off the lighter and followed the oily trail left by the cart's wheel. It guided her deeper into the complex, to a swinging glass door labelled *Technical Lab* which she unlocked by swiping Moore's keycard.

On entering, the first thing Cassie saw was DI Quinn's body lying against a gigantic machine. His jacket and shirt were pierced with thin slits – multiple knife wounds – and saturated in dark red blood. Flies buzzed around his angled head.

Power was out locally, but a portable industrial floodlight shone on the silver mannequins. They were all present except Monique, in the Modern Woman poses the sadistic killer had copied.

Stay alert, Cassie. You don't want to end up like them.

She edged into the workshop, stretchy elastic stockings breaking the otherwise total silence. The tracks led to a gaping three metre wide hole with steel girder corner posts. Their jagged toothed edges were downright nasty, supporting a corrugated iron platform on four wheels below. A maintenance lift, and the oil trail ended at the concrete drop off.

Cassie knelt down and checked the sub-basement room: a dimly lit warehouse with wooden boxes, overburdened shelves, and sports equipment wrapped in polythene. She replaced the security card in her stocking and the plastic fragment between her teeth. Ignoring the horrible taste, she dropped to the lower floor.

The metal square vibrated upon landing, and the resonant echo took three seconds to fade. Cassie stopped and listened. To buzzing air vents and the distant drip of water, but no sign she'd been discovered. She gently blew her nose into the back of her hand, purging her nostrils of dust to suppress a sneeze.

Still holding the lighter, the lone teenager armed herself with the silver strip again and picked up the trail. The black wheel marks became fainter and further apart, but they remained a valuable guide in this subterranean maze of dirty passages.

At every junction, Cassie held out the mirrored plastic and used its convex surface to scout the path ahead. That slowed her progress, but this crafty killer might be leading her into a trap.

Where are you going, you psycho?

She didn't talk for fear of being overheard. The answer was a nondescript storeroom with large crates, wooden pallets, and a wheeled gurney hoist for lifting heavy equipment. Unremarkable except for the transport cart and a grimy, open barred floor grate.

From below, the sound of rushing water. A ladder descended into darkness. Was this a security flaw the killer had exploited?

One crate rested at a different angle to the others, like someone had moved it. Black scorch marks on the surrounding chipped concrete suggested recent excavation and welding work, although the metal itself was cold.

"You crafty bitch."

Hold that thought.

Monique's last words had convinced Cassie that Tamara Cole was the killer. With Quinn dead, they were the only people alive at Hexagon, but if the murderer entered from outside...

She chewed the lighter, keeping the shard handy even

though it made the ladder descent tricky, and stepped into ankle-deep brown water that permeated her stockings. The stench of garbage was overpowering, like the spilled contents of a dozen wheelie bins.

It was dark again, so Cassie ignited the flame. Sewage flowed along a circular concrete drainage pipe, down a barely perceptible incline. Shadows appeared and vanished in the flickering orange glow.

Which way had the murderer gone? She guessed towards the surface, and was relieved when she spotted damp boot marks on the curved sides that the water hadn't erased. In this narrow passage, two metres wide at most, it was impossible to be quiet, but the ambient noise should conceal her footsteps.

Faint beams of light marked a vertical shaft. Rainwater poured through a drain above, generating waves that crashed against the pipe. Rust covered the broken rungs and grate – a false hope of escape – so Cassie pressed on.

The tunnel curved sharply to the right. There was a third opening, wider than the others, and a supermarket trolley underneath. That couldn't be there by chance, but what was its purpose?

Cassie had reached a dead end, with the route ahead blocked by vertical bars. The room above was brightly lit, and the hook-ended ladder was shiny aluminium with an unblemished manufacturer's mark. She cupped her ear, but heard only the water surrounding her soaked feet.

Time to be brave.

She put out the lighter and stored it in her stocking beside the keycard. Armed with her plastic "knife", she climbed into the mannequin killer's hideout.

The owner wasn't in the five metre by six storage unit, but statues were everywhere. A headless mockup of Elena

Savikova – with an unbranded pink dress and ice skates – lay on its back. Raquel's kickboxer outfit was on another silver female figure, next to a bald swimsuit wearer and a brown-haired gymnast doing a familiar handstand pose.

That area was devoted to physical training, with a treadmill, weights, and exercise bike, whilst the opposite side – all business – had a writing desk, computer, and filing cabinets. Video monitors showed white noise, but the setup was identical to Brad's reception desk. Had the killer hacked into the Hexagon surveillance network?

Behind the CCTV screens were stapled blueprints for the entire complex. Every floor from sub-basement to director's office, with the notice board fully covered.

Cassie raced around the rough wooden workbench to the enormous sliding metal door and pulled the handle, grunting as she strained to budge it. *Locked.*

She vaulted onto the desk to peer through a small window with diamond wire mesh. Dirty glass and trickling rain made a depressing view, but there – above the warehouses – was the Hexagon Sports sign.

Was this Poppleton Business Park? The killer must be meeting someone outside, but who?

Cassie stepped down and saw a blonde wigged silver figure against the concrete wall, behind the rough opening she had entered through. A ghastly sight, its swimming costume and chest roasted black and sharp-edged hexagonal holes where the breasts should be. Exactly how the Loughborough caretaker had described the vandalised mannequin.

Around the neck was an oddly designed medallion: a polished onyx disc with a metallic pink outer rim and cross jutting out at the bottom. A bizarre variant on the expensive ruby-inlaid crucifix at the university.

Broken glass was laid out on a cloth-covered table. The remains of a six-sided plaque, similar to Tamara's welcome gift, reconstructed to form a cracked image. The Hexagon logo and name were too badly damaged to read, but the silver athlete was a swimmer.

"Gemma Bright," Cassie said. "You sick bastard."

Her assumption of the killer's gender had changed. She couldn't imagine a woman doing this – not even to a likeness – but if Tamara Cole wasn't under the mask...

Cassie froze. There was another mannequin in the corner. The only male design. Dressed in a smarmy blazer, silk tie, black polished shoes, and gold wristwatch.

This lair belonged to a misogynist who'd strangled three women and posed them out of spite. Four, assuming Tamara was dead. Make that five, if Gemma's "suicide" was the beginning of this twisted plot. And those were just the female victims.

Surrounded by such overwhelming evidence, there was only one logical conclusion. Vince Harris was the mannequin killer.

CHAPTER SIXTEEN

Unmasked

Vince Harris held his wristwatch up to the car's interior light. *Twenty to four in the bloody morning.*

Eager to conclude this shady business, he had called back and left a voicemail message, but there was still no sign of her. It was pissing it down outside, pitch dark, and shivering cold. He turned the heater on full blast, hoping to relieve some stress, but it only made him sweat.

Had this been a hoax? No, Tamara was definitely the woman who phoned just after midnight to arrange this impromptu meeting. An act of desperation by the arrogant American who thought she deserved to run Hexagon Sports.

Vince replayed their conversation in his head.

"Poppleton Business Park," she had said. "Unit 3B. Three thirty AM. Come alone."

No introduction, only a demand delivered in monotone.

"You better have a damn good reason for calling me." To

avoid waking his wife, Vince went to his private study and shut the door before continuing. "The board's decision won't change, and neither will mine. That stunt you pulled in the pool didn't frighten me. More of a flop than a splash."

Quiet taps in the background, very close together. A computer keyboard?

"Are you even listening?" he bellowed.

"Britain's golden girl would be worth a fortune to Hexagon, and Director Wilson agrees."

Vince almost dropped the phone. She couldn't have a recording. It was impossible.

"But only a silver at the Olympics," the younger Tamara said, "or worse, a doping scandal. That would tarnish the brand."

"A very promising brand," Wade Wilson added. "You're new to our company, so I'm willing to overlook this infraction. You have a lot to offer Hexagon, but a young and impulsive woman needs to understand how things work."

Then came the startled gasp from Gemma Bright. Vince remembered the uncomfortable sight of an old man squeezing a teenage girl's thigh under the conference table. Wilson always was a tactless liability.

"Don't you damn well touch me," she wailed. "How can you do this? I idolised you, Ms Cole, and you're asking me to cheat? All to make more money for the company? Do you have any idea what I'm going through?"

Vince sank into his leather chair, hand on forehead. The varnished desk reflected his anguished grimace. He closed his eyes in resignation. The director's job was all but secured, and he was about to incriminate himself.

"Think of this as a… career development opportunity." His words sounded so reckless in hindsight. "A business deal where everyone wins. Imagine becoming the Olympic champion and achieving your dream. But this only works if nobody questions your integrity, so accept our generous gift, clean up your act, and go win gold in Tokyo. You'll find being on Team Hexagon is far more rewarding than Team GB."

Then the line had gone dead. Tamara Cole had issued her ultimatum, and with that damaging audio file in her possession, Vince had no choice but to negotiate. Was her goal blackmail or revenge? Three hours later, he remained in the dark.

He stared ahead, watching the sweeping windscreen wipers and rain swirl through the headlights. There were no lamp posts on this isolated lot. He had borrowed his wife's less expensive car, but that still presented a tempting target for thieves. Police patrols were concentrated around the Hexagon complex, not the neighbouring industrial park.

Vince checked the door pouch where he'd concealed the steak knife. A recent purchase, its steel blade was dangerously sharp. Violence made him uncomfortable, but this had gone beyond word duels, and Tamara's intentions were unpredictable.

Had she recorded the meeting for insurance? Four years ago, they had been young hotshots: the newly recruited head of female sports, and a junior board member hoping to impress. But the scheming businesswoman was sharper than anyone realised, with a ruthless competitive streak that would destroy them both.

Vince didn't like exposing himself, but the arrangement with Monique had fallen through, which left him no leverage. The company executives had appointed him as managing director, but only by default. If the Olympic race fixing plot became public, he wouldn't only be financially ruined, but blacklisted and vilified.

Would Tamara really push the nuclear button? If she

was willing to breach a police curfew with a lunatic killer targeting models, anything was possible.

A tall, black-cloaked figure rapped on the side window. Vince rolled the steamed up glass down. In the darkness, he couldn't see his rival's face, but golden blonde hair gave Tamara away. That bitch was smirking – he was sure of it.

"Let's dispense with the games," he said. "How much do you want?"

She unbuttoned her coat and parted the flaps. Her champion belt, and those shiny medals she loved showing off, were unmistakable even in this low light.

"Okay, I get it. You've won. Satisfied?"

Without a word, the woman pulled a mobile phone from her pocket and turned on its camera bulb. Was she recording him now? He squinted, temporarily blind.

"You businessmen think you're invincible," Tamara rasped, hard to hear over the pattering rain.

She tapped the cellphone screen. A video played – Wade Wilson hanging from his office fan. He grabbed the climbing rope noose, kicking his legs. Then his limp arms slapped against his sides.

A muscular masked figure in black walked into view, pulling the cable. The mannequin killer.

"Hexagon scum."

More psychotic whispering as she replaced the phone in her pocket. Then Vince noticed the military knife she rotated in her leather gloved hand, far more deadly than the one he brought from his kitchen.

Tamara flung back her cloak to reveal rubber armour padding. She unclipped a tube shaped object from a second belt and released a ringed metallic pin with her thumb.

"It's you!" Vince exclaimed.

He turned the ignition key, but before the churning

engine started, the killer threw the grenade through the driver's window. Green gas emerged from a nozzle. Even with ventilation, smoke soon filled the interior.

A sweet, sleep-inducing smell. Vince couldn't stop blinking. He reached into the door pouch for the steak knife, struggling to hold it steady.

The murderess grabbed the blade – free hand protected by leather gloves – and easily snatched the weapon away. Everything spun as she stepped back.

Blonde hair blew across her mist shrouded face. He'd been foolish to think Tamara was merely a blackmailer. Was this insane woman planning to frame him for the killings?

Vince coughed as the anaesthetic filled his lungs. He fell on the steering wheel, barely registering the head bump as he blacked out.

* * *

"So, you and Raquel were close?" Lyle asked, cocking his head at the wall behind the gunman.

Pictures of the murdered kickboxer were stuck on the cream-painted plaster with Sellotape. Glossy printouts with no dirt or creases, which suggested the memorial gallery was added recently. Many photos showed a teenager with neater curly hair instead of dreadlocks, others an older and fiercer-looking warrior sparring with men. Happier times before the mannequin killer ended her life.

"You think I'll fall for that?" the skinhead grunted. "Relax. Cops are on their way. I'm sure they'll be interested in your story."

Rick hadn't budged since entering the secret room. Was he lying about the police? Probably not, but the club owner guarded the only exit. And he had that thick-barrelled gun.

"We're investigating the murders," Lyle said. "I'm a reporter."

"And here I thought you two were thieving scumbags. Your mate got anything to say?"

Dan had stayed quiet since things had gone sideways. Humour wasn't the optimal strategy, which explained his reluctance to crack jokes.

He eyed the firearm and shifted closer. Was he planning to jump the guy?

"You were her trainer," Lyle said, diverting Rick's attention. "She came for help, to fight back against her abusive father."

He remembered the story Cassie had read on the Internet and prayed he had the details correct. From the bruises and scars, the bald boxing coach was a seasoned fighter himself. One wrong word about Raquel could set this powder keg off.

"That girl was in trouble, and nobody did a thing." Rick raised his voice, but thankfully, his anger was directed at society in general. "Police dragged their feet, social services turned a blind eye. Highlight of her week was punching dummies in my gym, then she got good and learnt how to fight kids. Then adults. Built up her confidence until she taught that evil bastard a lesson."

Dan rotated a downward pointed finger. *Keep him talking* in unofficial sign language. His crazy plan to wrestle the gun away would get them both killed, but Lyle played along.

"So you saved her. I'm trying to save someone, too. The same person who did that horrible thing to Raquel is after Cassie now."

"That tiny gymnast, the one in the news. I saw the security video, what that guy did. Hate to break it to you, but your flimsy girl doesn't stand a chance."

Dan charged Rick, yelling as he grabbed the pistol. The buff trainer was taken by surprise, giving the overweight student a brief advantage. He slammed the weapon hand repeatedly against the wall, punching holes in the plaster. Foam spilled out, dust spreading into a thick cloud.

Lyle approached the two struggling men, swerving to keep out of the firing angle. His friend was losing the struggle, arms yielding as the tough skinhead fought to regain control.

The onlooker had to do something, and a well-placed kick knocked away the weapon. Rick thumped Dan in the stomach, with enough force to send the knackered student careering into a surveillance monitor. Its glass screen broke from the impact.

Lyle grabbed the dropped pistol and took aim.

"Don't move!"

The skinhead ignored the danger and charged right towards him. Dan recovered and punched the sprinting Rick, and Lyle followed through with the handgun butt.

The double blow was an unstylish knockout. The kamikaze club owner fell through the open mirror, landing face down in the secret entryway.

"Was that guy nuts?" Lyle asked.

He couldn't bring himself to kill a man, but what if he had?

"Figured he wouldn't shoot," Dan said.

"You figured? That some messed up gang banger shit?"

"Well, I wasn't about to leave the heroics to you and Cassie. I better hold on to that."

Lyle happily relinquished the firearm, then he realised Dan was grinning.

"What's so funny?"

"You scared shitless. Trust a public schoolboy to think

—"

A distant blaring siren grew closer. Both men jumped over the fallen Rick and legged it back to the boxing club entrance, almost slipping on the rain-swept steps outside.

Lyle's car was still parked across the street. Dan impatiently egged his friend on as he unlocked the door. By the time they started the engine and sped away, blue lights flashed at the junction behind them.

"Call the police," Lyle said, tossing Dan his cellphone.

"We could turn around and explain things to them? In case you hadn't noticed, we committed an assault, a burglary, criminal damage. Soon as the club owner gives them our descriptions, we're toast."

"Then don't say who's calling! Just tell them there's a lunatic bitch on the loose at Hexagon."

* * *

The information was all in the killer's files. Land Registry documents confirmed the storage unit had been purchased two years ago in Vince Harris' name. Photocopies of a drainage network map had the sewage tunnel highlighted. A closer look at the Hexagon complex blueprints revealed security cameras represented by hand drawn boxes, and estimated fields of view marked by colour shaded cones.

Everywhere Cassie searched, she found more evidence. Each Modern Woman model had her own cardboard folder stuffed with photographs and typed surveillance notes. There were pictures of Elena's apartment, the boxing club exterior, a motorcycle workshop – presumably Monique's side business – and a rural Yorkshire estate only Tamara Cole could afford. Cassie's dossier was thinner, with only recent newspaper clippings and gymnastics competition records.

Enough data to reconstruct Vince's entire plan and concrete proof of his guilt. So why did Cassie doubt herself? Because it was too perfect. A meticulous killer would never leave such an obvious paper trail.

What about the computer? She moved the mouse, expecting to see a password prompt. Instead, there was a suspiciously unlocked Windows screen, and audio manipulation software loaded with a sound clip.

Cassie clicked the play button, and the vertical position marker scrolled rightwards across the waveform.

"DC Moore reporting in. All clear."

Her voice sounded drone-like, almost robotic, as if the murdered detective had been reanimated as a talking corpse.

"There's nothing to report... Same as usual... Will be glad when it's over... The models are sleeping safe and sound... Stop worrying."

Cassie pressed pause, grateful to silence the creepy snippet recital. How had the killer recorded all those phrases when the cops were only assigned last week?

Her cellphone rang. She reached for her coat pocket, then realised she was wearing the leotard. But that was definitely her disco themed ringtone.

She traced the lyric-free song to a grey plastic tray on the workbench. A bright rectangle shone through an oily rag covering the bulky contents.

Cassie lifted the blackened cloth and retrieved her stolen phone. There were two more, possibly taken from other models, mixed in with an acetylene welding torch and goggles, claw hammer and chisel.

She answered the incoming call. It was difficult while holding the plastic mannequin piece, but that crude dagger was her only defence.

"Lyle! Thank God."

"Took the words out of my mouth," he said.

"You need to warn the police."

"We've tried. They insist everything's okay, and to stop making prank calls."

"Don't forget to tell her about your criminal record," Dan butted in.

Cassie ignored him and checked the computer screen. She clicked an audio icon labelled *AI-Gen* which brought up an empty text box, flashing green underscore cursor, and circular cropped image of DC Moore's face.

"The detectives are dead," she said. "So is Monique."

"All three of them? Are you sure?" Lyle sounded surprised.

"Pretty damn sure since I saw the bodies, but I know why the police think everything's fine."

"Because they're idiots?" Dan suggested.

They must have her on speakerphone. On impulse, she typed two sentences on the keyboard and pressed the enter key.

"I'm DC Moore, not an AI generated voice. Trust me."

"Holy shit," Lyle said. "Copy our speech. They can do that now?"

It went quiet on the other end, leaving only background noise: a travelling motor vehicle and raindrops striking glass. Cassie pictured the two men gob smacked.

"Remember that USB stick we found in the director's office?" she asked. "Behind the conveniently unlocked door? Under the stand, left at an angle?"

"The recording of Tamara and Gemma Bright," Lyle said. "What are you getting at?"

"What if someone planted it to implicate Vince Harris?

Clues for the police to find? And there's a shitload more in the killer's hideout."

"The killer's… Where the hell are you?"

The car engine noise became louder, and Cassie realised she was hearing two different vehicles. Light shone under the closed unit door, brightest at points roughly a metre apart.

"Headlamps," she said. "I have to go."

"Cassie, what—"

She ended the call and powered down the cellphone.

It was too dangerous to keep. The murderer might notice its absence, and who could she contact? The police would never believe a fantastical story about an AI generated voice. Lyle and Dan, aware of the situation, were on their way to Poppleton. After weighing the options, she returned the phone to the tray and replaced the oily cloth.

The engine noise faded, and the headlights vanished. A car door opened.

Cassie closed the filing cabinet drawers and willed the computer screensaver to reappear. It did, just as someone inserted a key in the lock.

She sprinted to the tunnel hole and jumped, twisting into a spin to face the ladder. The gymnast snatched the central rung with her free hand. Her feet dipped into the wastewater below, making the tiniest of splashes.

Metal grated – the door sliding back. Quiet footsteps, too far away to be inside the storage unit.

Cassie peeked over the shaft and saw a tall blonde in familiar black attire and body armour, stood by the gloomy outline of a parked vehicle. *Tamara Cole.*

The amazon dragged an adult male from the passenger seat, lifting him without the slightest grunt or stumble. A suited, charcoal haired man that could only be Vince Harris.

Cassie's instincts had been right. The real killer was setting him up as a patsy.

The purpose of the bizarre objects along the underground route from the Hexagon complex – the supermarket trolley, the gurney hoist in the sub-basement storeroom, the oily-wheeled cart – became chillingly clear.

Tamara would use them to transport her unconscious captive to the main building and then somehow frame him. It must have been Harris who called the masked murderess in the reception area, but their early morning meeting was a trap.

Cassie stepped down into the dark drainage tunnel. She needed to escape before the killer discovered her. She kept to the side, where the water was shallow and she could feel the concrete, and retraced her steps around the bend. Past the rusty ladder and exterior grate, to the "back door" access shaft.

A splash behind her. Tamara must have dropped Vince into the pipeline. Narrow, focused light shone across the curved section. This had become a race for survival.

Cassie climbed up into the Hexagon tower's sub-level. It would take a while to raise Vince's body on the wheeled hoist and transfer it to the cart, even for muscle woman Tamara. Time enough to make it to the upper floors, hide, and consider her options.

The oily wheel marks were faint near the storeroom, so Cassie had to rely partially on memory and made a few wrong turns. Distant squeaking – the gurney chain? – gave her extra impetus to hurry.

Cassie felt the crushing weight of anxiety lift when she reached the maintenance platform. She sprinted down the corridor, footsteps muffled by her stockings, and pressed the up arrow button.

No power.

She looked for a switch, only to find an activation keyhole. For a key she didn't have.

What now? It was too risky to wander blindly along these similar-looking passages. Down here in the labyrinthine basement, she'd be easy prey for the murderous Tamara.

The three metre climb to safety wasn't impossible. Jagged corner post "teeth" and the platform guardrail were poor footholds, but the only realistic path to the technical workshop.

"You conquered the uneven bars," Cassie said. "Let's do this."

She placed the plastic shard between her lips and vaulted onto the horizontal metal pole. A spike was chipped off, and another blunter than the rest, giving her space to insert her foot. A large crack in the concrete wall was deep enough to reach into.

Cassie removed her stocking – the one without the stored items – and twirled it, lassoing the highest jagged edge. The tooth cut right through, but the tough elastic held.

She pried apart the slats of a rusted vent grille to create a gap for her fingers. Then she straightened her bare leg against the steel post and rested her inner knee on the dull point. Her stockinged foot slotted – just about – into the wall crack beside her other hand.

In that achingly stretched climbing position, Cassie reached for the edge above. Her worn stocking ripped as it caught on the crevice and tore lengthwise up her leg. She escaped a nasty cut, but the dislodged security keycard fell through the hole into a dark corner.

No time to go back. A light along the corridor. Tamara was coming!

Cassie pulled herself up, teeth biting harder against the plastic shard. She climbed into the floodlit room above, panting with exhaustion as she rolled onto the concrete.

Somehow Brad's cigarette lighter had remained with her, trapped under the folded nylon. But the skeleton key was lost, and the locked workshop door an impassable barrier.

A clunk from below, then a powerful whirr as the maintenance lift activated. Cassie looked for a hiding place.

The machine in the corner, behind DI Quinn's body.

She rearmed herself with the fragment and rushed over, ready to clamber into the long contraption. Then she saw the dead technician encased in silver plastic.

Though Justin's face was horribly contorted beyond recognition, his geeky glasses made a distinct impression. On the smooth chest, Cassie's reflected mouth was agape in shock.

Through the shelves, she spied a dark human figure rise from the sub-basement. Without thinking, she ducked behind the Modern Woman statues. Ironically, it was her own handstand posed likeness she used for cover.

Cassie listened for movement, but heard none. The murderer's shadow raised one hand, revealing the silhouette of the keycard. They tossed it away, and the spinning plastic rectangle bounced out of sight.

The killer yanked an insulated cable, cutting power to the floodlight. Footsteps in the darkness, moving closer.

"You can't escape."

The whispering psycho had her trapped, unless…

The mannequins.

Keeping low and pressed against the lower shelf, she straightened her silver statue's legs and laid it flat. She ignited Brad's cigarette lighter and wedged it under the neck to keep the flame burning.

Cassie retreated behind a crate stack and watched shadows move on the floor. But the murderess' black shape approached from her side. Too late, she noticed the leather choker drop over her head.

Remembering footage of Raquel's murder – and how the strangulation device worked – the would-be victim spun around before the killer could snare the hooks with her wrist rings.

Cassie lashed out with the shard, aiming for the neck – a weak spot not protected by those rubber pads. The murderess grabbed her weapon hand, leather glove squeezing until the plastic broke apart.

The wounded gymnast screamed in pain as a curved bit stuck in her palm, funnelling blood. Unarmed, she couldn't prevent the masked attacker sweeping her legs.

She fell back into the crates, landing among spilled fiberglass mannequin moulds. Limbs and torsos rained down. A chest section bashed her skull, and throbbing resounded in her eardrums. Strewn yellowish objects appeared on fire, capturing the wavy orange lighter flame.

The crazy-eyed killer knelt down on Cassie's body, trapping her. They pulled the leather straps directly to tighten the choker.

Cassie felt the noose constrict her windpipe, an unbelievably tight, neck wringing squeeze. She resisted the impulse to claw at the collar. All the previous victims – far stronger women – had tried and failed to escape Tamara's chokehold. She needed a different plan, but what?

Elena's toppled mannequin was within reach. Cassie pulled off an ice skate and swung at the murderer's neck. Another attack on the weak spot. The blade sliced through the cloth, revealing feminine Caucasian skin. But the crimson stain on the shoe heel had come from her wounded hand.

Faint from lack of oxygen and blood loss, she fumbled and dropped the boot. It slid out of reach.

Show me your face, bitch.

Determined to die fighting, Cassie bent her knees and used her inverted feet to flip the mask's side catches. The released black plastic fell off, clattering on the floor.

The mannequin killer was a woman, but it wasn't Tamara Cole's features illuminated by the orange firelight.

Monique.

Cassie's eyes were playing tricks on her. This had to be another hallucination.

The smiling murderess transferred both leather straps to one hand and pulled back her cloth cap. Brunette hair – not blonde – unfurled to recover its natural shape.

But Monique was dead. Cassie witnessed her murder.

Or did she? Images of past events flashed before her.

The staged video filmed from a tripod. Fake choking sounds over the phone Monique planted. Four – not five – mannequins in the killer's hideout. The silver "corpse" in the gloomy director's office that must have been a decoy. A blonde wig disguise to fool Vince Harris. Had she cloned Tamara's voice with the software?

So many questions. Not enough strength to think.

"Relax," Monique said. "You're about to become the big story."

Cassie's vision darkened as oxygen starvation took its toll. The unmasked killer smiled as everything faded to black.

CHAPTER SEVENTEEN

Killer Setup

Another inverted perspective, only this time Cassie was powerless to right herself. Her legs were horizontal and at full stretch, lined lengthwise along the conference table. A concrete foundation block held down her zip-tied wrists, and wires were fastened to the ceiling fan brace and a brass lamp above the door. The steel cables were hard to inspect without straining her neck, but cold metal loops secured her ankles.

Cassie's skin was damp from perspiration, and she hadn't yet been spray painted. As her vision sharpened, she saw herself performing the same leg split handstand on the television. The Modern Woman promotional image and upside down *COURAGE* header came into focus. Like the other victims, she had been posed to match her photograph.

The prisoner turned her head towards the door. It was propped open by the wheeled cart Monique used to transport her unconscious victims. At the other table end, the masked murderess sat in the director's chair, silently mocking her captive.

"Nothing to report," DC Moore said. "Everything is normal here. Will be glad when it's over."

A welcome voice from outside – except it wasn't her.

"You're talking to a dead woman!" Cassie wanted to scream, but her lips were sealed together by an adhesive strip.

She fought against her bonds, but her legs wouldn't shift, and pushing the rough concrete block only tilted it slightly. A sudden pain reminded her of the injured hand, now crudely bandaged with grey backed duct tape.

"Don't sound so grumpy," an unknown male said. "It's nice and warm inside, while we got Yorkshire weather to put up with."

A half second of static, then silence. Monique walked in holding a radio transmitter and audio recorder. She placed them on a corner table and stepped before the screen, her ruby red lips twisted into a near-permanent smile.

"That takes care of the police," she said. "Now for the meddling student reporter."

The unmasked killer wore biker leathers, her jacket unzipped to expose her muscular yet shapely physique. Skin tight leggings, revealing underwear, and heavy boots completed her Hexagon model persona. Without the body armour, the tall brunette was considerably more feminine in appearance. But no less deadly, and her white surgical gloves were ideal for a murderess.

Monique smirked as Cassie looked at the silent, black-clad figure in the chair.

"You'll have to excuse Vince. He's still working out how I managed to screw him over."

The gleeful psychopath removed her patsy's mask and pulled back the cloth cap. She ran her fingers through his dark hair and stroked his skull. Visibly shaken, the director stared up fearfully at his tormentor. Cassie noticed steel cables wrapped around the body armour, and his mouth, too, was gagged by duct tape.

"He was convinced I was *his* tool," Monique said, squeezing Vince's chin. "Every time we spoke, I sensed his dick harden. Money and sex are all these parasites want from us. Wilson, Cole, and him all thought they could outsmart me, but in the end, I screwed *them.*"

She ripped the grey strip from his mouth and wiped away the glue residue. Then she released him and stood back.

"You lunatic bitch!" he yelled. "You think I'm going to beg like those girls? I'll kill you!"

Monique walked casually out of Cassie's view, returned with a flat knapsack, and dropped it on the director's desk. Metal scraped as she drew her combat knife. Unsheathed, its serrated blade had a nasty glint as she stepped before Vince. Faced with a lethal weapon, all pretence of resistance crumbled.

"Wait," he pleaded.

"If I freed you and gave you this, could you go through with it? I let Tamara choke me, but that hypocrite lacked the killer instinct she always boasted about. One of her many lies."

"What have you done with her?"

"You actually care? Let's say she had to settle for silver."

Cassie – forced to keep silent and watch events unfold – recalled the spray painted corpses of Elena and Raquel. Monique's statement had a chilling implication.

"Damn you," Vince said. "You won't get away with

this."

"Why not? I spent four years planning for this moment, leaving a trail so they'll blame you for everything."

"Nobody will believe it."

But Cassie had seen the planted evidence in the hideout, and knew the story would stand up to scrutiny. The killer had left a horde of clues pointing to Vince's guilt, and his open hostility towards the Modern Woman line made him a plausible suspect.

"The reporter agrees with me," Monique said. "She knows how easily bullshit sticks."

"So you kill her, dress me up in your clothes, and make it look like I died in a struggle. Then you miraculously escape and become the hero. Is that your plan?"

"Well worked out. Do you know what else I learnt while doing my research?"

Monique spun her blade, its tip on her gloved index finger. Bright lines sped across Vince's sweaty face.

"Forensics," she said. "The longer before a body is found, the harder it gets to estimate the time of death."

The murderess gripped the knife handle and grabbed Vince by his hair. He opened his mouth to scream, but she struck first. The thrust blade penetrated deep into his neck.

Cassie's sticky lips tasted adhesive as duct tape compressed with a sharp intake of breath. Blood sprayed from Vince's wound, coating the steel. Monique released the weapon. Runny, dark red liquid trickled on the conference table.

"So the order of events doesn't need to be precise."

The director's chair shook and eventually fell back against the desk. Vince slumped, padded armour covered in spilt gore. Choked gurgles became sporadic wheezy coughs, then he stopped moving.

Monique reached behind the body, unfastened the cables, and tipped the corpse unceremoniously onto the floor. It landed somewhere below the table's edge.

The murderess took a tripod and cellphone from her rucksack and set up her recording equipment on the desk. Light shone on Cassie from her front left. This footage – unlike the falsified death scene Monique shot earlier – would be very real.

The killer pulled away Cassie's gag, and she finally spat out the soggy glue.

"I'm your grand finale," she said. "What makes me so special? You murdered a Ukrainian refugee, and an abused kickboxer any decent young woman would aspire to. You staged your own death, killed Tamara."

"Don't preach their innocence. Every model that signs a contract with Hexagon is scum."

"Including yourself?"

Monique ripped the torn stocking – still on Cassie's leg – and pulled the shredded nylon strips through the ankle loop. The killer pressed her victim's bare thighs, smirking as the cables held firm.

"You're their hero, Cassie. People idolise you, so I'll turn you into a shiny silver idol. Hexagon's image of a perfect woman, a defining pose they'll show around the world. The company will never stop paying for their betrayal."

That connection to the past again – but what was Monique's motive?

"Gemma Bright," Cassie probed. "She never committed suicide. You murdered her."

"Kill someone I *loved?* You call yourself a reporter? The clues are obvious, but you can't see them. Society is so ridiculously blind."

The infuriated killer stomped off and returned with the

silver paint spray. Air hissed, and Cassie felt liquid cool her shin. Monique rubbed the reflective coating and spread it out. The transformation from human to mannequin likeness had begun.

Lovers? Assumptions fell apart and a new story wrote itself in Cassie's head. Gemma Bright had committed suicide, after all. The female sex medallion in Monique's hideout symbolised an intimate bond between two women. Did she blame Hexagon for what happened four years ago?

These questions were immaterial. Cassie needed to escape from this dire predicament, but she'd been upside down for minutes. Her head felt heavy, and concentration lapses were becoming frequent, so keeping the killer talking was the best play.

"That video you sent me. The police were meant to find the phone, to corroborate your false story. Just like Gemma's audio recording, or was that fake, too?"

"No. Tamara really was a cheating backstabber. But I've been wondering. How did you escape from your room?"

"Never give a gymnast access to uneven bars. Did you forget? I'm your model of courage."

Monique smiled and spray painted Cassie's other leg, coating her thigh in a layer of sticky silver.

"Getting Elena's pose correct was gratifying. Beating Raquel, a competent boxer – that was rewarding. Watching Tamara as she realised I'd outfoxed her was pure joy. I even relished remaking myself in Hexagon's image, and smashing that foul mannequin to pieces."

The deranged woman reached under Cassie, paint-stained gloves shining in the cellphone light. She dragged her bouncing leather choker across the table by its straps.

"You asked what made you special. You're an annoying bitch who nearly ruined four long years of planning."

Monique lifted the collar over Cassie's inverted head and closed it around her neck. Not airtight, but enough to feel the additional weight.

"Choking you will be the perfect climax."

Preparations were almost complete. The mannequin killer was about to claim her final victim.

* * *

"Try them again," Dan said. "It's a trick. A fake recording."

"Sir, our logs show three similar calls from this number in the past twenty minutes."

"Because you won't listen! The detectives are already dead. The killer is… Forget it."

Lyle's passenger threw the cellphone on the dashboard, looking up for divine intervention, but the cushioned car roof probably didn't provide any.

"They're in denial," Dan said. "Guess police call handlers don't read science fiction. Maybe we should try a different approach. The whole psycho killer AI generated voice story is too intelligent for these assholes."

He folded his arms and gazed through the side window.

"Just realised how crazy it sounds. I am sane, and this is really happening, right? Please tell me *you're* still alive."

Lyle drove in silence, Rick's handgun clamped between his legs. 04:18 on the radio's digital clock.

Pre-dawn Poppleton was a ghost village with empty country lanes and darkened cottage windows. Everyone was fast asleep. Except Cassie fighting to survive in the Hexagon complex, and stubborn cops who couldn't care less.

The storm had abated. A quarter hour had passed since a thundery rumble, and the intermittent rain spits were tame compared to the torrential downpour they had experienced in York. But that hadn't lifted the gloomy outlook.

The club owner's comment about Cassie's small stature had stayed with Lyle – because it was the truth. With his girlfriend physically outmatched, he prayed her remarkable courage, resilience, and quick thinking would be enough.

"Slow down," he said as they approached Hexagon Sports. "Try not to spook them."

"You might want to put the gun away. Just a thought."

Lyle, feeling incredibly dumb, placed the weapon under his seat. Not the glove compartment, because they would have to open that if an officer asked for a driving license or identity documents.

He stopped near the front gate and lowered the window. There were four police vehicles parked outside and six officers in Kevlar vests and hi-vis jackets. An increased presence since yesterday evening, but their body language was relaxed.

A butch, sandy-haired woman crouched to check the car interior. "You need to turn around. Complex is closed."

"There's a killer in the building using…" Lyle took Dan's advice on board. "Special voice software to fake radio transmissions. You have to break the door down, send for reinforcements."

"Special voice software?" Her response was laced with scepticism. "This a wind up? Suppose you'll be saying everyone's dead next. Hope you louts are proud of yourselves. Move on before I arrest you for wasting police time."

"Call the detectives and try to have a normal conversation with them. Then it'll be obvious who's wasting time."

Lyle felt a prod above his hip. Dan looked towards the gatehouse, where a grim-faced officer eyed them suspiciously and gripped a lapel-mounted radio. He exited the small building with another cop. They approached, splitting into a pincer formation.

"We've been made," Dan said.

Thanks to that intervention, they definitely had.

Lyle reversed at speed. His friend reached under the seat, grabbed the pistol, and aimed through the windscreen. The butch woman – half way to the driver's door – backed away, hands out wide.

"Wonderful," Lyle said. "Now we're armed and dangerous."

"Luckily, most police aren't in this country."

Tires screeched as he swerved backwards round a bend. He changed gears and accelerated along the road to Poppleton. Actual tarmac and white painted lines, but still a single lane.

A glance in the rear-view mirror showed two vehicles in pursuit, blue lights flashing above. Siren wails increased in volume as they closed to within a few hundred metres.

There was a sharp turn coming up around the corner of the chain-link fence. A high risk plan formed in Lyle's head. He unbuckled his safety belt, collected his cellphone off the dash, and shoved it in his inside pocket.

"Give me the gun. And take the wheel."

Dan handed over the weapon and squashed onto the driver's seat. "I won't ask what the hell you're doing, but good luck."

"You too."

Lyle unlocked the side door, holding the cloth-wrapped grip so it wouldn't open too soon. His passenger assumed control, foot on the accelerator in readiness.

Immediately after the tight turn, the reporter bailed out, rolled into a soggy ditch that softened the drop, and laid flat. Sirens blared as the two cars roared past. The police disappeared into the night, chasing the decoy.

Lyle stood up and brushed down his dirty jacket. The muddy firearm took some hasty cleaning, but kept its polished shine. He'd thank Dan later – if he survived.

It was still dark, but the Hexagon Sports sign and upper office lights identified the tower. And tall skyscrapers weren't a common sight in Yorkshire.

I'm coming, Cassie.

First, Lyle needed a way in. Some cops hadn't chased them, so the front entrance would be guarded. He jogged along the side fence in hope, then sprinted in optimism when he noticed a bent back section.

Someone's raincoat draped from a sharp wire. The clear plastic was thoroughly wet, contradicting the now dry weather. It must have hung there for hours, if not longer.

Had Monique left this behind? That made little sense. The cops had assumed she was a potential victim, so she was already in the building. Somebody else had broken into the complex, but who?

Grateful for the mystery person's help, Lyle ducked through the hole, careful not to snag his clothes on the dangerous severed links.

He had breached the perimeter, but was still stuck outside the tower. There were fire doors, but no exterior handles. The front entrance was too exposed, and the lowered steel shutters prevented entry by ground-floor windows.

An annexe extended from the main building – perhaps there was an access point the police overlooked. No, those emergency exits were also sealed.

A ladder to the roof.

Solid-looking metal rungs, lower section raised, horizontal rings every two metres. But how to reach it?

Lyle wandered the grounds, searching aimlessly. A trash dumpster was against the wall, a large commercial variant on wheels. Perhaps an improvised platform would provide enough extra height.

The bin was practically empty and the ground well watered after the storm, which eased the push to the ladder. Lyle slammed the lid closed, climbed on top, and jumped. His fingers touched the lowest rung of the extendable part. On the second attempt, he managed the grab.

Sorry for doubting your ability, Cassie. Hang in there.

He smiled at his own joke. She made those bar moves look easy, but scaling a brick wall with no mortar gaps gave him a newfound appreciation for her talent. After the hands only first rungs, there were steps to rest his feet on, and the climb became much easier.

The roof was constructed of hexagonal glass panels fitted in steel frames. No skylights, and the enormous room below was pitch dark. There had to be a way inside.

Lyle rushed about, almost slipping on the damp, non abrasive surface. One pane sunk underneath his foot. He rubbed the window and detected the tiniest of rough cracks.

He stood on the metal boundary and banged the panel repeatedly with his elbow. Then he remembered the gun and used its butt instead.

Lyle yelled a battle cry – more out of frustration than necessity – and continued to hammer away. The glass shattered, and fragments fell into darkness. Faint plops – was that water below?

Warm air blew on his face, and he smelt chlorine. He was on the roof of a swimming pool. A vulnerable chink in

Hexagon's security, but few intruders would antagonise police, sneak through a chain-link fence, push a commercial bin, and enter via a high glass ceiling.

Lyle tucked the gun into his belt, kicked the sharper pieces off the steel frame, and jumped feet first into the unknown.

Wind rushed past until he landed with a loud splash. The water was lukewarm.

Weighed down by his clothes, he surfaced and swam towards the nearest reference object. The female statue was lifelike, bare silver legs reflecting ambient moonlight.

Then – even in heated surroundings – Lyle sensed a shiver run down his spine. He climbed from the pool and activated his cellphone light.

Tamara Cole stood in her Hexagon swimsuit, upraised arms secured to the lower diving board with a steel cable. It was a delicate balanced death pose, with the single wire linking two wrist rings and no bindings on her ankles or body. Spray painted like the earlier victims, but one key difference was the murder weapon: a gold medal decorated champion belt pulled tight round her neck.

The murderer had drawn a word on the hexagonal poolside tiles, between two marble columns, in the familiar corporate logo font.

SUCCESS.

The Amazonian blonde wasn't the mannequin killer. They must have been right about Monique. Had she got to Cassie too?

Lyle took a phone snapshot of the corpse and checked the picture gallery. Flash photography gave the American a silver glow, but let the ignorant cops deny this evidence. An ex-Olympian celebrity posed in her own company's swimming pool.

He selected that image and the previous one that showed Monique and Gemma Bright socialising in a York wine bar. They were behind two businessmen who were the subject of the photo, but clearly identifiable.

The years old social media post revealed a link between the dead swimmer and motorcyclist model that couldn't be coincidental. Were they friends? Lesbian lovers? Whatever their relationship, it provided a motive.

Lyle sent an e-mail with a very brief description, then checked the map he'd downloaded in the director's office. Hopefully, the police would respond, but until then, he somehow had to find Cassie – and the murderess – in this sprawling complex.

* * *

Monique finished spray painting Cassie Simms' left foot. The teenage gymnast looked away, but there was nothing she could do in those restraints. Both her legs now had a reflective silver coating, resembling the hollow mannequin in the basement.

"You're doing all this because of Gemma," Cassie said. "Would she want this?"

The diminutive reporter was more defiant than the others. Facing death, she still refused to scream. That would change once the choker tightened. Even the fierce and competitive Tamara spent her last moments begging for mercy.

"Don't presume to understand our relationship," Monique said. "You could never appreciate how it felt to be valued as a woman. I discovered my perfect soulmate, and in return, I offered that lost soul loving comfort a mother couldn't provide."

The killer grabbed Cassie's hair and pulled down until her already rigid leg split handstand pose stiffened. Finally, the irritating girl yelped in pain.

"The Lord does not look at the things people look at," the captive said under great strain. "People look at the outward appearance, but the Lord looks at the heart."

"Religious nonsense. You think preaching to God will save you?"

"Samuel. Chapter sixteen, verse seven. That quote was on Gemma's memorial plaque at Loughborough. The mannequin donated by her mother after you destroyed the original. You burned her swimsuit and smashed the breasts. What kind of woman does that?"

"Exactly." Monique laughed over the hissing spray can nozzle. "The inscription is so damn perfect. If only the uninformed mother – or the clueless reporter before me – understood what it meant."

She applied paint over Cassie's face, forcing the model to close her eyes. That idiotic question confirmed it – the girl was as ignorant as her employer.

Monique had recreated the Loughborough mannequin as a shrine in her hideout, a motivator to remind her what Hexagon's lies stole from this world. The destruction of her own likeness – that Vince insisted on keeping – worked to frame him. But she also hated the person she had become.

It was demoralising to join this company as a model after they abandoned her true love, but screwing over powerful men and playing corporate jerks against one another made up for it. The highlight was watching Wade Wilson choke in this office while listening to her pre-recorded commentary. That abusive bastard had no inkling his sexual "conquest" had returned in her masked killer guise to strangle him.

Vince's fingerprints were in the business park hideout, planted by pressing his hands against the workbench and broken plaque. The steak knife would be found in the storage box with the models' stolen phones. Physical evidence to ensure a post mortem conviction.

Monique rubbed more silver paint in with her surgical gloves, spreading it over Cassie's lips and inside her mouth. That made her cough violently. The killer smoothed the reflective coating over her victim's chin, neck, and upper chest, reaching under the leotard.

"To men like Wilson and Vince, we're property and sex objects. To Tamara, money makers. Success at any cost. And to this country? They hailed Gemma Bright as their cherished hero, then transformed their icon into a villain when it suited them."

Monique brought over the backpack, placed it on the conference table, and removed the hand stapler and newspaper clippings she had prepared. Broadsheet and tabloid photos showed Cassie, mostly in the meticulously copied handstand pose.

"I've got a new fan," the feisty girl said.

"Now they can reprint those with an updated image and learn that any icon is fragile."

The murderess stapled the paper cutouts over the wall-mounted photographs of Vince Harris until all seven were covered. The gold frames were perfect for the final painted word. But first, she would show Cassie the two videos.

"Tamara wanted the world to remember Hexagon's modern women. They certainly will."

Monique pressed the remote control to start her edited footage. Music played over the speakers. The promotional reel ran, with model shots replaced by their silver painted bodies.

"This is Tamara Cole," the narrator said. "And I'm here to introduce my new brand. Let us celebrate the Modern Woman, and her contribution to sport. Elegance."

Elena Savikova was a pathetically easy kill. That flimsy Ukrainian thought she was safe inside her York apartment. But with the power off, she blundered into the closet where the masked killer waited with her choker.

What was that dripping? Water streamed down Cassie's forehead, collected beads falling onto the table. *She was crying.*

"Elena," she groaned. A soft, whiny, and pitiful plea.

Monique wiped the tears away, adding extra shine to the paint. At long last, Cassie had broken.

But the killer didn't need the weeping commentary. She paused the video and replaced the duct tape over the gymnast's mouth. Play resumed with the kickboxer posed on the bench press.

"Toughness."

Raquel Valdez offered some competition, but those fancy moves were useless against body armour. Monique still remembered the fighter's expression of terror as her confidence waned. A superior opponent had beaten the cocksure woman, and she knew it.

"Success."

While the models were under the effects of the sleeping gas, the killer transported Tamara to the swimming pool area and secured her wrists to the diving board. Strangling her with that arrogant gold medal belt and watching her kick helplessly was worth the years of waiting. The swimmer was unworthy of her Olympic title, so how fitting that her death resemble a fish suffocating on dry land.

Monique had deliberately omitted *Athleticism* – the false victim the heroine raced to save. Cassie's escape was a nasty surprise while filming the fake attack, but thankfully, she inputted the wrong code to the director's office. That gave the masked killer enough warning to alter the scene, dim the lights, and pretend to strangle the mannequin.

The footage in the phone's memory would fool the police. In the shots, there was insufficient light to tell the posed "woman" was a decoy from a distance. Since Cassie was meant to be dead already in this changed timeline of events, the camera was pointing away from the table and angled so the window would reflect the television wall side.

Monique would later paint herself silver. Then record herself in the mannequin's position. A loose wrist restraint pin would "accidentally" fall out, allowing her to reach forward off screen to grab the knife. Edited together, the model and murderer would appear to be two different people.

With the gymnast's death scene added and timestamps modified, the videos would be consistent with Vince murdering Cassie, only to be killed in self defence by his fifth and final victim. Attacks hours apart, but given the illusion of occurring within minutes, and in reverse order.

As the screen went dark, Monique removed the adhesive tape from Cassie's mouth.

"You're sick," she said.

So unimaginative. No wonder she hadn't figured out the secret.

"You live for stories, so I'll give you the scoop. This will go viral in the coming days. Hexagon was already finished, but when the world learns the full truth, this wretched company won't even rise from the ashes."

The killer started the second video – the autobiographical account she had viewed many times, but never shared.

Her handsome lover appeared, short blond hair neatly combed. The climbing rope noose hung above. His black suit, trousers and tie were creaseless and perfect for a funeral.

"My name is George Bright," he said. In a deep, masculine voice. "Six months ago, I was diagnosed with gender dysphoria."

CHAPTER EIGHTEEN

The Tragedy of Gemma Bright

George Bright had considered boycotting the BBC broadcast of the Tokyo 2020 Summer Olympics opening ceremony, but he wanted to see treacherous Tamara one last time. The Team USA flag bearer and poster girl had thrown him under the proverbial bus. Now the audio file would bury her career and Hexagon Sports along with it.

The event's title was a misnomer, because it was July 2021. Even the Greatest Show on Earth had been impacted by the COVID-19 pandemic. Nationwide lockdowns had disrupted athletes' planned schedules and thrown training timetables into chaos. Months of physical exercise in isolation and socially distanced pool sessions – and for what?

To please the British public? The media pundits and their damning judgements? A tall stack of newspaper articles was on the kitchen counter, with attention-grabbing headlines such as *GOLDEN GIRL QUITS THE RACE, THE FUTURE IS NOT SO BRIGHT,* and *SINFUL SWIMMER IN HIDING.* And the ridiculously simplistic *HOW COULD SHE BETRAY US?*

George had laid that clipping on top. After he ended his life, the tabloid press could eat their sanctimonious words. Their "traitor" was male, ineligible to compete in women's sporting events, and their media darling Tamara Cole a lying cheat. How would they react to that?

"Lebanon," the ceremony announcer said.

There were no cheers in the near empty Olympic stadium, only yells of delight from the waving competitors. George added another pencil mark on his notepad, bringing the marathon tally to 203 countries.

According to online research, there were 206 nations in the parade. He had watched from the start, when Greece led the traditional showpiece. Team GB entered early at number 27. In Japanese order, only France and the hosts followed the United States, but the agonising wait was almost over.

With the time difference, it was afternoon in Britain. Drawn opaque backed curtains blocked out the sunlight, but the fifty-inch television added colour to the geometric patterned carpet. A Victorian grandfather clock ticked in the hallway, a reminder of a luxurious but hollow former life as Gemma, the national sweetheart. Outside, girls laughed innocently on the village lane, yet to encounter the harsh reality of adulthood.

Before the fallen champion was crucified in public and quit her sports science degree, her fellow Loughborough students were jealous that she owned a bungalow in Woodhouse Eaves. The Hexagon modelling contract and multiple fashion endorsements had funded a short-term mortgage, but with those cancelled, lawsuits and repossession loomed. Shared budget accommodation or the celebrity goldfish bowl everyone wanted to piss in – who was worse off now?

"The United States of America."

The official Olympic announcement – in three languages – brought George back to his leather couch. Among the black attired contingent, two athletes in white jackets carried large national flags. The camera focused on the statuesque blonde figurehead.

"There's Tamara Cole," the BBC commentator said. "America's pool queen. Nine golds in her glittering career. She's competing in only one race in Tokyo, and aiming for the perfect ten, but who isn't thinking of Gemma Bright and what might have been?"

Like her compatriots, the legendary swimmer wore a blue face mask with white stars. Strong enough to carry her banner single handed, she had an aura of invincibility, but nobody was untouchable.

George switched off the TV, straightened his tie, and enabled the mobile phone camera. The spotlight was on him, but he wasn't afraid. Nervy Gemma had hated the British media circus and couldn't handle video interviews, but this was a new man. His tailored suit fit perfectly, and the loosened shirt collar helped with ventilation. Without a restrictive bra, his aerated chest didn't feel so clammy.

No prepared speech – George's abridged life story would come from his heart. He looked into the tripod-mounted phone on the Ottoman coffee table and rested his hand on the closed Holy Bible beside him. The New International Version was an eighteenth birthday present from his Christian mother. While he had never shared her religious devotion, the hard bound tome was a welcome companion on his final journey.

Would she understand his choice to transition? That

was unlikely, but George prayed the Lord would forgive her. She could never throw this sacred text away, and the highlighted verse – Samuel 16:7 – would hold a new meaning for her in the mournful days ahead.

"When did I first feel different?" he asked aloud.

It took many anonymous online lessons to shed the feminine voice, and replace it with a hoarse, male-sounding dialect. But he needed more than trimmed hair and a wardrobe change to convince his audience.

"At fourteen, I had a crush on my best friend Louise. I couldn't concentrate in class when she blew kisses behind the teacher's back. All the boys found her attractive, and I envied them. When I talked to my mother, she dismissed my feelings as jealousy. Don't mind her, you're the beautiful one. I was a sporty tomboy, and my teenage crisis would pass. I didn't dare suggest I felt love."

George recounted details that any transgender male would relate to. Teen Gemma preferred trousers to skirts but never admitted that to her girlfriends. Many times, she feigned interest in handsome shirtless celebs when sexy women caught her eye.

The third tallest pupil in a mixed private school, older hunky lads on the swimming team resented her for humiliating them in the pool. On a daily basis, she heard comments about her small breasts and hushed whispers of "she-male" in the corridors. But no matter how bad things got, she never cried. Only feeble ladies did that.

Accepted on a scholarship to Loughborough University, the media championed the rising star as an Olympic medal prospect. Baby faced Gemma fit their condescending image of female athletes, and Hexagon insisted on formal evening wear at publicity galas. High heels were clumsy to strut about in and fawning assistants took forever to apply superfluous makeup. Perfumes might please posh women, but she couldn't wait to wash away the vile scents afterwards.

"The other students all hated the rich model," George recalled, sipping from his water bottle. "The greatest thing about the pandemic was studying online, but loneliness took its toll. I started slacking, making excuses. Eventually, I braved an appointment with my doctor, who confirmed my worst fear. That I had dysphoria."

That wouldn't be a surprise to listeners, since he'd begun his video with that revelation, but speaking about the diagnosis gave him goosebumps.

"He advised a gender change, which would mean giving up my dream of Olympic glory. Or I could play along and suffer as a silent, obedient woman. I thought my life had no direction. Until I met Monique Garneau."

On that fateful Saturday evening in York, *Carlo's Wine Bar* was quiet. Licensed premises had only partially reopened following the pandemic lockdown, and other patrons in the middle class establishment were mainly wealthy stockbroker types. Hopefully, they didn't follow women's sports.

The photoshoot at the Hexagon complex had taken all day. Gemma's sleek swimsuit emphasised her muscles and flattened her chest, but the marketing team had insisted she remove the cap. Keeping still while smiling for the camera would have been easier without long blonde hair itching her shoulders.

"You're Gemma Bright, aren't you?"

The bartender – a tough-looking brunette about her age – had seen through the ocean blue dress and clawed hair accessory "disguise". Her plan to spend a relaxing evening in anonymity had been scuppered.

"Yeah. That's me. Britain's golden girl."

Gemma stared down at the walnut counter, readjusted her platform shoes on the high stool, and took the ribboned gold medal out from under her clothes. Her dominant victory in the two hundred metres breaststroke at the European Aquatics Championships had caught the nation's eye and made her some bookmakers' favourite for the Olympic title. More pressure and expectation – it never stopped.

"Mine isn't so glamorous," the bartender said.

She held out a black stony textured medallion, maybe obsidian or onyx. The circle's outline was pink and shiny, with an undersized wire cross at the bottom.

"The gender symbol for female."

Gemma wanted to appear enthusiastic, but this venue was depressing and her white lie obvious. Pendant lights cast a sepia glow over fake medieval-style brickwork, overpriced menus written in chalk, and racked vintage wines. The glass of sour French Chardonnay she had ordered was half-empty.

But the woman behind the bar intrigued her. The server's buttoned beige uniform was tight around her athletic figure and toned thighs. Above average height with arms better suited to manual labour, she was a tough character in ordinary surroundings, and her shiny red lipstick was token gloss.

"Not everything is as it first seems," she said.

The bartender gripped the black disc firmly and rotated the cross anticlockwise. A central section between two almost invisible grooves turned three eighths of a circle. With a seductive smile, the woman twisted the medallion around to reveal its other – blue rimmed – side. Then she pulled the intersecting line up to form an arrow shape.

"Nor is everyone."

A faint wire where the cross piece used to be, but the transformed symbol represented the male gender.

Gemma drunk her remaining wine. Bitter liquid poured down her throat, but the parched dryness remained.

The brunette pushed away the empty glass and took her speechless customer's wrists in a soft, comforting hold. Their eyes met in mutual understanding.

"It's okay, Gemma. I've watched you on television. You're at ease in the swimming pool, but not in public. When you almost tripped at the Young Sports Personality award, the commentators put it down to nerves, but we both know the real reason. Long silk dresses and heels don't suit that manly body of yours."

It was no use pretending – her secret was out.

"How did you guess? Have you always been…"

The bartender pulled her catch closer. "A woman? Yes, but not that choosy when it comes to sex. Perhaps it's fate that we met. I'm Monique Garneau. We're closing soon. Where are you staying?"

"*The Majestic.*"

"A high-class hotel, for a high-class sportsman."

Gemma snatched her hands away. This was an unreal situation, and events were unfolding far too quickly. Had the masculine reference been intentional?

"I'll call a cab," she said.

Monique leant forward and rested her elbows across the counter. She stretched her hair, releasing it in clumps.

"My ride's out back. There's space for two, and a lonely person needs company. Someone appreciative to confide in."

Gemma lifted the black medallion off Monique's shapely breasts and reversed the process to convert the sex symbol to female. It was inappropriate to act intimately towards a stranger in public, so why was she reaching for the server's nipples? The tiny bumpy impressions were faint on the uniform, but visible.

The bartender grabbed her wrist, a sudden move that made her drop the disc. Caught in the forceful grip of an offended woman, she swiftly repented.

"Sorry."

Perhaps it was alcohol, but Gemma's thoughts were racy and free of moral inhibition. The aromas of myriad wines – fruity and earthy – mixed into a resolve sapping concoction.

Was that a valid excuse for blasphemy? She recalled the occasion she spoke the Lord's name in vain after Sunday School. Her mother – a wrinkly long haired woman in a plain white dress – scolded her before the parish vicar. Rubies inlaid in a silver crucifix necklace reflected an ashamed blonde girl.

"Lead us not into temptation," Gemma mumbled, hands clasped together.

"Oh, don't misunderstand me. You've done nothing wrong, but we should continue this in private."

Absolution banished the unhappy childhood memory. Monique poured another glass of wine, which the nervy customer gulped down.

The analogue octagonal clock above the bar ticked towards eleven. Patrons' loud conversations were an indecipherable chorus of partial sentences, irritating background noise that wouldn't stop. After last orders had been served, Gemma finally escaped and met Monique in the outside parking area.

The "ride" was a sleekly designed black and silver motorcycle, as racy as its owner, who had changed into an unzipped leather jacket and crash helmet. The odour of wine had been replaced by her oil stained jeans. She was a muscle woman in a man's world of high-powered engines and machinery.

The bike's seat was a tight squeeze for two people, so Gemma clung on to Monique's waist as they zoomed through the streets. Her blue dress fluttered behind her, and the headwind chilled her unprotected thighs. Lights became blurry trails of white and the speedometer dial was way over the legal limit.

"Shouldn't we slow down?"

Gemma's plea went unheeded, but Monique was an excellent rider. Sharp corner turns and zips through slowed traffic came naturally to her, and they arrived at *The Majestic* within two minutes.

The five-star luxury hotel was among York's most prestigious, an Edwardian building near the rail station and historic city walls. Rooms cost hundreds of pounds per night, but Gemma was a Hexagon Sports model on official business, so the company had subsidised an overnight stay.

"I don't remember how we got upstairs," George recalled on camera. "Only that the porter, some foppish guy in a red cloak and top hat, gave Monique an odd glance. She wasn't *The Majestic*'s usual customer, or even a usual woman."

Before the executive suite door closed, the biker had stripped off her jacket. Her nipple outlines were more noticeable against her sweaty black tank top. The motorcycle boots came off next, then her leather pants.

The half-naked Monique walked round the navy blue upholstered armchairs and stroked a tulip in the coffee table vase. She turned, fell back onto the double bed, and spread her legs invitingly. Long brunette hair framed her shoulders. Softly illuminated by spiral-based lamps, the provocative temptress lay in wait.

"Why so hesitant?" she asked. "Don't you find me attractive?"

Gemma hadn't moved from the oak-panelled threshold. She stepped out of her awkward platform heels and removed the formal dress. With that burden lifted, she approached the bed. Slowly to begin with, but growing in confidence.

"Check my jacket," Monique said. "The inside pocket."

Gemma followed her instructions, but the only interesting item was a transparent brown plastic container with a flat cap. It was crammed full of digestible capsules, and someone had written a single word in black felt tip: *Testosterone.*

Drugs? Is she serious?

"They're not prescription, and even if they were, I'm an athlete. This is an illegal substance. If they test me positive, I'll be banned from competing."

"I've followed your career for a while, and read the papers. You're in York for a publicity shoot. They don't screen for that, and who cares about a women's race? It's time to accept who you are, and reap the rewards."

Gemma stepped closer. The cap popped off, disturbed by her twitchy thumb. Pills shook about in the container she couldn't hold still.

"If you're nervous," Monique said, "let's take one together."

The brunette parted her legs further, making more room on the spacious bed. The reluctant model knelt down in a sitting position, her bare feet curved around the duvet's edge. Her thighs rubbed against her sexy companion's.

Monique removed a capsule from the bottle and placed it between her glistening lips. White crystalline powder appeared as the shell dissolved.

Gemma, unable to resist any longer, grabbed the beautiful woman's neck and kissed her. As they exchanged bodily fluids, spiky crystals got mixed – and swallowed – with saliva.

Monique reached behind the swimmer's back, unclipped the bra, and tossed it away. Unshackled of feminine attire, the bare chested man let sheer impulse drive him.

He grabbed the tank top loops in his clenched fists and pulled. Elastic stretched under his relentless grip as he forced the underwear down her body. He clutched the athletic biker's wrists and threw her onto the duvet. Then he licked her perfectly rounded breasts and...

Gemma sat up, spitting saliva out in revulsion. She let go of the sweating woman's arms. Had she just...

"Most men's dicks are flaccid disappointments," Monique said. "When it's implanted, I imagine yours will be much harder. Then you can truly fuck me. I can't wait for that."

"A gender change operation? I... hadn't thought that far ahead."

"Relax. Allow a woman to dream. With those pecs, you're halfway there already."

Gemma felt her upper body. Had she – he? – been in denial?

Monique flicked away the container and selected a testosterone pill from a heap spilled over the duvet. She forcibly parted Gemma's lips and threw it inside.

Manliness and the irresistible desire to screw this gorgeous woman returned. But she wasn't interested in him. The topless beauty had spotted the open suitcase, and the glass object among the women's clothes.

"Don't touch that!" he yelled.

Monique kicked aside the panties and cocktail dress to

expose the six-sided plaque. She lifted it up, obscuring her face behind the thick material, silver swimmer image and lettering.

GEMMA BRIGHT. His preachy mother had given him that name, but the Hexagon Sports logo – and false representation – was the real blasphemy. He staggered to his feet.

"Look at this design," Monique said. "This is how the world sees you. So fragile, so... feminine. They want to make you into a pretty doll. A girl's toy. Lovely, beautiful, gentle Gemma."

"Stop saying that name!"

He punched in fury, his clenched fist connecting with the etched text. The strong-armed brunette didn't move an inch as the glass plaque broke into pieces and fell away to reveal her delighted smile. Chunks of the shattered hexagon landed around them.

He wanted to grind the swimmer motif to dust beneath his bare foot. Then his calm lover took his bloody hand and wiped it clean with a pair of panties. She tossed the dirty garment aside and swept forward into his welcoming embrace.

"Doesn't that feel better? Now you've relieved that stress and accepted your identity, let's go back to bed."

The sex that followed must have been intense, but the combination of wine and drugs left hazy memories of fondling the naked brunette and miming penetration. When morning came, Monique – and all her belongings – were gone.

Gemma had a severe headache. Was last night a fantasy? Had her alter ego really bedded a woman? Then she noticed the hexagonal plaque fragments stacked neatly on the coffee table, and a sharp pain in her bruised knuckles. It all happened.

She needed a long shower to rinse away the sweat. The bathroom was en suite with wavy patterned tiles, a reminder she still had another session of swimming costume photos to pose for. She had overslept, but her limousine pickup wasn't until this afternoon.

No soap among the toiletries – had the hotel staff forgotten to include it? Warm water and body lotion would suffice.

Gemma stepped into the glass cubicle and noticed the phone number written in red lipstick diagonally across her nude chest. If anybody else saw it…

She turned on the shower and rubbed her skin with the sponge. It took a few minutes of furious scraping – and cursing – to erase Monique's message.

Did that crazy woman think an impulsive one nighter made them lovers? That the transition was real and not role play? The presumptive mechanic was a drug-taking psycho who'd taken advantage of a vulnerable drunk loner. She could go to hell.

But Gemma's mouth had kissed Monique and sucked her breasts. The shower might cleanse her body, but not her mind. She wrapped herself in a bath towel and returned to the main room.

The bedside table drawer was open, illuminated by the sunlight that crept under the drawn curtains. An indented golden cross shone on the Holy Bible's cover. Freely distributed by Gideon's International, most hotel chains had discontinued the practice, but *The Majestic* still offered the Lord's teachings to its guests.

Gemma slammed the drawer shut and opened the drapes to let in daylight, but that only invited more soul searching. To the northeast, rising above the city rooftops, were the towers of York Minster.

The gothic limestone cathedral was centuries old, a British national landmark and tourist attraction. A place of worship, it offered counselling and spiritual guidance. The repentant teenager needed those, even though she had abandoned the Christian faith years ago.

She changed into unisex clothes – tracksuit bottoms, shirt and a loose denim jacket – and tucked her blonde hair inside a beanie hat. The mask was for viral protection in crowded places, but it covered her face from her nose to chin. In the closet mirror, Gemma saw an unknown person with focused eyes.

Nobody would recognise her. She didn't even resemble a woman.

The Minster was a fifteen-minute walk from *The Majestic*. A taxi would have been quicker, but a scenic stroll along the medieval wall trail, over the River Ouse and through the peaceful city centre allowed some thinking time. Last night had changed Gemma irrevocably. She hadn't only destroyed the Hexagon plaque with that punch. Her own identity had crumbled.

Sunday worship was in progress when she arrived at the cathedral. The half capacity congregation was spread out along angled wooden pews. Piped organ music filled the cavernous nave as those gathered boisterously sung hymns. Many people had removed their face masks for the communion service.

Gemma walked down the central aisle, head bowed in respect. On a school history trip, a tour guide had claimed the "stone" ceiling was actually painted wood, but the grey texture between the gothic pillars appeared rough. At the cruciform junction, the masked guest turned away from the southern rose window towards the Five Sisters.

The stained glass arches in the north transept were dedicated to women who died during World War I. The female remembrance theme was ironically appropriate under the circumstances.

Gemma listened to the droning music and choir singers. Accompanied by the peaceful and relaxing melody, the row of coloured windows was almost hypnotic.

"Is everything all right, my son?"

An old man's voice – probably the Minster's duty chaplain, since the Archbishop of York was leading the service. That was a relief, because speaking with an ordinary priest was nervy enough. There was acceptance behind the concerned greeting, even if he had simply assumed the visitor was male.

"I have sinned in the eyes of the Lord." Bright spoke in a deep tone that the mask muffled further. "I should feel ashamed, but I do not."

He didn't turn around. The chaplain might question his gender upon seeing his soft skin.

"This isn't a catholic church," the reverend said, "or a confession booth. You don't need to say anything unless you wish, but I'm here to listen."

"Society expects much of me, and has mapped out my future. But I must take a different path, one that will shatter their dreams. When they look at me, will they see a monster? A freak who betrayed them?"

Bright felt a reassuring hand grasp his shoulder.

"The Lord does not look at the things people look at. People look at the outward appearance, but the Lord looks at the heart."

A Bible quote. The visitor didn't know the chapter or verse, even though he should, but he would consult the book in the hotel room when he returned. Reassured there were no sins to forgive, he had renewed purpose.

"Thank you for your kind words, Reverend. My path is clear now, but I should tell you my name. It's George Bright."

That was the defining moment of transition, when he first accepted his identity without question. For the benefit of viewers, he described the afternoon swim photo session, where he attempted – but ultimately failed – to hide his testosterone use. Then came the revelation in the director's office.

"There was no chance Hexagon would approve my decision to withdraw from the Olympics," George said. "So I recorded the emergency meeting on my phone, expecting them to try emotional blackmail or threats. While the audio wouldn't be admissible in court, it would give me insurance in case they denied the conversation and sued me for breach of contract."

He omitted to mention Wilson's predatory thigh squeezing antics. The microphone picked up the female gasp clear enough. Gemma wasn't the only model the sleazy director had assaulted, and many dark truths would come out in the investigation.

"Then Tamara Cole suggested we cheat in Tokyo, that we collude so I would win gold. I was her legacy, more important than the perfect ten or fair play. Suddenly, instead of revealing my secret as intended, I had evidence of an Olympic fixing scandal. Don't believe me? I'll let the pool queen speak for herself."

George removed the audio player from his breast pocket and placed it on the Ottoman. Legally obtained or not, their voices would be authenticated. It was sufficient proof to end all their careers.

"For a female athlete, victory isn't enough. To be

celebrated, she must be perfect in body and mind. Adapt to what society expects."

He paused for effect. Those were Tamara's exact words, her closing argument of that seismic boardroom meeting.

"I was supposed to lie for money and fame. How could someone like that ever understand? After that, my decision was an easy one."

George summarised the events that followed. The change of name was done by deed poll with two solicitor witnesses, and he requested they keep his gender identity secret until he revealed the truth.

The Olympic withdrawal – with no official explanation – led to mass media speculation and a convoy of news vans camped in Woodhouse Eaves. In isolation, George watched Tamara Cole give a press conference, flanked by Wade Wilson and Vince Harris.

"We regret to confirm Gemma Bright's contract with Hexagon Sports has been suspended pending investigation. It has recently come to our attention she may have used performance-enhancing drugs. We are in complete shock, and reiterate we had no prior knowledge. We will co-operate fully with the UK Anti-Doping Agency, and issue a statement once they publish their findings. Until then, we cannot comment any further."

Light bulbs illuminated the deceitful woman's face, and George shut off the television in disgust. Without a urine sample, Tamara had no physical evidence, but Hexagon's reputation and profits were all that mattered. Those liars would engineer a guilty verdict.

George spent the following week locked in his home as the media frenzy reached fever pitch. With the Olympics scheduled to begin within days, Gemma's imaginary drug habit was the hot topic. But that was a different person, a confused girl who made a stupid mistake. The infatuated biker had left phone messages asking to meet again in York, but he ignored them.

"I realised my life was over," George said. "The press, my family, Hexagon – none of them would accept me as a man. And Monique only wanted to satisfy her sex craze. I changed my name, but I would never be free of Gemma's shadow."

With past and present identities matching in the parallel story timelines, it was easier to refer to "her" in third person.

"Whenever I could, I snook out for supplies and newspapers. It's amazing how much rubbish they talk. I mostly stayed indoors, but there was one last thing I needed to do before recording this video."

The mannequin of Gemma Bright at Loughborough University was an affront, a silver plastic mockery with oversized breasts and exaggerated hips. Blonde wig strands were cleaner than any human hair could possibly be. The display's sole purpose was to market Hexagon Sports' branded swimsuit. An outdated Olympics tie-in, this special edition had Team GB colours and markings.

Dressed in a black hoodie, face mask, and gloves, George stood before the false woman. It was late evening during the summer holidays, so nobody spotted the ex-student enter. The sports centre management hadn't removed the mannequin from the entrance hall, but only because the drugs investigation was ongoing.

George placed his mobile phone vertically on a nearby shelf and configured it to record video. He opened his rucksack, took out the stainless steel crowbar, and smashed the glass. No alarm sounded, so he could relax while he doused the costume in cooking oil and set it ablaze with a struck match.

The flaming outfit filled the damaged display with grey smoke. A detector above beeped, a whining noise that would fetch security. But there was enough time to watch Gemma burn.

Fire ate through the left shoulder strap, leaving loose material, which George hooked away with the crowbar's curved end. With those horribly inflated breasts exposed, he grabbed the head to steady the mannequin and swung at the domes. Both fell apart under repeated attacks. Plastic fragments rattled about in the hollow, mutilated figure.

George pulled out his spray can and added a message to the vinyl floor in the same reflective silver as the cursed statue. A six-sided character font to match the scorched company logo.

BEAUTY.

He didn't require altered body measurements to possess that trait.

The metallic letters captured the firelight and appeared to burn in front of the blackened mannequin. The two black holes hammered from the torso, enclosed by orange-yellow cinders, were crudely hexagonal.

Security staff waving electric torches sprinted down the corridor, but George escaped with the cellphone video in the confusion. They would be preoccupied with tackling the blaze. If there were cameras on campus, the police might link him to the arson attack, but they would struggle to identify the masked vandal.

How would the world react? George didn't know. He only hoped his story would make a difference, and with Gemma Bright's grotesque image destroyed, he would be accepted for who he was.

CHAPTER NINETEEN

Model of Courage

The video ended with George hanging himself. Almost dreamlike, he climbed atop the couch and inserted his neck in the climbing rope noose. He stepped forward and didn't struggle as his legs swung and then stabilised between the sofa and table.

Technically, the recording stopped after the cellphone memory expired twenty-three minutes later. The remaining portion was a depressing still of her peaceful deceased lover. Since Monique had no wish to watch that, she switched off the television screen.

"You found the body," Cassie said. "And altered the scene to make it appear the drugs rumours were true. You kept the audio file of Tamara and the Olympics fixing scandal for yourself, then used it to turn the conspirators against one another. That broken plaque – you took it as a momento. What else did you do? Steal the legal documents of the name change? Dress your boyfriend in women's clothes?"

The gymnast had remained silent through George's video, showing a surprising amount of respect. Now the girl had more annoying questions, but her deductive reasoning was correct.

The budding reporter had guessed nearly everything, except the duplicate house key Monique had made with a soap impression. George had been too concerned with recounting the York Minster episode to mention missing hotel room cosmetics.

With access to a bike mechanic's workshop, forging a copy from the mould was straightforward, and finding the home address of a celebrity athlete was equally trivial. A kinky sex session and a few beers were enough to loosen a male fan's tongue.

"You're not denying it," Cassie accused. "George Bright's dying wish was that the world hear his story, and you concealed the truth. So instead of a transgender man, they got a cheating swimmer high on testosterone. He died with a female name, betrayed by a crazy stalker who pretended to love him."

Monique stomped towards her prisoner and backhanded her face. The steel cables and ankle restraints that held her in a leg split handstand moved, but only slightly. The ensnared model could talk all she wanted. With her wrists bound to the concrete brick, there was no escape. The murder weapon was inches from her hands, but beyond her grasp.

"You don't understand what made George so special," Monique said. "Neither did Tamara. She didn't even remember her own hateful words when I quoted her at the meeting."

The killer pulled the choker's leather straps, tightening the collar around Cassie's neck. The defiant girl stayed tight-lipped, but her forehead creased under the pressure.

"I've experienced desire before, but never passionate love from someone who society cast out. I knew George was suffering from the media exposure you reporters thrive on, but instead of surprising him with a home visit, I walked in on his corpse."

Monique released her hold to let Cassie breathe, and collected items together on the table. The intact stocking, its ripped cousin, a second silver spray can to paint herself with later, unused cables and restraints. The preparations were almost done.

"Surprise him? Seems George didn't appreciate your sex therapy and dumped you. Probably figured you were a psycho."

Cassie's stubbornness only increased the killer's desire to strangle her. The plucky heroine posed on the same table where Tamara Cole broke Gemma's heart and cemented the transition – it was poetically perfect.

"Sharing the video with the press would have let Hexagon off the hook," Monique said. "They would have claimed the race fixing recording was a fake, painted George's story as the lies of a troubled teen who cracked under pressure. Let the world believe drugs were the reason, because they weren't ready for the truth."

"What gave you the right to decide that?"

"George needed somebody with a killer instinct to see his plan through. When I watched the silver mannequin burn, that was my inspiration."

"So you joined Hexagon and planned a murder spree for four years? That's called obsession."

"The circumstances had to be right. I wanted something

that would destroy Wilson, Harris, and Cole, and forever ruin this lousy company. Then that bitch came up with Modern Woman. She chose my victims for me. Her idols she hoped would replace George became symbols of her inflated ego. Let the public mourn their new sweetheart as I mourned him."

The killer carried the spray can to the vandalised picture wall and depressed the nozzle so hard the hissing paint sounded like a roar. She added an angular letter to each stapled newspaper clipping, drawing lines through Cassie's face wherever possible.

The aerosol was empty when she finished, but the fifth – and final – single word message was written in gleaming silver.

COURAGE.

* * *

Lyle's decision to download the Hexagon Sports complex map could yet be crucial. The interactive scrolling blueprints provided both light and direction.

Instead of wandering corridors in darkness, the drenched student located the junction box – inside a forced open substation room – and swapped fuses to restore power to the ground floor. Some mid-level offices would be without electricity, but the immediate priority was to locate Cassie.

En route to reception, Lyle received a call. He answered quickly so the ringtone wouldn't announce his position.

"Is this Mister Norton?" a posh-sounding man said.

"Yes."

"Detective Chief Superintendent Hanson, Major Crimes Unit. Your photo of Ms Cole certainly got our attention. We all thought it was a crazy wind up at first."

Lyle moved at pace, already irritated by the laid back attitude. Was this guy for real?

"Well, it wasn't. Two of your squad are probably dead, and my girlfriend's next on the list, so drop the small talk. Now you've woken up, mind telling me how to open those damn shutters?"

That triggered a flurry of activity. Hushed chatter and radio traffic suggested Hanson was in a busy control room, not on site in Poppleton. A bureaucratic commanding officer in a police headquarters bunker wasn't much help.

Lyle still had the gun, but it was soaking wet from his rooftop dive and swim. It seemed functional, but the equipment test would come if – when – he confronted the murderer.

He cautiously entered the entrance hall. Wary of a surprise attack, he kept turning as he stepped around the dividing wall.

The guard's strangled body was behind the reception desk. That would have shocked Lyle a week ago, but with all the murders, he suspected only Monique – and hopefully Cassie – were still alive.

"Mister Norton. You there?"

The woman's friendly voice was far more reassuring than her patronising boss.

"Listening."

"Can you access the emergency controls?"

Lyle checked the surveillance screens. Red error message boxes flashed everywhere, but one flickering monitor showed the murderess holding Cassie prisoner in the top floor office.

His girlfriend's stretched legs had a reflective metallic silver sheen. The killer had posed her last victim in the trademark handstand, with the leather collar around her throat.

"Mister Norton, can you release the lockdown?"

Lyle typed on the keyboard and flicked switches, but the security system was completely wrecked. Monique must have sabotaged it to lock everyone inside the building.

Fried components and severed wires stuck out from the open access panel. It could take hours to repair the extensive damage, even with expert advice.

"No," Lyle informed the woman. "Not in the time we have. I'm going to save Cassie."

The lady provided unhelpful instructions to remain in the foyer until a special armed unit arrived. But the lone rescuer powered down his phone – it was a hazard now.

He checked his inside jacket pockets. The Stanley knife and wire cutters he pilfered from the power room were basic stuff, but any tools that might sever the killer's steel cables or leather choker were potentially vital.

Lyle headed for the lift and remembered his girlfriend's strategy when they had searched the offices.

"Get off one floor down to evade detection. Thanks, Cassie."

She had minutes – perhaps seconds – to live. He knew where the action was happening, but Monique Garneau was a psychopath who killed without mercy. She wasn't wearing her protective armour, which gave him a slim chance to succeed.

The police were trapped outside the shutters, and being directed by a buffoon, so Cassie's only hope was a bold man with no plan.

* * *

Cassie inhaled as the mannequin killer clutched the choker straps. In the television screen's reflection, she saw hexagonal letters sprayed behind her posed body. Struggling against the steadfast cable setup had only wasted energy, and with no apparent means to escape her restraints, the situation seemed hopeless.

"The model of courage," Monique said. "Defiant to the end."

Cassie stared back at her tormentor, determined to remain strong. But she instinctively opened her mouth as the murderess pulled the strangulation collar tight. The pressure on her windpipe increased as Monique stretched her arms apart and shifted closer.

The inverted director's office faded in and out, with only the merciless killer remaining consistently in focus. Choked into silence, Cassie heard straining leather over her weak gasps for air. The thin edged plastic zip tie cut into her sore wrists. Physically shattered, her flexing fingers didn't even wobble the concrete weight.

Visions of silver painted women flashed before her, mixed with Modern Woman mannequins of Elena, Raquel, Tamara, and the deceptive Monique. Exhausted from being in the same position for so long, Cassie couldn't distinguish real-life models from their likenesses.

Then she envisioned her own murder scene: a leg split handstand before the hexagonal styled *COURAGE*. She floated over her limp corpse, as if inhabiting a disembodied ghost.

"Don't move!" Lyle yelled.

Her upside down boyfriend held a wet gun to Monique's head. In her dying moments, the victim had imagined her heroic lover saving the day. Cassie stopped struggling and smiled.

The killer released her grip on the choker. A sharp intake of air preceded extended coughing. Cassie could breathe again. Did that mean this bizarre last minute reprieve was happening for real?

"You can't kill me," Monique boasted.

Lyle pushed the pistol into her temple. "You sure about that?"

Cassie concentrated, blinking to correct her vision. Where had he found the weapon? And why the hell would he hesitate?

"Shoot…" She was too tired to finish the sentence.

"He won't. Because he's a spineless wimp, not even one thousandth of the man George was."

The murderess turned to face Lyle, surgical gloved palms flat as if inviting him to fire. She tossed back her black hair and pressed her forehead into the barrel. At close range, a headshot would be fatal.

"But I'm glad you're so pathetic. You can watch your lover choke to death, like I had to."

Her eyes shifted slightly right towards the conference table. What was she up to? Cassie saw blue lightning flash on the underside of her reflective painted leg.

"Lyle!"

The yelled warning alerted her boyfriend to the impending danger. Monique pulled the electroshock device from her backpack, but he struck first and pistol whipped her hard across the face.

The killer's eyes rolled upward until only white ellipses and blood vessels showed. She staggered back, knocking equipment off the table. She fell onto the big screen and slid down, unconscious. The inactive stun gun dropped from her gloved hand.

"You all right?" Lyle asked.

"Quit pampering me. Either kill that crazy woman or get me down, but do it before she wakes up."

"That's not as easy as you might think."

Her boyfriend stowed the handgun in his belt and removed a Stanley knife from inside his jacket, finally showing some initiative.

"Should I tell you not to move?"

He inserted the slanted razor between Cassie's hands and sawed at the plastic strip.

"Only if you'd like a punch in the face later," she said. "Thought Dan was the team comedian. Where is he?"

"Leading the police on a tour of Yorkshire. Hope he's okay."

Lyle's dusty cutting tool was feeble compared to Monique's combat blade, but he made good progress. The severed bond sprung loose and slid off the table.

Cassie was partially free – though the wrist ache remained – and could move her upper body. Her liberator stowed the Stanley knife back in his pocket and pulled out some wire cutters. A lousy idea, since the steel jaws wouldn't even fit over the cables, let alone break them.

"The locking bolts," she said. "On my ankles. See if you can— Watch out!"

Monique rose behind Lyle, the undamaged stocking stretched between her closed fists. She wrapped her makeshift garotte around his throat and twisted it to create a tight noose.

Taken by surprise, he dropped the wire cutters and elbowed his attacker repeatedly in the stomach. The barrage of forceful blows made the powerful brunette grunt, but her stranglehold didn't loosen. Even without protective armour, Monique was a formidable adversary.

Cassie stretched sideways towards the ceiling fan. She

groaned in pain as she reached for her ankle restraint, but her only reward was coating her fingertips in more silver paint.

It was hopeless. She could barely reach her kneecap.

The dangling leather straps of the choker, still around her sore neck, brushed against the table. Restrained in the leg split, she could only watch while the killer dragged her captive along the carpet.

"Use the gun!" Cassie shouted.

Monique piggy backed on Lyle. She trapped his forearms and waist between her thighs. The Stanley knife, which for some reason he chose over a firearm, fell from his clumsy grip. The murderess kicked it away with such ferocity it skidded under the wheeled cart.

Cassie tried to unbind her other ankle – the one pointed at the entrance – but that was also beyond her grasp.

Lyle winced in the killer's crushingly tight squeeze. He flung her back onto the television screen with enough impact to crack the plastic. The psychotic woman simply laughed and twisted the stocking tighter.

Chairs toppled over as the struggling boyfriend bulldozed his way towards the doors. Cassie's outstretched leg was right in front of him. If Lyle freed his arms, he could release the ankle restraint.

He slammed his head back into Monique's, dazing her. That gave him an opening to bite the locking pin and yank it out.

The hinged ring fell open and swung through the open doors. Supported only by the ceiling fan wire, Cassie dropped onto the conference table. A hard landing that took her breath away, but the situation demanded a speedy recovery.

The murderess screamed in fury and somehow twisted

the stocking knot through another revolution. That was too much for Lyle, who passed out, dragging Monique down with him.

The dazed gymnast clambered to her feet. The steel cable linking her ankle to the fan support jerked tight. She tried the locking pin, but her greasy painted fingers slipped on the unyielding bolt. Unless she released it, her movement would be restricted to a few metres in radius.

Below the table's edge, Cassie saw her motionless boyfriend. Monique pulled the pistol from his belt.

"You somehow broke free," she said, standing up, "and Harris shot you. Then I stabbed the murderer with his own knife, but sadly, he strangled Lyle to death before all that. You're a reporter. Think the public will buy the story?"

"Not a chance in hell."

With the killer outside Cassie's range, defiant words were all she had. Monique grinned and aimed at her.

"Straight through that pure heart of yours. This is for ruining my perfect pose."

She squeezed the trigger. Cassie expected a loud bang followed by sharp pain and eternal darkness, but there was no gunshot. Instead, a science fiction sound effect played.

"God damn toy!"

Monique threw the imitation firearm away and marched towards Vince Harris' bloody corpse. The knife in his neck...

Cassie jumped off the table and knelt to retrieve the blade. The murderess got there moments later and shoulder charged her. With that athletic build, a petite gymnast was easy to knock aside.

Monique flung the director's chair against the desk in anger and grabbed her bloody weapon. She rose and slashed at Cassie, who arched her body just in time to evade the glinting steel. A straight line of red spots sprayed across the gymnast's leotard and vandalised picture frames.

The killer feinted a knife attack and went for the choker strap with her empty hand. Cassie had forgotten about the leather noose but successfully deflected the grab with her forearm.

She ducked right. In the narrow aisle cluttered with executive chairs, there was little room to manoeuvre.

To negate the height disadvantage, she vaulted atop the table and leapt over Monique's whooshing side swipe. A fierce low thrust made the gymnast retreat. Her bare feet teetered on the wooden edge, but she regained her footing.

The killer grabbed the stretched wire. That disrupted Cassie's rhythm, and she stumbled sideways onto the director's bouncy leather seat. She back hopped to a safer position as the murderess circled the table. Attrition would be the deciding factor, and Monique had far more energy.

Underneath the ceiling fan, the steel cord had wound into a double loop that Cassie almost tripped on. She backed away and looked for a weapon. The stun gun and Stanley knife were out of reach. Which left nothing except...

An insane plan – requiring precision, composure, and a huge amount of luck – but it was her only chance.

Cassie took up the cable slack, skipped back, and sprinted towards the director's chair. She somersaulted forward, the coiled wire in her clenched hands. Ignoring the stunned Monique, she used the surface as a springboard and punched off.

She had performed vaults many times, but never under such tense circumstances, with hardly any run up and improvised equipment. The dangerous play brought her within inches of the ceiling fan blades, but she avoided a collision.

In mid flight, the gymnast dropped the wound cable over Monique's head, and half twisted to land crouched on the table facing the killer.

Before the murderess worked out her strategy, Cassie pivoted on her unrestrained foot. She split her legs between the wooden edge and a picture frame. The steel wire was at full stretch, with the noose tight around the brunette's neck.

Monique's angry yell suddenly became a choked gasp. She slashed the cable. Her serrated blade bounced off with a harmless clink. Further swipes were equally ineffective. Cassie prayed the grating ceiling fan brace would hold under the enormous stress.

Monique ditched the knife and grabbed the cable two handed. Somehow, her immense strength was enough to make Cassie's foot shift. Her squeaky heel left a paint smear along the table's edge. Her bare feet lacked traction, and the noose round the killer's neck loosened.

The murderess smiled triumphantly. She was winning the contest of muscle power.

Another cable pull made Cassie wobble. She needed more leverage. There was a brass wall lamp between the pictures, but grasping at that would upset her balance. The swinging choker straps bounced off her leotard, giving her an idea.

Cassie unwrapped the collar and flung it at the light fixture. The circular loop snared it, and the gymnast gripped the dual leather strips tight, nesting her hands inside the brass hooks.

The steel cable creaked as Monique fought to free herself. More stress noises from the fan support and lamp, but the killer's efforts were getting weaker.

Strangled gasps became more desperate. Monique clawed at the thick wire. She kicked empty air and stared at

Cassie in hatred. Then, after a long struggle, she stopped moving.

Every muscle in Cassie's body strained under the extra weight, but she kept her bent pose to ensure that the psycho was dead. When police officers with automatic weapons stormed the director's office, the embattled teenager had almost passed out.

A helmeted man in an armoured vest looked at the silver painted gymnast. Legs spread between the conference table and frame, holding a leather choker around a wall light. Thinking about it, the sight must have seemed utterly ridiculous, but posed women with reflective skin were nothing new in this case.

"She's with us," Lyle said, dashing over. "The good guys."

The cop relaxed a little and lowered his gun.

"And we've got one hell of a story," Cassie added.

She dropped to the carpet, easing the tension in the cable.

Monique's body collapsed on top of Vince Harris. Her gloved hands were completely still, and brunette hair locks shook under the released steel noose.

The mannequin killer was dead, and this terrifying ordeal was over.

CHAPTER TWENTY

Perfect Ten

The Hexagon Heroes exhibit was the new centrepiece of the lobby, between the entrance and reception. Shiny silver mannequins were no longer in vogue, replaced by human likenesses with natural skin colours. An attempt at rebranding, but the company's future remained in doubt.

The chief executives were all dead, and their shady dealings exposed. George Bright's incriminating audio and Olympic conspiracy were public knowledge, and few had sympathy. Which explained why Cassie had been asked to give a speech.

"We gather here today to remember the fallen champions. I survived to tell my story, but many others did not."

Reporters representing major media outlets – from the UK and overseas – surrounded the six statues. Camera bulbs flashed and a cluster of extended microphones competed for her attention.

It was a sizeable crowd and sombre occasion, but a beautiful day outside. Golden sunshine added a radiant glow to her smart casual wear. Cassie looked less sporting with untied hair and formal trousers, but the professional clothes suited a company spokesperson.

"We should commend Detective Inspector Quinn and Detective Constable Moore for their bravery. On behalf of the University of York and Hexagon Sports, I offer my condolences to their relatives and know I also speak for their colleagues at North Yorkshire Police."

The mannequins wore the same outfits their real counterparts died in, but Cassie resisted the impulse to cry. She was the designated hero, thrown into the spotlight with a memorised speech. It was usually Prime Ministers and royalty who addressed the nation, not student reporters. Eyes around the world were on her – talk about pressure.

"Elena Savikova came to Britain to support her family, so I've asked the company to make a donation to the Ukrainian refugee fund in her memory."

That triggered a round of applause, which Cassie acknowledged with a pause. The statue had the figure skater on a false icy looking surface with one leg raised behind a glittery yellow outfit. The funding request was essentially a demand given the political pressure, but this public address was all about diplomacy.

"Raquel Valdez taught me a thing or two about self defence," Cassie said. "An important lesson that anyone can become a hero. Her personal abuse story will strike a chord with many, and she will be missed."

More clapping, and she spotted Rick – the club owner – behind the reporters. Things were still tense between him and Lyle over the break in, which explained her boyfriend's absence.

Cassie waited for the chatter to die down before she continued.

"Justin West was a technician, but his daring antics to confront a murderer and destroy her surveillance hack proved vital. This allowed my rescuers to pinpoint my location, otherwise I would not be standing before you today."

Only a few claps, reluctant and spread out. Hexagon's mannequin maker would be proud of his tribute, even if the clean-shaven chin and combed black hair were complete misrepresentations. Beside the elegant Elena and a kickboxer in fighting gear, an everyday man in jeans and a chequered shirt lacked impact. But his contribution wouldn't be completely forgotten.

"And then there's me," Cassie said sheepishly. "Not much to say about that. If you want further information, I guess you'll have to watch it on the news."

Her joke invoked laughter from the audience, and provided an excuse to avoid personal details. There were enough of those on the BBC website profile.

Hexagon had respected her wish, and dressed the mannequin in an ordinary red leotard. Company branding was toxic in the post-scandal era, and Cassie wished to remember her humble roots.

"I'll hand over to the acting director to make an official statement," she said.

A smartly attired woman took Cassie's place. Grateful for the cordon manned by security staff, she left the imaginary stage and walked around the dividing wall behind reception.

Lyle stood proudly in the shade, with the smiling Dan by his side. The two men weren't formally dressed, but a welcome sight after the artificial pleasantries and schmoozing.

"See you're both taking cover," Cassie said.

Dan straightened her suit collar. "The Hexagon exec look doesn't really suit you. Six heroes and we didn't make the cut. Don't think wanted criminals are on the official guest list, but we managed to sneak in."

"Thought the police dropped the charges."

"They decided not to pursue them because it wasn't in the public interest. They still got the burglary, assault, and resisting arrest crimes on file, so they can reopen them once the fuss dies down. Rich boy will be just fine, but me? Might be a good idea to do community service. Know any companies hiring security guards?"

"Cynical as ever," Lyle said, prompting a mocking bow from his friend. "You never told us. How did you work out that gun was fake?"

"It's the details. No safety catch, a flat-bottomed handle with no loadable clip. And Rick wasn't too bothered about being shot. Kinda obvious, but Lyle was shit scared."

"We're not all gangsters, you know."

"Ex-gangster. But it fooled the cops and the psycho killer."

Cassie peeked around the divider. The new acting director was still talking corporate drivel, and some press members were chatting amongst themselves now the main event was over.

"So, Hexagon Corrupt Limited has recognised transgender athletes," Dan said. "That's progress."

He pointed towards a double mannequin display between the lifts. Gemma Bright, in her branded swimsuit, stood back to back with short-haired George in his black suit and tie.

"External pressure," Cassie said, "but they're still thinking of George as two different people, and haven't accepted him as male. That should tell you something."

Lyle placed his arm round her waist. "Baby steps, but at least he's been exonerated. Releasing the video transcript broke the legal loophole and allowed George's solicitors to go public with the name change. Real dumb they couldn't say anything until now."

"And the Olympic betting scheme put the last nail in Tamara Cole's legacy. You've probably noticed they've removed all traces of her, Vince Harris, and Wade Wilson. Denial is the new strategy."

"More an age old strategy," Dan said.

Lyle tapped on his cellphone and showed them a news report. The image was of the silver statue at Loughborough, but the background was the main entrance hall instead of a side corridor.

"The student population are more forward thinking," he said.

Cassie zoomed in on the picture and realised the swimmer's design was flatter chested with short blond hair. The jewelled crucifix remained from the original display, and also the Samuel Bible quotation.

That ex-forces coach who labelled Bright a snowflake was in shot, looking away from the camera in disgust. The cleaner had a beaming smile, though.

"They misinterpreted the message as being about drugs," Cassie said. "When it was about a struggle against gender identity. Pity the mother never knew."

Lyle hugged her tighter. "But she still loved her child. Enough to insist on restoring the memorial when everyone else wanted to abandon a shamed drug addict."

"She would have been proud of his decision. To give up

an Olympic dream and risk public anger was an enormous sacrifice. If only Gemma hadn't trusted Monique. That's what started this whole thing."

"The hindsight paradox," Dan said. "What if? If only… Maybe… Just accept Monique was a crazy psychopath, that awful shit happens, and move on with our miserable ordinary lives. We still got our media degrees to finish, right?"

Cassie smiled and led her boyfriend towards the lifts. Dan trailed along, nervously glancing back.

"You know a back way out of this place?" he asked her.

"A few fire exits, if they're working now. And an escape tunnel through the killer's hideout. Take your pick."

"Perhaps using the front entrance and risking the angry club owner isn't so bad?"

The noise receded as they turned into a side corridor.

"I'm thinking you deserve a perfect ten," Lyle said.

Cassie shook her head in dismay. "Not a great saying these days. That's what they called Tamara's gold medals."

"So we need a new champion. Got one right here."

"And the system has changed since 1976, when Nadia Comăneci did it. The press made that blunder with their headline about me. They should do their research. There's a code of points for gymnastics now."

"This women's sports history lesson is truly fascinating," Dan interrupted, "but it's a figure of speech. I think your boyfriend's saying you're awesome."

Lyle kissed Cassie on the cheek. "For bravery, stopping a serial killer, and that sheer badass takedown I slept straight through, you get a perfect ten."

ABOUT THE AUTHOR AND PUBLISHER

Andy Phillips was born in Oldham, England. He holds a PhD in Applied Mathematics and a BSc Joint Honours Maths/Physics degree. In a varied career, he has worked as a scientific researcher in the USA, a police intelligence analyst, a data analyst, and a higher education teacher.

From a very young age, he became fascinated with strong female characters — whether good, evil, or somewhere in between — that appeared in action, science fiction, and thriller movies. His favourite era is 1990s direct-to-video, back when VHS tapes and rental stores were still a thing. Determined to tell stories of his own, he wrote five freeware interactive fiction games, and later founded the publishing imprint *Action Girl Books*.

His novels deliver fast-paced tales of action, suspense, and danger, including multi-faceted plots, high-intensity scenes, and cinematic storytelling. He thrives on creating strong heroines and complex villainesses, often pitted against each other. Drawing inspiration from books, TV, and film, he hopes to inspire others to be creative, too.